UNDER COVER

THE SECRETS OF THE FOX WILLOW QUILTERS

A Novel by Mary Jo Hodge

Dedicated with love to
Charles C. Hodge

and to Quilters everywhere and their Partners
who smile when they step on a stray
needle or find thread snips in the soup.

PART ONE

THE QUEEN BEES

Chapter One

"Next Stop: Fox Willow"

The slob seated next to Amelia had been feigning sleep. Amelia knew this was just a pretense to keep leaning on her. At last the crowded bus was pulling into a town. Her ticket was for a city still 100 miles away.

"What difference does it make now," she decided. "If he doesn't get off here, I will."

Amelia badly needed a shower and to regroup. She had been on one bus or another for four days and three nights. Either on a bus or in some morbid bus station waiting for one!

As they pulled into the station, the man put his hand on her thigh, suggestively.

"It'll be dark in a few hours."

These were the first words he had spoken to her since moving up to take the seat by her. At that stop - a hundred and twenty miles back - he had stood in the aisle waiting for the elderly woman to leave. He even assisted the woman, lifting her bag from the rack above. Then he had squeezed quickly beside Amelia.

"Ride buses often?" He had questioned as soon as he was seated. Amelia had ignored him. She had ignored each of her several seat mates over the last days. She wanted no one to remember her – no one to ask questions.

Amelia would have changed seats. However the bus was crowded.

The people boarding were blocking the aisle. More had arrived than those who left. People were hefting large suit cases into the upper compartments. Some even struggled with cases for musical instruments. By the time all were boarded there were no empty seats. Two children were snuggled in beside a Mother in a two-seat space. One boy was sitting on the floor of the aisle.

Amelia hated the presence and smell of the man. The implication in his observation about the coming darkness was crystal clear. As soon as the bus pulled into its designated parking slot, Amelia picked up her sweater. She had draped it over her legs several stops back. The skirt she was wearing was short - too short! She slipped her arms into the sweater, being careful not to touch the man.

"You aren't gett'n off here, are you, Dolly?" the cad asked. "Come on – be a sport, go one more stop it least. I'll treat you for the night somewhere else. This little burg is dry – no bars, no liquor, no fun."

Unbelievably he was blocking her way! Amelia actually had to call out to the driver.

"Driver, please. This is my station. Let me out please!"

The bus driver sized up the situation quickly. He came over and helped her with her small bag. The moocher started to follow her out, but the driver stopped him.

"You stay right here, you hear me? I see a big guy out there who has come to meet her." Even as he spoke the bus driver stood blocking the cad's view until Amelia could get inside the station.

Amelia hated the tight, slutty clothes that Greg favored. Greg got enjoyment from embarrassing her. Maybe she'd put enough time and enough miles away from him that she could shop a little. She never wanted to get on another bus, but she would soon, happy about it or not. Greg would not stop looking for her. At least she could dress like she wanted to and feel decent for a change.

After washing up in the bus station Amelia found a phone booth. The Yellow Pages promised three motels and one bed and breakfast. Though small, Fox Willow seemed to be a prosperous enough town with lots of restaurants and a variety of boutiques.

It was late afternoon and the food counter at the bus station was closed. She didn't mind. She was sick of the bus station food anyway. She needed a place to stay and take a bath before she did anything else!

Outside she found that there were no taxis around. She had seen the three motels from the bus window earlier. They were certainly out of walking distance. Amelia walked a block in the direction of a drug store sign.

Amelia had grown up in a city. She found it fairly easy to follow the street layout in this picturesque town. It was laid out in squares, all rotating from a central square formed by a park. Children's playground equipment and several benches were the focus of one corner. A band pavilion highlighted another. The streets all ran north and south or east and west from the center park. The most outstanding aspects of the park were two statues, which adorned the North and South sides of the green space. From where Amelia stood one looked like foxes playing with their kits.

Facing the streets that divided the stores from the park, she saw boutiques and some eateries. Amelia recognized some of the names from the Yellow Book. Uncle Sam's Soul Foods was right next to McLarson's Pub and Grub. Next was a small jewelry story that seemed to split space with Hazel's Hair Haven. A furniture store and a chain drug store with a nationally recognized name completed one block of the square. The street signs heralded this particular roadway as 'Main Street'.

'Church Street' ran at right angles from the far corner of the square of businesses. Amelia turned and walked down the opposite side, toward the band pavilion. Here, she passed a US Post Office, a Farmer's Mercantile Bank, and a pizza place. Pausing, Amelia admired an intricate quilt in the window of a fabric store. The boutique that she came to next promised a great sale for two days only. This brought Amelia to the corner of Church and Willow Streets. Eureka! Willow Street, according to the Yellow Pages, was the thoroughfare on which she would find the B & B.

Amelia soon came within sight of a lovely old Victorian house. It took up much of the block. The stately dwelling was painted in shades of the palest lavender, with deep purple trim - lots of it. In places the trim was supplemented with narrow strips of gold. The structure was three stories high at it's center-most expanse. To either side of this - likely the original portion of the building - gabled additions spread like wings of a swan in flight. The windows were of leaded glass, in colors of yellow and lavender. Three stone chimneys reached skyward from each wing; smaller versions of a much larger chimney serving the central edifice.

The sign in front of the house was neatly lettered.

"Gems and Jams"

Proprietor: Ruby Fentasia.

Amelia had a pang of jealousy that she tried quickly to will away. This Ruby was a lucky woman. Amelia wondered if the proprietor could possibly know how lucky.

Taking a deep breath Amelia tried the door. A bell tingled as the massive, walnut masterpiece opened. Stepping into the lovely foyer, Amelia stood mesmerized. She stood face to face with herself. The ornate gold framed mirror showed a tired and flustered woman. She looked 20 years older than her actual age of 28. Shaking off the entrancement of the mirror,

Amelia's eyes fell on a guest book. It lay on the marble-topped table underneath the mirror. Two stiff, Empire style love seats braced each side of the table. Looking down at the floor Amelia noticed that the rug was oriental in beautiful shades of beige, deep blue and maroon. Catching her breath, she called.

"Hello, anyone home?"

"Coming! Hold your horses!" She heard the reply and sat down on the nearest divan, exhausted. She ignored the guest book!

A smiling woman appeared around a corner, drying her hands on an embroidered, lace-edged tea towel.

"Hi! As you probably saw on the sign outside, I'm Ruby Fentasia. Sorry to tell you we don't have anything for you tonight. Most of the rooms here are let monthly. Those reserved for overnighters are a mess. My cleaner just quit. She ran away with her boyfriend. Who knows if she'll ever be back. I had a quilting bee most all day! I don't know what to say. The motels are about a mile out of town; you could try them. They're on the access to the Interstate."

"I know," sighed Amelia, acutely aware that this beautiful house would be more than she dared spend at any rate. "The bus that I was on just passed them. Is there a taxi service?"

"No, not since Clem died. I suppose I could clean out one of the rooms for you," Ruby said, looking at her watch. "I'm expecting a couple of friends over for tea in just a few. You could join us and then I'll clean the room afterward."

The doorbell tinkled again!

"I'm a mess," exclaimed Amelia, seizing a possible opportunity. " Let me clean the room. As a matter of fact, I'll clean two. It sounds like you have more guests arriving!"

A man appeared with a woman on his arm. They were dressed in expensive business clothes and looked as travel-weary as Amelia. They must have been traveling all day. The man was carrying a heavy suitcase.

"But I can't just let a stranger clean the rooms," Ruby began. She stopped in mid-sentence as she saw the man who came forward. His tone of voice left no doubt that he was a man used to giving orders.

"My wife is pregnant! Is there somewhere she could lie down. I'll pay extra for quick service. We have a busy night ahead."

Ruby sighed.

"Take her to the parlor. I'll see what I can do about getting a room ready right away!"

She caught Amelia by the arm and rushed her to a closet filled with clean linens and towels.

" I'll grab the vacuum. Bring plenty of sheets and towels - king bed size." Ruby ordered. "We slip the comforters inside clean sheets - it takes five sheets for each bed."

Amelia filled a convenient wicker basket. She followed Ruby past the dining room. They entered a hallway that looked like a wide corridor of a movie theater. Instead of movie posters lining the walls, this hallway held unique watercolors.

"What gorgeous art work," Amelia exclaimed, amazed.

"Many of the guests who come here are fledgling artists. They often send me a gift when they return home. That's why they are all so different." Ruby hurried along as she spoke.

Ruby ushered her new assistant into a spacious chamber with private bath attached. Also, there was a separate walk-in closet - or perhaps it was intended as a dressing room. The sheets were crumpled on the huge king bed. Together they made quick work of changing them. While Ruby vacuumed, Amelia dusted and straightened a small anteroom containing a writing desk and high intensity lamp. Together they had the suite ready in 20 minutes flat.

"Your room is just across the hall," Ruby said. "Don't bother checking in. You just saved my hide. That man is running for the Senate. He's supposed to speak at the high school gym tonight. I never thought he'd stay here! But I wouldn't have wanted to turn him away . I would've been the talk of the town!　　　　Amelia got more linens and walked into the room across the hall. Her eyes widened as she saw the beauty of the room. The bed was canopied with white draping silk. It looked like a cloud floating in the center of the large room. There was a writing desk on one wall and an ample chest of drawers. The private bath had both a shower and a tub, the latter rigged with water jets. There was even a French bidet. Amelia had never seen one before.

Tears came to Amelia's eyes. Ruby probably thought the couple would prefer a king bed to this double, Amelia mused. Otherwise, she would have given them this room.

Before she changed the bed and ran the vacuum, Amelia took off all of her dirty old clothes. Throwing them in the bath tub to soak later, she turned on the shower as hot as she could stand it. For 20 minutes she let the hot water relax her. She used the soap and the complimentary shampoo, washing her hair three times. Still she didn't feel clean. As she came out of the bathroom wrapped in a huge towel, she noticed that Ruby had been inside. Just inside the door Ruby had hung a maid's uniform.. A note was attached to the collar.

"You don't have to wear this if you don't want to but I thought you might need a fresh change of clothes. It looks like you didn't bring any real bags with you unless you checked them at the bus station. I knocked, but you didn't hear me. The invite to tea still stands."

Amelia thankfully threw the towel in the now empty wicker basket and stepped into the clothing that Ruby had provided. Without the apron it didn't look too much like a uniform. She didn't really care. It was clean and a decent fit!

She was close to exhaustion.

"I think I could sleep for about 20 years," Amelia thought, looking longingly at the fairy tale bed. However, Ruby had been nice to her; she really deserved a thanks. She might even need more help! Weren't there other rooms that were vacant but not cleaned? A candidate for the Senate would probably have an entourage.

"Maybe if I open those curtains and let what light is left inside, I can shake off this sleepiness," Amelia decided.

She was immediately awestruck by the view! The elaborate damask drapes had hidden a sliding glass door. Opening it, Amelia saw a small patio arranged so that it served this room only. Walking onto the patio she could see a lovely garden spreading for about 80 feet beyond the house. Wisteria in full bloom draped sturdy trellises, framing the rose garden in front. A cutting garden could be seen further on, proudly showcasing asters, indigo, delphiniums, dahlias and daisies. There were other blossoms Amelia could not identify from her door. Beyond the gardens, steep mountains reached high into the sunlit sky.

Further to the right, stone patio tables and outdoor bar-b-q cookers were arranged in artful arches. Comfortable lawn chairs were placed in a circle around two different fire pits.

Ruby was hanging lanterns even as her guests were arriving.

With tears in her eyes Amelia unlocked the gate of her little patio and walked over to say thanks and offer her help.

"Oh, Hi," Ruby greeted her new employee. Well, at least a Johnny-On-the-Spot helper. "Meet Pearl. She is one of my best friends. You should see the embellishments she comes up with for art quilts." Suddenly Ruby realized she did not even know the name of the unexpected guest turned even more unexpected maid.

"OK", thought Amelia quickly. "We have a Ruby and a Pearl here at the 'Gems and Jams B&B'. I shouldn't try for so precious a gem. Maybe a fake gem - I know!"

"Nice to meet you, Pearl. You're best friend could be mine, too. Best shower I've had in days!" she had been improvising as she conjured up a name.

"I'm Crystal," she said lightly. "Crystal Williams."

The two women shook hands, each noting something furtive in the other's eyes. Something they would not have noticed except that it was so familiar. Something they saw each time they looked in a mirror.

Pearl broke the spell.

"We're in for a real treat. Ruby wants us to try out her new jam. She calls it 'Fenneled Figs'. I heard it made a great hit at breakfast this morning."

Recipe Taken from Ruby's Personal, handwritten notebook:(Recipes are in no-way guaranteed. Try them if you dare, but at your own risk of a clean-up nightmare.)

Ruby's Jam of the Day

Fenneled Figs

Gather the blooms from a fennel plant that you are sure has not been sprayed with insecticide. These flowers have a mild, anise flavor. If you like licorice, you will love this jam. If you don't; well chose another jam!

Ingredients:

30 Fennel blossoms (fresh or frozen fresh from your garden)

4 qts figs   3 qts sugar   1 sliced orange

Did you ever wonder what pioneer women did without oranges?

1 lime   1 cup water

Procedure: Mix sugar, citrus and water and place over heat, stirring until it spins a thread. Don't ask me to explain that. If no one showed you how to spin a thread when you were little, you had a deprived childhood. Maybe a neighbor will take mercy on you. If not call home bureau or the local quilt guild. They know all about threads and will teach you to quilt. Then you'll be too busy to make jam. Why are you making it anyway? They sell it at all the grocery stores.

In case you are still there stirring, when that little thread creeps down from your stirring spoon, remove from heat and take out citrus fruit.

Stir in figs and blossoms. Cook -yes stir - until it is thick and your arms are tired. Call that good and use it for syrup if it doesn't spread properly. Also good on chocolate ice cream!

Isn't everything?

Suppose somehow you stirred too long and your mixture is hardening like rocks. When that happens to me, sometimes accidently, sometimes not - I make all day licorice lollipops!

Take a cleaver and attack mixture! Be aggressive! Chop out about a fistfull and place on waxed paper. Keeping paper between your hands and jam, insert a popsicle stick and mold around it. I like to give my lollipops hour glass figures. Some people just butter their hands and go at it, but I can warn you – this will ruin a good manicure.

Lick and enjoy! Ruby

Chapter Two

Fatal Impulse

Somewhere in Colorado, 1958-63

Pearl had buried her secret as belonging only in her past. Only she knew what had happened on that ski slope long ago. She was only twelve when her mother brought Brad to live with them. Twelve and ungainly as a young colt. Brad made fun of her awkward control of her fast growing body. He insisted on hugging her - way more often than just hello and so long. Worse! He was a pincher.

When she complained to her Mom of the bruises on her arms, Mom intervened. He never pinched her arm again. Soon after he switched to pinching her butt. The first time he had found her alone in the den. Mom had not come home yet from work. Pearl was surprised that Brad was there so early.

"Stand up!" he demanded.

"Why?" she asked suspiciously.

"Your Mom and I are going to a movie. I'm meeting her for dinner first. Brought you a pizza - look in the kitchen."

"Oh, well thanks!"

"Stand up and hug me good-by, you little minx."

Pearl shrugged. Might as well do as he says so he'll just go.

The hug was more like a punitive squeeze. The pinch was long and hard; right on her butt.

"Don't you dare go showing your Mom where I'll be pinching you now," he blurted, squeezing harder. "If you do you'll be really sorry. I'll leave bruises everyone will notice and maybe a black eye or two. Do you understand?"

Pearl didn't answer. She was trying to pull free, when he pinched her butt again, even harder this time.

"I asked you a question? Do I have to take my belt to you to get an answer?"

"I understand," Pearl conceded. "The alpha dog speaks," she muttered under her breath, as he loosen her and was turning away.

"What did you say?" he demanded!

I said, "Thanks again for the pizza."

He slapped her lightly and left.

Brad was charming to her friends and the best of all substitute Dads in front of others, especially Patricia, Pearl's Mom. Patricia thought the sun rose and set with Brad. Occasionally he would disappear for a week or two. Patricia fretted, varying from anger to tearful outbursts. Pearl hoped he wouldn't come back. Secretly, she gave him a new name -'The Jerk'! Surely her Mom would give him the boot if he did return.

Patricia received him with open arms, apologizing for whatever she had done to keep Brad away. This continued for months; then years. As Pearl turned Sweet Sixteen he was still there, very deeply entrenched in her Mother's affections.

At sixteen Pearl's figure had matured to the point that she attracted lots of attention. Greg began making sexual overtures. She spent most afternoons after school at a friend's or in the library. There was no way she was going home earlier than her Mom would get there from work.

Mom approached her, asking if she wasn't old enough now to start dinner. "I could leave a casserole in the fridge and you could put it in the oven, for example," Mom elaborated.

"Maybe after I finish this term paper, Mom. It requires lots of research. I go straight from school to the library. I only have the two hours before the library closes."

"Well, then - in a few weeks?"

"The paper is due the last day before the December break. Then I'll have a lot of studying for exams. Probably February?" Pearl would have to think of more excuses then. She had no doubt of The Jerk's intentions as soon as he found her alone.

The largest present under the tree was labeled to both Pearl and her Mom. Inside were three matching ski parkas and a packet of travel information. The Jerk had come up with a ski trip for three during the February break. Pearl couldn't hide her delight. She skied almost every Saturday in Winter - riding on the school's special bus to the resort fifty minutes away. She had never skied in the Canadian Rockies - the place The Jerk had chosen. He had booked a chalet with two bedrooms.

Pearl had never seen him ski; she knew her Mother was a beginner. Most likely he was, also - he had never mentioned skiing before and this was his fourth Winter of nosing in on her previously carefree family life.

Brad was more cunning than she had bargained for or she would have played sick and stayed home! The lure of a ski trip was great, but nothing like her repugnance for the man.

The first morning he signed Mom up for the week -long lesson package. He then announced that no one should ski alone in an unfamiliar resort. Mom would be with the class, while he and Pearl would be partners.

"Why don't we sign up for classes, too?" Pearl suggested.

"I don't think that many classes fit in my budget," he replied. "Tell you what. If I can't keep up with you we'll consider day lessons tomorrow."

Mom was all for this plan. "With lessons, maybe by next year I can go with you two aces," she laughed.

The first day went remarkably well. They explored intermediate slopes all morning, getting a feel for the condition of the snow and for their comparative skill levels. By afternoon they were comfortably taking the expert trails.

They met Mom for lunch at the main chalet - soup and hot dogs.

At 4:30 they met Mom again at the class assembly point. "I'm starved," she announced. "Are you still game for that "Pub and Platter" place we passed on the way up this mountain yesterday?"

"You two go," Pearl suggested. "I'll get a pizza here and take it back to the chalet. Give you some time together." Mom was delighted, but Pearl saw a wicked look flash in The Jerk's smoky grey eyes.

The middle of the night was when it happened. The Chalet he had chosen had a layout that separated the two bedrooms much more than the adjoining rooms at home. Pearl's room was off to the right of the entrance foyer. The room was designed as a second bedroom for the portion of the Chalet they rented. It could also be leased as a third bedroom for the suite next door.

Pearl was roused from sleep when she felt her breast being gently squeezed. As she started to cry out a hand pressed over her mouth.

"Hush, it's just me. Go back to sleep!" His voice was a hoarse whisper.

Wide awake now, Pearl could feel the length of him in bed with her. His erection was pressing against her behind; his right arm reaching around to cover her mouth.

Pearl drew her legs closer to her stomach and lashed out with both at once, kicking his shins.

"You bitch, I'll fight with you, but not where your Mom will hear!

You can't win you know. It's only a matter of time."

Brad stormed out!

As soon as Pearl heard the door close, she got up and dressed in three layers.

Then she went straight to the small kitchenette. She brought the biggest knife she could find and put it under her pillow. The lock on the door to her room was mysteriously broken, but she brought a chair and tilted it under the knob. She wondered if this really ever helped keep others out. Carefully, she balanced her ski boots on the chair. At least if he tried to come back in, she would hear a warning noise.

At 11:00 A.M. she was bouncing through the deepest moguls she had ever skied. Looking down from the top she had almost passed the slope by, almost until she heard his chant behind her.

"Scaredy cat! So you're scared of all kinds of bumping around! I'll teach you about bumping in bed. The trail here to the left looks like it will take us over to the bunny hill. It's just made for you!"

Zoom! Off she went! The extra adrenaline pump his words had invoked gave her just the amount of guts she needed for a slope like this.

Panting she reached the bottom. Looking up she hoped to see he had taken another route, but he was halfway down. He was skiing cautiously, stopping every few feet. Suddenly she felt an urgent need to get away from him.

The trail signs indicated a traverse that led to another chair. Consulting the small map provided by the ski area, she saw this chair went even higher up the mountain. From the top there was a choice of several trails. She would get away at least for the day!

He caught up with her sooner than she expected. On leaving the chair lift she had made a poor choice. This route from the chair had brought her to a trail meant primarily for Alpine skiers - a virtually flat trail along the mountain top. From here there were three choices.

The first choice was going back to the chair and choosing a better slope from there. Trekking uphill would be no fun. A second choice was to take the cross country trail. The map showed this winding around for miles. It would take all day without Nordic skis.

The third choice proved no choice at all as Pearl skied closer. She had expected a difficult ski over a rim; then a groomed expanse for traversing. Instead she found a cliff - the edge of which was only about a foot from where she was standing.

Choosing option one, Pearl noticed a shorter way back up to the main trail leading from the lift. It was steeper but formed a hypotenuse, angling back to her left and intersecting the main trail closer to the lift. As she struggled up the incline, herring boning energetically, Pearl saw 'The Jerk' speeding by on the path above her.

He called to her just as she reached the top of the rise. His voice was insulting; mean.

"You crazy bitch! When I catch you we're going straight to the chalet. An afternoon there alone with me is just what you need! You could have killed us both! Where the heck do we go from here?"

He had just pulled up at the edge of the cliff, skis parallel to the rim. He glanced over his shoulder, looking down.

"Hell!" he shouted.

"Sounds like a plan," she called back loudly.

Without forethought, but as swiftly as a hawk sweeps down on it's prey, she sprang forward, using the rise she stood on like a springboard. She did a quick turn as she reached him; just in time to push him off the cliff and stay on the edge herself. Adrenalin flowing, she scampered back up the rise she had just left, not daring to look back.

She breathlessly reached her Mom halfway through the break time allowed by the classes.

"He took a slope too hard for me," she improvised. "I thought he'd be here waiting."

Patricia did not consider that Brad was hurt. He had never made any long-term commitment to her. She accepted this with bitterness.

"He's found a ski bunny! Well, we aren't leaving!" Patricia had remarked. "He's paid for our week and we are having fun! One of the women in my class has a son about your age. He wants to drop out of his lessons. I'll introduce you at the pig roast tonight and you can partner with him."

Pearl just wanted to go home, but she dared not act out of character. She would try skiing with the boy if that would please her Mom. Pearl was immersed in a mixture of anxiety and joyous relief.

When their week ended, Patricia half expected to find Brad at home. She never suspected he was in harm's way until the news came, weeks later. The heavy snow that night would have prevented the ski patrol from a thorough search even if he had been reported missing.

The March thaw had facilitated the discovery of his frozen remains. Routine search helicopter crews spotted his ski pole on a rock outcropping, pinpointing the probable search area. What was left of the body indicated a broken leg. The death was ruled accidental - freezing after an injury prevented him from seeking shelter.

From the location of the pole and body, no one even suspected a long fall from the cliff. An ungroomed slope, not included on the ski maps, veered off the cross country trail just a few feet from where Pearl had made her choices. Called "The Wall of the Devil" this slope had once been groomed for daredevils. Now off limits, it's very prohibitions attracted a few skiers. This old trail wound down to the bottom of the ravine. It was a challenge, even for experts, and many broken bones had resulted from the headstrong who dared try it.

Everyone assumed his death was an accident - he had taken the daredevil slope. Newspapers covering the event noted he had won a number of slalom events during his late teens. This would be the type of skier who would respond to the challenge of the unmarked trail.

That Brad had gone down a quicker way, no one even considered. There was no inquiry.

Chapter Three

Dangerous Undertaking

Fox Willow, USA

Amber was the oldest of Ruby's inner circle. Her soft, knowing eyes told of a lifetime of sorrow. Crystal thought she had never met a lovelier, more stately woman. Amber's carriage was erect, her smile genuine. Her rosy-blushed skin belied her 52 years. Amber's hair still showed signs that it had once been a rich auburn. Now, the white streaks outnumbered the auburn, but the entire effect was beautiful - unique to Amber!

Pearl had quickly felt a kinship with Crystal. She shared with Crystal the basics about the other quilters. Through Pearl, Crystal soon found out that Amber had been a widow for only a short time. She and Ruby had been close since the week Ruby arrived in Fox Willow. Now, each with no family in the area, they were almost inseparable.

"I doubt those two have a single secret from each other," she remarked.

Little did Pearl know.

Each woman in the Fox Willow quilting bee had her own closely guarded secret! Amber had hidden hers long before most of the others were born. If one looked carefully and deeply into Amber's eyes, one could see it there. From this secret came the sorrow that mellowed Amber. Her secret had taught her to cherish every day. It had taught her that safety was never a sure thing; that caution and forethought alone could lead to safety. Even that was not a sure thing.

"Fate has its say, and fate is fickle," thought Amber. "Where did this new one come from? Why has she come to tea in a maid's uniform? She isn't a spy - spy's have a purpose for joining a tea party. This one acts like a small child. She can't even believe she is at a garden tea party. She is scared half to death and trying to hide it."

Probably Ruby had known this girl in some former time and place.

"I'm being overly suspicious," Amber thought. But still she could not chase away her sense of foreboding This Crystal even smelled of danger!

Countryside, Occupied France, WWII

Amber grew up in France during World War II and the time of Germany's occupation. She was only 10 when her family became involved with the French Underground. Unavoidable circumstances led to the part Amber came to play. Now the oldest member of the quilting bee, she still kept the secret that she had harbored for so many years.

Yes, she had been involved much more than she liked to remember. Who knows which side she was on who she helped hide. Certainly not Amber. She couldn't tell the difference of who to hide from and who to help. Her family was doing both - usually at odd times like the middle of the night. Back then Amber wasn't even Amber. She was Suzette and had been from the time of her birth until the escape from the occupation forces. Escaping meant leaving behind the important things. Things like friends, family members, dog, roof over head and most of all one's name - one's identifiable self.

Suzette's Mother tried to keep Suzette in the dark about the happenings all around her. Suzette had eyes though and she had ears. She knew about the comings and goings in the middle of the night. The hay wagons were filled with straw so that people could hide underneath. Suzette had seen some of these people. She had played with the children.

From her bed she had heard stories of the parents. Stories no child should hear.

The quietness of her father and brothers screamed at Suzette. The stealth with which they moved about in the night - the whispering - the mysterious errands. Together these left Suzette trembling in her little bed. Very early one morning these errands left Suzette alone in their three room country house. This was unusual but it had happened before once or twice. When Suzette heard someone at the door she thought it was her father. She ran from her bedroom to greet him. Instead of her father she saw a tall man not much older than her eldest brother. He was dressed in traveling clothes which looked to be Swiss to the young girl. She had seen picture-books of mountain climbers and she associated the kind of clothing this man wore with a mountain climber's garb. He had pants that were gathered around the ankles in a band instead of hanging loose and free. He boots were quite a bit more substantial than footwear any member of her family possessed.

Suzette did not know whether to be frightened or to welcome the man. She spoke only French. He was speaking some language she could not identify. Suzette had no idea what he was saying.

"Who are you?" she kept repeating.

"Where is your father?" the man asked, this time in fluent French. "I must see him."

Suzette feared for her father's safety and for her brothers, too. Something about the man made her frightened. He was a danger to the entire family. Suzette just knew it!

Suddenly he fainted, falling to the floor. Suzette ran to him. He was bleeding from a cut on his head. She quickly got a rag and held it to his head. She brought warm water from the teapot to rinse his forehead. The cut was behind his hairline and she couldn't see how deep. Little did she know of such things at any rate.

"What happened to you? You are bleeding everywhere," Suzette exclaimed.

He mumbled something. He was incoherent! Suzette was alarmed. He was speaking another language now. She was sure it was German. It was the language the soldiers spoke when they strutted through the streets.

Eventually she understood. He was asking for a drink. Suzette rushed to get water but he pushed it away. He wanted something stronger, he demanded , this time speaking in French.

"So perhaps you want cider." Suzette ran to get hard cider from where her father kept his supply. The man drank his fill directly from the jug and leaned back against the table. Surely he wasn't going to try to sleep there.

"You must go; you must go now," she said.

"No! No! I am staying here," he said. He took his gun out and put it across his lap. The girl did not know what to do or how to react. She left the man sitting on the floor and ran outside. She must look for Jules her middle brother. Jules would know what to do. He should be here somewhere. He had been tending a birthing mare earlier the previous evening. Perhaps he was still in the barn. Perhaps he was the family member who was supposed to be with her.

Suzette found Jules sleeping by the exhausted mare. The new colt was softly nudging against his mother.

"Wake up, wake up Jules, there's a man in the kitchen. He is bleeding."

"A man? What kind of man?"

"A scary man, I think. Maybe he is Swiss. He has Swiss boots. I'm afraid of him; he has a gun"

The two slipped back into their modest home and saw the man had fainted or perhaps was sleeping while still sitting on the floor. Jules sneaked up slowly behind him and conked him on the head with an iron skillet.

" Oh, he was already bleeding. His head was wounded." By this time Suzette was frantic.

Jules was searching the man's pockets.

"This man is a spy. We must get rid of him." Jules tied the spy's feet together. He then pulled the scout's hands above his head and tied those also. "We must do this quickly. He is a German scout; more may be coming here. When he sees them he can report us and have us killed . We must hide him well because he will be missed."

Suzette was still perplexed.

"I do not understand," she pleaded with her brother.

"The scouts travel ahead of the soldiers. They are in disguise so the locals will more likely trust them. Others will come after him. They could be close. Was he bleeding when he arrived? Often they come on horseback. Perhaps he was injured in a fall."

Jules fetched a mattress and they used it like a stretcher. Luckily the family stallion was still in the barn. Father had taken one of the mares, but left the stallion and the mare who was birthing. Jules made a stretcher that could be pulled by the horse, using the mattress. He rigged a harness so the horse could drag the mattress down the heavily furrowed fields. With some difficulty, they got the man on the mattress without waking him.

" Where shall we keep him? What shall we do with him?" Suzette wondered anxiously.

" We must keep him hidden until we can ask father. Father will know what to do."

Jules and Suzette guided the horse to the old graveyard about a mile and a half from the house. Next to it was an ancient outhouse that had not been used for years.

"Maybe we should put him in there, Suzette." Jules knew it would be difficult as they would have to lift him up and over the seat itself. There were tangled vines growing through cracks in this weird structure.

" Then he will die down there," contributed the frightened Suzette. "How would he ever get back out?"

Jules looked quizzical.

"Maybe that's the point; maybe we shouldn't want him to get out."

" That is barbaric," sputtered Suzette. "Let's not do anything until father comes. We don't even know for sure if he is an enemy."

Jules reluctantly agreed, thinking he could come back to get the man in the privy with the help of one of his brothers. Suzette was too weak to help lift him; she had been of little use just dragging him onto the mattress.

The man was already beginning to recover so Jules quickly tied a kerchief tightly around the man's mouth. It wouldn't do for him to be heard screaming. Jules pulled the spy into a wild blackberry thicket .

"When father gets back with the wagon we can load him on it and find a better hiding place," Jules assured Suzette. They both straddled the horse's back and headed for their house. As they reached the road, which gave access to the house by wagon, Father and Georges were arriving from the other direction.

"There is no time to explain right now," Father said. "We have to leave our home now, immediately. The Germans are on to us. Your mother, along with Calvin is waiting about a mile and a half from here. Run in the house and get whatever food and clothes you each will need. You might have to carry it on your back pretty soon, but at least we can put the food on the wagon for now."

"But Father, what about the man we captured?"

Suzette's voice trailed off in the wind. Her father was already dashing for the barn, calling back to Jules as he did so.

"Hitch the stallion to the wagon, Son," Father called to Jules.

"We'll put the one about to give birth on a lead. She can walk behind us, without a heavy load to pull."

"The filly came a couple of hours ago," Jules called back.

"Come and help me then. We'll have to put the filly in the wagon for now. Otherwise she might slow us down. We'll try her walking when we pick up your mom and your brothers. It's good we have the horses and wagon! They'll wreck our house and take everything they can carry on their backs. If we stay, we sure won't need anything though. We'll soon be six feet under if anyone even bothers to bury us. We've got to get out of here."

Jules sighed. Even if he could get his Father to listen there wouldn't be time to go back to the old cemetery.

"Why didn't I kill him while I had the chance?"

Once in the wagon he and Suzette could bring the others up to date. He helped his Father and Georges get the filly onto the wagon. There was no need to put a lead on the mare. She would follow her baby.

"At least we have something left," Father said. "We can sell the horses for passage to Canada or the US. If we can just get across the border in northern France we'll all be fine."

Holland, 1944

Three weeks later the family had arrived at the outskirts of Amsterdam. They were down to one horse, having sold the others for bribes to cross the border out of occupied France. They had high hopes of being transported to England in the near future, with the help of the Underground. If not they could always go further North.

Friends of the Underground gave the signal. The family gratefully followed their directions to a safe house. Here they received bad news.

A Scout who happened to be a cousin of an important man in the German secret police had been found tied up near an old cemetery. His assignment had been to infiltrate the underground. The spy described his experience in great detail.

The German spy's story, as related by the Dutch friend of the French war refugees.

"Instead of staying on the roads, I cut across several fields and a small forest. Both my map and compass assured me I was saving at least a day. All was going fine until a snake struck my horse. The horse reared crazily and threw me off. I hit my head on a huge stone. I couldn't stop the bleeding, so the next farmhouse I came to I stopped to get assistance. I also hoped to get lodging there. I was in disguise, so I didn't think anyone would suspect me of even being German.

I was still miles away from the area which was reported to be a stronghold of the Underground. This part of the countryside was considered compliant. As a matter of fact, if my information was correct this same household had supplied horses for our officers just a few weeks before. They had thrown in a big fat hog! I still remember the delight with which some of the officers told about the feast they had with roasted pig.

It was almost dawn when I arrived at the house. Instead of finding the horse trader and a hearty welcome, no one was there except a frightened girl. I would estimate her to be about nine or ten years old. I felt I had nothing to fear from such a little child. I had barely made it on foot to the house as my horse ran away when he threw me. I suppose he had gone wild with the pain brought on by the snakebite.

I had no choice but to get some rest and hope her father showed up soon to supply me with a fresh horse. Even if no one else came I could probably find a mount in the barn. First, however, I needed rest. My head was pounding and I had not eaten or drunk anything since my horse ran away with my supplies. I unharnessed my gun and held it in my lap, partly to frighten the girl and make her comply with my wishes. I had come to the conclusion that it was highly suspicious that a family would leave such a young girl alone through the night.

The next part of my report is sketchy; my memory for the next several hours is a blur. The girl brought me a jug of something that could have only been hard liquor of a homemade sort. I was reminded of the stupid movies of American hillbillies. The mixture burned as it went down my throat. At the time I felt it would be helpful to ease the pain in my head. Looking back I may as well have been drinking turpentine. It made me sick and woozy.

I passed out on the floor of that farmhouse. I don't know how long I had been asleep when I felt a blow to my head. It was as if someone had dropped a cannon on my head. The searing pain lasted only seconds. I was out like a light.

When I finally woke up, I was lying in a Blackberry thicket. The fruit smell was strong and further aroused my already intense hunger. The sun was high in the sky. I couldn't move my arms or legs, and soon discovered they were tied with rope.

The child I had thought harmless must've had some help. However, I had seen no one except her. Undoubtedly, she hit me with some solid object, adding to the injury my head had already endured. While I was unconscious, she could've tied my feet and hands. I must believe, however, that she had help getting me from the house to my location amidst the berries. The only other possible alternative I can think of is that the liquor she gave me caused me to forget the events of the next few hours. In the back of my mind, I remember her cooling touch. I know she had bathed my first wound with warm water and stopped the gushing blood. My efforts to do the same had been futile. The continuous bleeding had caused me grave concern. It had occurred to me then that the girl would make a great servant. After my mission, I would consider coming back for her.

Perhaps she could've gotten me on a horse if I had assisted her in walking out the door of that small dwelling. She might have led me to a waiting mount. As I thought about it, I remembered a dream of smelling a horse. The smell topped off the effect of the bad liquor, and I thought I would be sick. Also, I had a vague recollection of bumping along on rough ground and hearing a horse neigh.

I don't know if she intended that I have food; thus left me in the Blackberry thicket purposely. I could not use my hands or feet the way they were so thoroughly tied. However, the scarf that she had placed around my mouth had fallen loose. I scratched up my face terribly in the process, but I could gather blackberries with my teeth and eat my fill of them. The blackberries kept me alive. It was three days before I was found.

The Dutchman continued his disturbing news.

"The spy's report concludes with an explicit description of your Suzette. When this henchman was found by German troops, the Blackberry thicket was beside a cemetery. Most of the markers were quite old, but they copied the surnames on every one that was legible. They took this list of names to the school and cross-referenced with girls who met the Scout's description. They even went back to your farmhouse and found a photograph. She is accused of attempted murder, assault with a deadly weapon and disloyalty to the Third Reich., thus treason. Any one of these means certain death. What's more, this spy is the nephew of a man very high in the pecking order of the Gestapo. There's a bounty on Suzette. It is doubled if she is brought in alive! We must get her across the border immediately. We are making the arrangements for her."

"Never mind, Father, we will all get to America." Suzette did not want to be taken off by strangers to go ahead of her family .

"It isn't safe for you to wait here with the rest of us." Father was insistent. "Your brothers and I can split up and travel in pairs. There are no descriptions out and no photographs of us. Perhaps Jules should go with you, as he helped you with the man. They may secretly know about Jules, but just not be saying."

"If anyone goes with her, it should be Mother. They will both be safe in America. I came up from behind when I hit the man in the head. He cannot possibly know of me. The only thing I regret is not throwing him into the old privy. He would be dead by now and we wouldn't have to worry - not any of us." Jules was shaken.

"It is true that Suzette is too young to travel alone. If one of us does not accompany her, we will have to trust to our friends that we hardly know. If the persons arranging the transport will agree, Mother would be my first choice to go. However, it must be Suzette's decision. Daughter, it is not your choice whether to go ahead or not. You must go! We will give you the choice of who will go with you."

"That is so unfair, Father. How do I know who to choose? I love all of you. Perhaps you are wrong about their not knowing about the rest of us. We left other photographs in our house, not just ones of me. They will be looking for everyone in our family, if for no other reason in the hope that whoever they find will tell on the rest. Why can't we all stay together? That is what I will vote for – togetherness for ever. If we separate now we may never see one another again.."

They all knew she had a good point. Father agreed to talk to the Dutchman. He came back the next evening, and was closeted with Father.

" It is all settled," Father said. "They have a helicopter coming in for Suzette tonight at midnight. She will go directly to England and leave there within 24 hours for Australia. In Australia she will be given a new identity and sent to America. In that way if they trace her from here to England, they will spend years looking in Australia. "

" I don't know how to tell you the next part. Suzette was right in that the separation may be for a very long time. They do not even know the identity they will give Suzette in Australia. It is as yet undecided. The Gestapo have inventive ways of making people talk. It is felt that it's better that none of us know exactly who Suzette will be called or where in the Americas she will go. The Dutchman thinks Québec in Canada, but he is only guessing that because we are French," Father continued.

"There's room in the helicopter for Suzette and one of us. Suzette was right; she shouldn't have to be the one to choose. Everyone put their name in the hat, and I'll draw."

Each of Suzette's brothers took the proffered slips of paper and wrote. Each wrote the name of their mother. For some unknown reason, this is just what Father had expected. Suzette refused to put a name in the hat. She would not choose one of her family over another. She knew that it would be close to a death sentence for the ones not chosen. They wouldn't be going to all this trouble to send a helicopter for her if there was a possibility for the others to leave soon. She had grown quickly in the last few weeks. Her acute mind was on red alert.

Suzette was crying. Georges came to her. He had been the brother she was closest to in so many ways.

"Don't cry little Suzette," he said, "we'll make a game. Every year on your birthday, contact the biggest newspaper in the Canadian capital – Ottawa. How does that sound? Put an ad in the personals asking to buy a horse named Billy Gray. Remember that old song, we made up to sing around the camp fire?"

"O Billy Billy - ole Billy Gray! If you weren't a billy goat, we'd have fun today!"

Suzette couldn't suppress a smile.

"I was four years old. I could write a better song now."

"Billy Gray is perfect," said Jules. "Gay Billy Gray, come play with me today," he sang, remembering the words a tiny Suzette had spun out of the blue. You can leave an address. Better still. Don't newspapers have a procedure to contact an advertiser anonymously? All of us who can will answer back. Somewhere in the answer we'll say, we don't have a horse by that name, but we do have a billy goat. That way you'll know it's us, for sure."

Suzette was somewhat cheered by this game. Deep in her heart she knew it was just that, however, a game. She said goodbye with a sad heart.

Mother was more cheerful, more optimistic, more naive. She has always wanted to visit the Americas. Once they were in Australia they were given options as to where in the Americas to go. They could've chosen Brazil, the Vancouver area of Canada or several places in the US.

"Let's choose New Orleans," Mother had said. "The city is half French. Besides, they have a big tourist industry there. It would be easy for me to get work. We'll find a great French restaurant that will be happy to have my culinary skills!"

Suzette did not care where they went. She was still sad. She could only console herself with the thought that just her being with them might put her father and brothers in more danger. Mother tried to cheer her.

"It's not as if it is your fault. You're not the reason that we moved that day. Remember your father came home to get you, Jules and anything you could grab quickly. We had cast our lot with the French underground months before and done it willingly. We had been discovered knew our time was up. You are the only one that was an innocent in all of this. You did not choose to join. We did not even ask you how you felt about our joining. We decided you were too little! That is what is unfair."

"Your father and brothers and I knew exactly what we were doing. When we took the first step to help our neighbors we sealed our fate. The first people we helped smuggle were the Cohens from right down the road. You must remember Amy Cohen? Georges was always sweet on her. They're happily settled in America now and will be glad to help us if we become desperate. I think we can make it alone though, don't you?"

"We were warned in Australia that the Gestapo has far-reaching arms. I think we should try to make it on our own. Anyway, the Cohens will never have heard of Amber and Alexia Davies. Maybe this war will end and we can all get back together safely. How many different people did you help get away?"

Mother pondered.

"Including the English and American fighter pilots that were shot down, I would say at least one hundred. There were a good many that I am not sure. They got past our area of control, at least. But we didn't always hear if they got back to England.

Jade was addressing Ruby.

"Opal cannot come this afternoon after all," Jade was saying "Olivia fell and broke her tooth playing soccer. Opal has to take her to the dentist right away"

"Oh, I'm sorry to hear that," said Ruby. "I guess you'll just have to meet Opal some other time. Olivia is one of her daughters. Hopefully she'll be OK. Opal makes up the rest of our quilting bee", explained Ruby.

"I had a special treat for Opal. Just last night I finished a big batch of Lavender-Green Kiwi Jam."

"Just pass it over here," Pearl urged. "For once the rest of us will get to try it!"

Jade and Amber were laughing over jams and their favorites of Ruby's fruit and floral concoctions. Really, Crystal wanted a way to excuse herself, but she felt uncomfortable breaking into the conversation. Then Ruby made escape almost impossible.

"Since we're not waiting for Opal, let's sit down and have our tea." Ruby pulled out a chair for Crystal.

"Here sit next to Jade." Ruby suggested. "You'll really love her when you get to know her."

As Crystal looked at the exotic woman she caught her breath. Jade's black hair shone with the luster of a raven's wing. She had wide-set eyes the color of the ocean and skin the color of almonds. Her bone structure was as if chiseled by a master sculptor with high cheek bones and classic nose.

She listened as Jade described their quilting group. Then she began asking Crystal such questions as,

"Have you ever made a quilt? Do you like quilts? What are your favorite patterns? This was like talking in some other language to Crystal. She didn't know a Lone Star pattern from a Log Cabin.

"Well, Ruby will show you some. She has some beauties in her private rooms. They come mostly from the South; made during the Civil War days and before. Also, Amber has the most gorgeous quilts and she can tell you the history of each and every one. Her favorites are quilts that use house patterns. Farmhouse scenes surrounded by pieced houses she makes by the dozens. Mostly wall size quilts. She rotates these for display in the window of her real estate offices. Opal collects antique quilts. She likes traditional patterns done in jewel tones. Pearl is more into art quilts. She loves winter landscapes, but her abstract winter scenes are to die for - especially the kaleidoscope snow flakes!

"And you? What are your favorites, Jade?" Crystal found she really wanted to know.

"Me? I like anything quilted, even clothes. Quilts with ocean scenes I guess are my favorites. I like making lighthouses - you know, beacons for the weary. Each lighthouse has its stories about ships in trouble who are guided into harbor safely. Just don't get me started on ships! The patterns for ships can be dull easy or so intricate even the best quilters have a challenge. Even harder is the Mariner's compass."

Crystal thought as Jade talked about quilts and their pasts, that the women of the guild seemed to have histories of their own. Jade's deep set eyes revealed something more mysterious than just living in a small village and quilting once a week with friends.

Pearl interrupted Crystal's thoughts, explaining all the things Crystal could be involved with during the coming week.

" I will be staying just for tonight, I believe." Crystal confided.

Ruby overheard.

"Please don't go tomorrow. I have a full house of tourists coming this weekend. As I told you my maid ran away and I don't know when she'll be back. I think she's eloping!

"Not only that, I'm completely out of Merry Blackberry Jam. You were so helpful today. I thought surely would be here at least a week or two. I can offer you the rooms you are using, breakfast, plus minimum wage and kitchen privileges. "

"I do need to go shopping," Crystal said. "I lost my suitcase; someone took it a few stations back. I have almost nothing but this maid uniform you gave me and what I was wearing when I came. I also need to find a Laundromat."

"I'll take you shopping right after tea," offered Pearl. "We'll go to my boutique. I'm having a great sale right now; both clothes and shoes. I make the selections myself. I go twice a year to New York City right after the new fashions come out."

"If they're designer clothes I can't really afford them," Crystal replied hesitantly.

"Designer clothes, my foot. They're off the rack, but they're beautifully done ripoffs. Now I'm getting excited to show you. Let's go right away. You can pick from all kinds of styles. I have everything from designer jeans to ball gowns and bathing suits."

"Well, thanks. I would love to go with you." Crystal couldn't remember when she had last chosen her own garments.

Pearl had waited for her at the corner drug store once they finished at the boutique. Then Pearl drove her back to the B& B. Bone weary, Crystal changed to her long granny gown- one of her new purchases. She slept more deeply than she had slept for many years.

Ruby's Jam of the Day

Lavender-Green Kiwi

Ingredients:

8 Kiwi, peeled and sliced 1/8th in thick

1 2/3's cup lime juice

½ cup unsweetened pineapple juice

5 cups sugar

2 three ounce packages Pectin

1 compacted cup lavender blossoms

Procedure:

Make a cool glass of lemonade and sit it by the stove.

Adjust unit on stove to medium heat -NOT medium high; err on low side

Combine juices and sugar in large saucepan, place pan on adjusted unit of stove and   STIR

"

Stir until sugar is dissolved. You may drink lemonade while stirring.

Blow 3 kisses into mixture and remove from stove, adding kiwi and lavender, Return to stove and stir some more until mixture begins to boil. Stir harder and count 60 seconds. 1001, 1002, etc.

Let cool while you take a shower or, if lucky enough to have a pool, go for a swim. Add pectin.   Use the cutest jam jars you can find that actually will work with sealed lids and -well, if you don't know the drill from here, look in the pectin package.

Taste and hope this turned out ok. If too syrupy use on pancakes.

If too thick, jab raisin sized pieces out using two spoons and serve as taffy. (This has the advantage of serving also as a hand-strengthening experience. If you have succeeded in creating taffy, wrap individual pieces in waxed paper. Save for treats on Halloween or in homemade pinata.)

Chapter Four

Island in the Caribbean,

Mid-40's to Mid-60's

The Caribbean island on which Jade was born was an ideal place to live. The sun was bright every morning with a sprinkling of rain usually between dawn and high sunrise. The sunsets and sunrises led to colors in the sky beyond the imagination. The white sandy beaches and crystal-clear azure waters were a paradise. A paradise for tourists and the wealthy, that is! Not so for many natives. Jade's family had few prospects. They were lucky to have one cow. They lived in a hut in the midst of all the splendor. Their hut was on a back street. Jade's parents depended on the tourist industry for their living. Her father was a gardener for a plush resort. Her mother cleaned for the same establishment.

Jade had six brothers and one sister. She and her sister were the most beautiful children in the entire island. From the time they were walking people who saw them would gasp. Before they could count to ten, their father set up a stand on weekends. Here, tourists paid him to take pictures of the children. These pictures were taken against the backdrop of his stand. An illusion had been created by an artistic friend. The stand was made to resemble the front of a wondrous, island restaurant. There appeared to be a thatched roof and a doorway framed with lovely Tahitian carvings. This was just a facade; the carvings were on very thin wood and easy to move on the back of the cow from the hut two blocks away.

Tourists were fascinated by the faces of the girls and came in no small numbers to take their pictures. Some commented on the poor clothing but others were happy because of the contrast it made with the girl's lovely faces. One tourist wandered to another stand along the week-end market place. She returned with an entire bolt of blue batik fabric. "Take this and make the children dresses to wear. I'll be back next week-end and will expect to get photos. The blues in the batik match the azure in their eyes."

The girls' Mother made each a shift dress, making sure they understood it was only for market days. More tourists were attracted as the fabric reflected not only the blue of the children's eyes, but the ocean and sky. Soon the picture taking sessions garnered more money than their regular jobs.

Jade grew up looking into the shining eyes of strangers. She was told to smile and be warm and friendly toward them. Never was she to fear the tourists. She somehow avoided the gangly stage of growing-up. Her Sister had bad teeth and could no longer smile for the cameras of the tourists. It is no wonder that by the time she was 12 Jade was comfortable, almost forward, with strangers. She looked about eight and talked with everyone she met. Her beauty was slow to mature. Tiny for her age, Jade passed for a young child until her sixteenth year. Suddenly, her feminine attributes emerged, then exploded.

Chicago, 1965 - 70

When Jade was eighteen she was absolutely striking - from head to toe. A tourist from Chicago courted her, offering her father money. He claimed they would marry back in the states so his family could attend. He whisked her away with promises of a beautiful wardrobe and a lovely home.

This man she knew as Duke Daniels provided the wardrobe, but had no honorable intentions. He introduced Jade to the world of prostitution. She did live in a lovely home where she had one room - a room dominated by an ornate bed. It was what some people considered the best red-light house in Chicago.

Jade hated this 'work'. She loved the beautiful clothes and the attention she got, but she hated being touched. Most of the men had bad breath or smelled unclean.. She fought back tears for the first day and tried to run away twice. She hardly got to the corner and was put on bread and water for three days as punishment.

Gradually Jade managed to adjust to the situation. An older 'girl' took Jade under her wing. Alice soon taught Jade to take advantage of the situation and to ask for tips in cash. She learned to flirt and to tease. If she behaved in the erotic way that Alice taught her, often the man would be satisfied prematurely. She danced before them, twirling scarfs. She touched herself provocatively. She made suggestive conversation while slowly helping the men undress. The more she perfected these skills, the less real intimacy was needed.

Jade shortly developed special customers -ones who only asked for her. Most of these came to watch her or to listen to her melodious voice as she told her wild stories. If a man shared a fantasy, Jade would spin a tale especially for him.

From her customers Jade heard many languages. She learned words that most girls her age had not even heard of. By the time she was twenty-two, Jade was fluent in English. French, Spanish and Italian. She had come to enjoy her "work", especially when she felt the power she could wield over so many. Her regulars brought her jewels and tipped well. For the next five years, Jade was content.

It was one cold Winter day when Alice said good-bye that Jade became alarmed. Alice was moving to another "house" at the urging of Madam.

"I always knew this would happen." Alice assured Jade. "The clientele is less gentlemanly, but I won't be out on the streets. Madam made it clear from the start that her establishment is for young women only. I've lasted longer than most; I'm getting close to forty." As Jade looked at the women who were in their late 20s, she began to see that they were no longer the most desired of the girls. She saw the hard look in her eyes, their sagging skin, their need to rest more and more. What will happen to them when they're in their 40s Jade wondered.

"Well, it's not happening to me!"

Jade began hiding a portion of her tips from Madam with the help of her most steadfast customer, whom she called Sean. It was accumulating in a safe deposit box..Every two weeks Sean bribed Madam to take Jade out, supposedly to entertain his visiting customers. Jade was supposed to be giving Madame a cut of the tips and spending the rest on clothes, perfumes and makeup. She set aside a little to report and share. But Jade's beauty was such that she needed no makeup. Her complexion was clear and the shade of warmed butter. Her cheeks were like ripe, softly mellowing peaches.

When Jade reached twenty-four, she ran away. Sean helped her once more. He loved her, she knew; but he had a wife and four children. Helping her get away to a new life was for him a kind of penance. He would miss her incredibly; but he would make the sacrifice and go to confession one last time.

Jade emptied her safety deposit box and took a taxi to the largest mall in the City. She had left her "work" clothes at Madam's, but had taken her jewelry. At the best shop in the mall she bought an entire wardrobe. She had heard one of her regulars talk about the cruises he had taken. Several of his fantasies had a setting at sea. Thus, she knew where she was going. She would pose as an independent woman of means and find a widower who would really take care of her and who would not demand that she sleep with other men.

Wise of the ways of the world now, Jade knew she could do this. She had manipulated many of her customers, flattering and coddling them so they became desperate to be with her. They were spending more than they should have dared, risking bankruptcy . Some wanted to come twice a week and would have come more except for Madam. Her policy allowed twice a week as the most with one "courtesan". Some wanted Jade to go away with them. Some had asked her to live in an apartment that he paid for and be his exclusively. Jade knew from all of these experiences that she could make a man care for her deeply. She could use her beauty and her skills in the boudoir to make sure that he was happy. But she wanted more. She wanted no wife or children making him feel ashamed or threatening her future.

Jade also knew the ways of protecting herself from conceiving a child. If she ever had children it would be with a man who she could respect. That man she was more likely to find on a cruise ship than in a brothel.

At Sea, 1966

The day after leaving Sean, Jade found a cruise ship that still had an empty cabin. She booked it immediately. She boarded proudly, showing off her newly purchased, unreasonably expensive luggage. They contained her new wardrobe - gowns and casual clothing chose to impress. She had dressed in white linen slacks and a sling halter made of raw silk. The jacket she carried over her shoulder was made of Cashmere and the same azure as her eyes.

Jade found that she was very popular on board. There were few men who were not accompanied by other women, however, none of these few were immune to her beauty. They made special efforts to visit with her and to dance with her in the evening. These men were young and viral and would have easily come to Jade's cabin secretly. She wanted none of that.

Jade discouraged even a hint that she was anything more than a woman of outstanding virtue. She quickly concluded that the unattached men were playing the same game as she. They were looking for lonely, rich companions.

There were two mature women in their 60s or 70s - Jade wasn't sure which. They were traveling together, sharing a cabin. These women took Jade under their wings. It was from them that she began to learn manners. Jade had never been exposed to the finer points of how to act in polite society. This was her first experience with proper behavior at the dinner table. She knew nothing of pouring tea and choosing the correct spoon. These two ladies had quickly seen through Jade's attempt at playing a lady. They at first were amusing themselves in the game of seeing how subtle they could be in their efforts to correct her. Jade's charm and good-natured receipt of their council soon won them over. Jade became their project..

These mentors, Ethel and Elinor, were thought to be sisters. As the two weeks rushed by, Jade began to suspect something quite different. She felt these ladies were very much in love with each other. Furthermore Jade was convinced they had been so for many years. They were not sisters but they were soulmates. The two were as one.

Whether this was expressed physically, Jade did not know or care. They were totally committed to one another in a way that was almost sacred. Jade wanted that kind of committed relationship more than she wanted to breathe.

When the cruise was nearing the end Ethel and Elinor invited Jade to spend time with them at their home in the Hamptons. Jade had made up some story about her mother just dying before she took the cruise. She was so filled with grief she had to get away from home. They insisted that if she came and stayed with them a few weeks that could help put her loss in perspective. Her sorrow would still be there, but she must decide what she wanted to do next in life. Jade's story that she had not worked before but had stayed home to take care of her ailing mother made them all the more sympathetic.

Eastern USA, 1966 -70

So Jade had a sort of coming-out experience in the Hamptons. Here she found dozens of men of means who were ready for a trophy wife. Some were divorced, some widows, - all rich and indulgent of a beautiful young woman.

Jade stayed with the two women for three months. During that time she carefully reviewed the attributes of the men that were available. In the whole three months she could not find one that did not have too much baggage to be a good selection. Also, even though they fawned over her, most of the men were in a hurry for a physical relationship. What they offered did not come close to the kind of intimacy Ethel and Elinor had with one another. Hating to keep depending on the two women for lodging and food, Jade thought that she would have go back to her funds and see if there was enough to book another cruise. Perhaps she'd have better luck this time.

"Oh, stay one more week-end," Elinor pleaded. "There's a lovely party this coming Saturday. We're shopping for new gowns tomorrow. Come with us to the City. It'll be more fun with three."

"Well, okay I'll stay one more weekend," Jade thought. She had little hope that the Saturday night gathering would bring her the kind of future life she had been planning. However, fate smiled on her. The tall, white-haired man caught her eye immediately. He was strikingly handsome - old enough to be her father perhaps, but in great physical shape. He was talking tennis when he saw her and stopped in mid-sentence. She saw right away that his interest was more than casual; more than just hoping for a lucky night or two.

Richard Grason had been traveling on business when he stopped to visit friends in the Hamptons.

"Just the weekend," he agreed to their genuine plea for him to prolong his visit. Grason worked for a senator in Washington, DC and had come to Virginia to confer with another lawyer. He needed a weekend off and visiting his old friends was a plus.

When Grason's eyes fell on Jade he thought of a dream that he had once. He had dreamed that an angel had come to him to make his life happier in his old age. This man had lived through deep sorrows. He had been widowed twice and had been left childless each time. There had been a couple of babies stillborn by his first wife before she died very young of pancreatic cancer. Heart broken he was reluctant to seek the company of women.

With the second wife he had taken the chance. He had met her at the height of his loneliness. This woman was younger than he was and very reckless. She loved to drive fast, to drink heavily and to party late. The marriage lasted only two years when he caught her in a compromising position   with her masseuse. He had begun divorce proceedings when she took his Rolls for a fatal drive. The coroner said she had been going at speeds of 110 when she left the road and went airborne. The car flipped over twice before landing at the bottom of a deep ravine. He estimated that her death was instantaneous.

That was twelve years ago and Grason had never again thought of marriage, outside of the dream. But one look at Jade told him that if he were a younger man he'd think of it now. When the gathering moved from the cocktail area into the dining hall, Jade just happened to be at Grason's side. The host had announced open seating.

She looked up at him with her deep azure eyes.

" I think I have lost the two ladies I was with. Are you sitting with someone?" she asked

"I am now," he said gallantly and ushered her to a table where his friends were seated with another couple.

"May I introduce you to my new friend, ah —"

" Jade,"   she said " Jade Dobson. I'm here visiting Ethel and Elinor Whitehall."

Gibson prolonged his stay in the Hamptons and took Jade for a long ride the next day. They discussed politics, religion and all the things that people aren't supposed to discuss when they first meet each other. Grason found in this woman an intelligent and interesting conversationalist. She not only was beautiful and desirable but she could hold up her end of any topic he selected. Certainly she was well read, even though not well-traveled   He was amazed at how few places she had been and wanted to show her the world.

Jade managed to spin the story she'd told so often since on the cruise ship. She had lived with an invalid mother. Once her mother died she discovered there were liens against the house. Losing her home she garnered what she could and booked a cruise. She'd never forget her mother's death and the hard illness that could only have ended in sadness.

Since Jade had practiced this story so much it came out naturally. Jade was almost believing it herself. Richard Grason asked Jade how she would feel about coming to Washington, DC and getting an apartment nearby. He said that he could help her look for work. Jade sounded skeptical saying that the only work she had done had been caring for her mother. Perhaps that would qualify her for work in a home for old people. Grason knew of a perfect situation. He had a friend who had just recently been diagnosed with terminal cancer. The condition was deemed inoperable and sadly the man was going downhill fast. He wanted to remain in his home, but needed a live-in companion to make this feasible. Currently he was paying three shifts of nurses, plus double-time for week-end care. Grason's friend wanted someone to read to him and to help him enjoy these last days of his life to the extent possible.

Jade had nothing better to do, any way. Of course she didn't tell Grason that. So far he had not approached the question of sexual favors. He treated her with respect and great warmth.

The next morning she boarded his private plane, amazed at its lush interior. Jade had never flown except the one time from the Caribbean Island to Chicago. This had been in a crowded coach where she was squeezed in between the man taking her 'home' and some stranger who smelled of rum.

Upon reaching the Washington, DC area, Grason arranged for a hotel suite for Jade. She feared immediately that he was going to expect special favors. Instead he arranged for a driver to take her to visit his friend.

"I'll meet you there, if that's all right. Jamison will be expecting you at 10:30 A.M. Some of the nurses find him grumpy, but if you can get past that I feel sure you'll get along."

Right away Jade liked this man. Jamison was in his 80s and still jolly with an ironic sense of humor. Instead of an interview, he asked her to read from Dickens and she did so. Although she had read every book in Madam's small library and many brought to her by her John's, she's never read Dickens before. She started with a passage that Jamison requested . Two hours later her voice was just about spent. She hadn't even noticed when Grason had arrived. She heard a chair scrape, and looked up as he was walking toward the door. He left with a wave.

The next day Jamison's lawyer came to talk to her in the hotel dining room. The lawyer was a middle-aged woman who seem friendly and kind. She asked Jade very few questions. She explained to Jade that Jamison wanted her to live in his house, but that she would have separate rooms and even her own small kitchen. An apartment had been added to the house long ago for a relative. She would need to check on Jamison every few hours and read to him late afternoons and after the dinner hour. He would have a nurse in for his baths and other necessities every morning. Three days a week a physical therapist would be there from 1-3 pm to keep the invalid as mobile as possible. Old friends had scheduled visits for the 4 days there was no physical therapy. Thus, she would be free every morning and until three in the afternoon. His meals would be delivered as would her breakfast and dinner. She would be required to be there seven days each week, unless she called the lawyer at least 48 hrs ahead so that respite care could be arranged.

Thus, for the next 18 months Jade lived in a beautiful house. She took her meals alone usually, but with Jamison when he felt like company. He ate very little and talked even less. However they spent every afternoon and most evenings with Jade reading to him from one of the classics. Often, he would interrupt Jade to recite a portion from memory in his hoarse whisper.

She asked if he would like to have her read poetry and he sent out to a local bookstore and asked for volumes of Tennyson, Donne, and Browning. Exhausting those they chose Keats, Longfellow and Poe. As his time became shorter Jade spent more and more time with Jamison. She bathed his fevered brow, soothed his bed-worn back with lotions, held his glass so he could better sip from it - even assisting with his bed pan though he had shied away from this for many weeks.

One day he motioned Jade close so she could hear him.

"My dear, it is worth dying to have met you. You have taken the loneliness out of my life. I had been like a hermit since my wife passed on. My books and my pipe and a few friends were my lot."

"Jade, it is time now to call Hospice. Your kind assistance is more than I would have asked of you. Just being here was all I expected. If you want you may leave now. There will be no happy days ahead for me. I'm close to the end. They tell me I will have times when I will be incoherent. I'll have to take more and more morphine for the pain. Already it has become almost unbearable. You can choose whether to leave or to go. You are too young to have to face the agonies of death."

"I did not come here to desert you. I came here to see you through until you go to a more glorious place than this. If you will let me stay, I'll do whatever the doctor tells me will work best. You can have hospice nurses on occasion and even daily if you need them. They can instruct me how to help you when they are not here."

Gratefully Jamison took her hand and kissed it formally.

"Thank you, Jade. That is exactly what I hoped you would say."

Meanwhile, Grason came frequently - at least twice a week. He spent the evening hours talking with his old friend or listening while Jade read. When Jamison grew tired Grason took over the bedtime rituals. Afterward, Grason and Jade spent the next hour to an hour and a half talking. The discussed everything from Jamison's deterioration to the Washington Redskins, the political campaign coming up soon, or the stock market's variability. Whatever they talked about was less important than the fact that they were growing closer to each other. Jade had so much respect and admiration for Grason that she was ashamed of her ploy and her charade. She almost told him her background but bit her tongue. She remembered too well a woman who had befriended her on her arrival in Chicago. She had disappeared a few weeks after Jade had come. One morning Jade saw her at the kitchen door. She was shallow faced and bone thin. Madam had thrown her out without a qualm. Jade knew Madam only cared about her "girls" if they were putting money in her pocket. Jade was determined that she would never be thrown out to the mercy of the streets.

True, Jade had family back in the island. She could go to them but what kind of life would that be. If she told Grason of her real-life she would have to talk about her family and how they took advantage of the way the children looked. Although Jade had enjoyed the attention of the tourists, many today would fault the parents. Often the tourists touched the girls, sometimes inappropriately, on the pretense of posing them to get the 'best light'. Jade had hated the cheek and arm pinchers and being 'positioned' with exploring hands on her rear. She hated to identify herself with this life of rags and scant meals. She'd worked so hard to remove the memories of this family. She wanted no part of trying to explain it to another human being. Even though she felt shame in lying, she could never tell.

By the time they moved Jamison to a hospital bed, he only had a day left. His will included a generous stipend for Jade; one that would set her free to do whatever she wanted for the rest of her life. Most of his money he had given to charities and some to a distant cousin. Jade could hardly believe the bequest he left her.

Encouraged by Grason, Jade rented an apartment near the house where she had been staying. She found work at home doing translations for members of the Senate. The referrals from Grason were invaluable. Over the next months Jade and Grason's friendship ripened. He had never once pushed for a physical relationships. Jade began to fear he was impotent or that he had guessed her past and feared a disease.

Jade had tears in her eyes the night he proposed on one knee with the ring in his right-hand and his left holding her's. Once engaged they began to spend nights together and found that their bodies were as compatible as their minds. Jade felt a new sensation. Her experience with people who she hardly knew had not prepared her for the same act when it was truly an expression of mutual love. The difference was like night and day; like precious as opposed to repugnant; like arousing and meaningful as opposed to 'just get it over with".

The respect that Grason gave to her body entranced Jade. His gentle touch, the time and care he spent making her fulfilled led her to virtually worship him. He had her heart, her mind and her body for the rest of her life.

Fox Willow, USA, 1970 - 80

-54-

They were married in the spring and the elections the next fall unseated the senator that employed Grason. He asked if she would be satisfied living in a small town. This is when they returned to his hometown of Fox Willow. He had a house there that he took her to visit. He offered to sell it and get a different one more to her liking or even to build. However, she immediately fell in love with the Cape Cod. It was nestled on two acres of land on the edge of the small town. The large kitchen had been designed by a gourmet enthusiast. The center island was as large as many a closet. A rectangular copper rack above the island held a myriad of pots and speciality cookware. An alcove in one corner sported a built-in breakfast nook.

"I may never leave this room," Jade said, breathlessly.

Gibson laughed.

"Maybe I should show you the bedrooms," he replied with a grin. "We'll have fun refurbishing them."

Grason practiced law for a few years in Fox Willow; then retired from his law career. He then spent most of his time with his computer writing memoirs or doing genealogical work on his family. He offered to research Jade's family. She encouraged him to finish with his family first before he got into the complicated process of hers. She hoped with all her heart that she could put him off doing this forever because, if not, she would have to make up her family.

Meanwhile, the year after they had come to Fox Willow, little Jimmy had been born. Their hearts were so filled with joy in this baby, Jade ceased to worry about the past and her shame. She knew that nothing mattered now more than the present and the future. They spent hours playing with the baby from the time he was born. Grason and his son were inseparable until Jimmy was old enough for school. Even then,

Grason fretted and thought of maybe home schooling the boy. Jade thought perhaps she should have had a second child because she was afraid he was spoiling this one. But a second child had not come and she thanked her lucky stars for this man and for the one boy whom she so dearly loved.

Chapter Five

Foxy Blues

Waking early, Crystal emptied the bags from Hudson Drug Store. She chose the carton of hair dye and got busy. Now, dressed in jeans with a relaxed fit and a black T, Crystal looked years younger. She was trim but demure. She had cut off 10 inches of hair and darkened the color to a rich brown. The cut she had devised herself – a side part with a tress on the left that almost covered her face. A page boy effect on the right and a neat point going to the center of her neck in back completed the look.

Crystal felt great. She still needed shoes – the heels she had left with would be replaced by sneakers at her first opportunity.

Crystal reviewed her new wardrobe. A second pair of jeans, this one black. One grey tweed jacket; one ensemble consisting of a mid-calf length yoked skirt with matching slacks and vest. This outfit was complemented by a light gray cotton shirt with a button front and pleats to either side of the buttons. She completed her purchases with two sensible bras and three pairs of cotton panties.

A bell sounded somewhere in the house. It must be time for breakfast. Crystal changed back to her maid uniform and slipped her feet into her hated heels. Ruby met her as she entered the kitchen.

"Can I help you serve?" Crystal asked.

"No, why don't you join the guests for breakfast?"

"I'd really rather not," said Crystal.

Noticing Crystal's hair color had changed , Ruby smiled

inwardly. She had felt that something was amiss when she saw Crystal traveling with only a light tote bag. She could understand if someone wanted to keep a low profile. Goodness knows it had been true for her for long enough.

"Then have breakfast in the kitchen with me." Ruby offered. "Occasionally I sit out with the guests, but there are plenty of people there today."

"The senatorial candidate and his wife aren't very sociable, are they?" Glancing in the dining room en route to the kitchen, Crystal noticed the couple had chosen a small table in the far corner.

"No, you'd think he'd be trying for votes every chance. I heard from two of our permanent guests, Gilda and Lisa, that his talk didn't go over too well. They called him arrogant."

Ruby sat down and Crystal joined her. They had a marvelous meal consisting of quiche, blueberry muffins and scones served with a delicious Blueberry Jam. This was followed by hot baked apples with the choice of milk or cream on top. Coffee and tea were freely available.

Two young girls high school age were doing the serving in the main breakfast room. Ruby left the kitchen two or three times just to check on her guests and to chat briefly. This was great for Crystal, as she preferred to be alone with her thoughts.

Crystal felt she might stay on in Fox Willow for a while. The friendliness of the women and Ruby's obvious need for help were the deciding factors. Crystal had planned to get lost in a large city but maybe a small town was even better. Greg could think of her choosing a city to hide in. He never would he think of her being a part of a 'one horse town'. In his arrogance he scarcely thought such places as Fox Willow existed. She could rest here and even earn money. Rather than spending her ill begotten funds she would put them away for when she really needed them most. She would live on what she could earn for the next two or three weeks at least.

"I need to drive over to a mall - it's in Jefferson City, about 35 miles from here. Would you like to come along?" Ruby asked.

"I'd love to if you're not going right away. I promised the owner of this establishment that I would fill in as ardent housekeeper."

Ruby laughed.

"Just what I wanted to hear. I was thinking that together we can get the rooms done before noon and stop for lunch on the way. There's a lovely little café just this side of Jeff City that has a great French cook. Amber loves the place."

Once at the mall Crystal found sneakers plus low-heeled sandals. She also purchased a sketch pad, pencils and a journal.

"You seem to have been lucky to find what you need here," Ruby said when they met at a large fabric store. "It's a pretty good mall. Some people in Fox Willow complain that we don't have our own."

"Most people who live in cities have a longer drive to a mall than you have," Crystal laughed. "Fox Willow is such a neat name. I've been wondering about it's origins."

"That's a good story for our drive home," Ruby suggested.

****

"Have you noticed those small hedges that I use around the herb garden and the rose garden? Those are the blue fox willow. Before you could call this anything except farmland for a few pioneers, erosion was a major problem, especially in the Spring. All the good loam had a tendency to wash downhill to the lake. One farmer went on a search in the bog lands and around them and found these shrubs growing madly.

He dug up all he could get on his wagon and planted them on his acreage. The effect was so significant that the man gave up farming. He grew and sold these shrubs which he called 'Foxy Blues'.

"A professor at the state agricultural school heard about their effectiveness for erosion control and came to visit. He identified the plants as Salix brachycarpa or 'Blue Fox' - so the old pioneer had really known what he was talking about."

"Did he say why the colorful name?"

"The new growth is always covered with fine, soft hairs. Next Spring you can feel it - to touch it's something like a pussy willow. The leaves are a bluish green as you can see now. In the fall the colors will be brilliant. Anyway, except for the erosion control, the town probably would never have thrived. Fox Willow was a natural choice for a name, since 'Foxy Blues' was an exclusive or so the fellow claimed."

Ruby was pulling the car into a driveway outside of town. A small shop with a welcome sign had been created by converting the garage.

"I want you to see some of the things people around here are making with willow branches - not just the Blue Fox variety, either."

Inside the shop Crystal admired a beautiful display of intricately woven baskets. She was even more delighted to see the sculpture created with dried willow stems. There were dolls, lamp bases, mobiles, and numerous other clever objects. Best of all Crystal admired the slender necked swans.

"Everything but foxes," Crystal remarked. "Do the sculptors in the park have a story, too?"

"Doesn't everything?" asked Ruby, pensively.

Ruby's Jam of the Day
Merry Blackberry

First of all, you need blackberries. Lots and lots of blackberries. The more blackberries you have the more jam you can make. If you don't have blackberries in your yard, join me and the majority of jam makers. We must search for them.

The best way to find blackberries uncontaminated with insecticides is to find a bear. Bear's love blackberries and they won't eat sprayed berries. When you find the bear, follow him until he leads you to his secret berry patch. Climb a nearby tree and wait. When the bear has eaten and ambles away, it is safe to come down and pick berries.

Hopefully you brought a very large pail.

Go home and wash the berries. Try not to eat anymore! Eating before washing probably means you ate an inch worm or two. If on a diet, count 1 protein consumed.

Weigh berries or just measure. For every cup of berries you need a cup of sugar. Put berries and sugar in large pot and cook with liquor described below.

A day or more earlier wash and snip some rosemary leaves from your garden; or 'borrow' from a neighbor if you've been too busy looking for bears to tend a garden.

For about 7 cups of berries I would use 3tbs. Rosemary. Boil in a small amount of water - just enough to coat bottom of pan and let sit off heat as soon as it has boiled. Since I would do this before I have found berries, I just make enough merry liquor for the number of jelly jars I have available. Any extra blackberries I can eat plain. Refrigerate liquor as it may take several days to track the bear. You can also freeze this for a luckier day in case you came away from the thicket with more scratches than berries.

Cheater's way: don't tell. (By the way, I would never do this, but some people just don't like to be around bears.)

Prepare liquor as described. Buy large jars blackberry jam at grocery. Remove from jars and measure portions to fit your loveliest jars. For each jar, stir in 1/3 teaspoon liquor. Seal jars the safe way or keep frozen til used.

Chapter Six

Home Enough for Me

Fox Willow, USA, 1980-1988

One month after arriving in Fox Hollow Crystal reviewed her finances. She had not needed to use one penny of her ill-begotten funds since her clothes buying spree the first two days. Not that she was concerned about cash flow. Crystal had planned her "run" carefully. She had saved three letters from credit card companies, offering cash using enclosed forms. Two days before she left, she had cashed all three for $2500 each. On the day she left, Crystal had opened Greg's safe. Not that he had ever given her the combination. For years she had secretly rummaged through papers in his "Library". She dared to do this only when he was out of town as he had forbidden her to enter the door. Once she found the combination she searched through the safe to become familiar with its contents. She took nothing, making sure everything was returned to exactly the place she had found it.

Every three months she repeated this action being sure to only do this when Greg was out of town. He had a lackey who watched her as she left the building, but fortunately he did not have cameras or any methods set up to watch her inside.

Six weeks ago Crystal had hit pay dirt. Something new was in the safe: tapes – video tapes! Once she watched them Crystal was quite sure of their value to her. Wisely she made copies, returning the originals. She packaged the copies in a bubble envelope and mailed them in the slot on the ground floor of their plush apartment building.

They were addressed to General Delivery, Daytona, Florida, Attention Elizabeth Powers. Ms. Powers had been her ninth grade English teacher. It was not a name Greg would know or guess. She had researched Post Office policy once when she was a freshman in college. If it was still the same policy, and she hoped it was, they would hold the mail for her for 12 months.

On the day she left, she went back to the house safe. Usually there were stacks of hundred dollar bills: each stack containing $2000. Thankfully, this day was no exception. Crystal took ten of the stacks, replacing all but the top and the bottom bill in the stack with newspaper and returning the altered stacks in the back of the safe behind the other piles of money. She hoped it would be some time before Greg would miss it.

Her first bus stop had been Datona Beach, Florida.

As the days passed Ruby became dependent on Crystal's assistance. Crystal was taking care of reservations now as well as helping with the cleaning. She soon noticed that Ruby was turning away people for the fall season. As Autumn wielded it's magic paintbrush, more and more travelers wanted to come to revel in the beauty.

"There's a mayor shortage of rooms," said Crystal. "I think you need the room I'm using more than you need my help. You can hire someone else to clean that doesn't need to live here."

"I've been putting off looking hoping you would stay or Fran would come back. You're right I could use the room," said Ruby, "But I don't want to lose you. There is an alternative. Amber suggested that you move in with her. She says that her house is so empty since her husband died, she feels like she's been relegated to a museum. You can share her house as long as you wish. Also, you can come here and work as long as you agree. Having you take care of reservations and accounting is a Godsend. If you can figure the taxes for me, that will be even better. I want more time with my guests and more time to make jam and to try new recipes for my muffins. I just have to get three days together to make more Natty Orange Marmalade."

Crystal had never thought of staying one place for more than a few weeks. This small village seemed a safe place; Greg would look for her in cities. She was sure of this! He didn't even think small towns actually existed except as suburbs for commuters. Also, she had work without having to show identification. Payment was in cash or in the barter system.

So it was arranged. Amber was delighted to have Crystal move in with her. Her loneliness since her husband's death had been almost unbearable. Another plus was having someone in the house when she took week-long trips to see her Grandchildren. If the house looked empty she was afraid of thieves. She could bear the loss of replaceable items like the TV - even jewelry. If they should find her old treasured pictures of her family in France - well Amber couldn't take such a lost. She had only two photographs; well hidden, but still ---

Crystal had a knack for bookkeeping and soon was doing Pearl's accounting for the boutique. Her years as a high school math teacher had been good ones before she had the misfortune to meet Greg.

Months sped by, stacking up like alphabet blocks - months growing into years. Crystal begin to wonder if Greg had even looked for her, after all. Perhaps the disdain with which he obviously regarded her led him to believe that she would return on her own, more docile than ever. She had felt from the first day she planned her run that he would find her eventually. She was gambling that her life between her run and her return would be so much better that his punishments would be worth it. To be alive and away from him even a few weeks had been worth the world to Crystal.

Her time in Fox Willow was beyond all she had hoped to find. Hidden from his outlandish demands, she was thankful for each and every day of every week. She could breathe and she could dress as she pleased. She could eat when she wanted to eat. If she wanted to be a little chubby around the belly, it was her belly. There were a few unmarried men her age and older in Fox Willow that looked at her as if a little flesh on her once poking bones was a good thing. She actually dated once or twice, even though she never wanted to be committed to a man again.

Crystal had opened a safety deposit box in the local bank. Most of the money that she had taken when she left Greg was there, yet untouched. So were the tapes that she had retrieved. Crystal had given information about the name on the account to Ruby and Amber. She told them nothing else of why she was there, or what she had left behind. No one asked and she offered nothing. She felt she was a teenager again, with two or three Mothers. She felt hidden in a loving den of thieves where secrets were held dear. A den where everyone needs each of the others. Where each has a secret that each guarded faithfully. No one knew the secret of any other; no one dared to ask for, in return, they might be expected to tell their own.

The six women called themselves the Queen Bees. They met weekly as many quilting bees do to sew charity quilts for children. No child under twelve ever left the nearby Children's wing of the Community Hospital without a quilt to comfort them. The quilts brightened up the hospital rooms of children with severe illnesses who had to remain for weeks and months at a time in this the sterile environment. In addition, the Queen Bees made sure each child had a quilt to cuddle with them and to take home, even if they were only hospitalized for a few days.

The ladies took turns visiting the hospital in pairs, leaving quilts in their wake as they went from room to room. They read books or told stories, often stories related to the quilts they brought with them. Crystal wasn't very good at piecework , but she was really great at making up stories. She soon had a story for every quilt that the Bees had ever made.

In one story a woman's churn was broken and she couldn't make butter for her family. Instead she spread cream on her husband's toast - thick cream straight from the cow's daily milking. When her husband objected, the woman insisted it was butter: that he needed new glasses. The children laughed at the woman's joke.

The Ohio Star block elicited a story of a time the stars were all in the heavens and none on the quilts. Bed covers were plain and somber, like the faces of children kept after school. Around harvest season, according to the story, you can see the stars at midday if you look carefully just about mid-afternoon. There was but one catch. As you looked up at the sky you had to sing out, "O HI O".

"You mean 'Hi O Silver' ?" Many children would shout!

"Oh, that would never work," Crystal insisted. "It has to be "O HI O". If you sang this just right at just the correct time of day, a star would fall from the sky and land right in your lap! When you had enough of them, they would pop right on that plain old blanket and make a beautiful quilt.

"And if you don't believe it, just look at your new quilt," she would end.

Summer nights when the stars are out and when you are outside; if the weather is warm, if the wind is blowing, think of the lovely Summer Wind. This blew an idea right down from the heavens. A young girl caught this idea and drew it quickly in the dirt. She called her Grandmother to come and look! The Grandmother had poor eyesight and could hardly even see her own feet looking down in the night. The child described the drawing to her Grandmother, careful to put in the details. Two nights later her Grandmother presented her with a small quilt; the blocks have been called "Summer Wind" to this day.

Since the Log Cabin was the Queen Bee's choice for their signature quilt, Crystal refused to make up a story for it. Instead, she asked the children to make up stories. They thought of Abe Lincoln, of Daniel Boone, and of pioneers when she said "Log Cabin . Their stories spun out like the threads on a spinning wheel.

Ruby's favorite pattern to make for the children was Sunshine and Shadow. She preferred to do it in yellows and deep blues. Sometimes, however, she used black and bright red. These colors delighted the children, but saddened Crystal. She saw Ruby's sunshine as blood red and her shadow as dark and foreboding.

Pearl, on the other hand, loved any and all butterfly patterns, as well almost as her winter landscapes.

"Butterflies are happier for children," she contended.

She had a great variety of patterns. Pieced butterfly patterns, outline patterns for quilting when the tops were all layered and basted, and close to a hundred applique butterflies. She preferred the old-fashioned applique butterflies which were outlined in the button stitch.

Pearl estimated that they had made ninety small butterfly quilts just since Crystal had come. They began sewing about ten in the morning and continued until about one. Then the local diner would bring them sandwiches . As soon as they ate they would go back to their quilting until their fingers were sore. They always said their farewells with happy hearts. Always for many years. Years that spun cobwebs in their memories and left them with a sense of carefree indifference to the dangers that had once so evoked fear at the very memories.

Ruby's Jam of the Day

Natty Orange Marmalade

This recipe combines the spicy, nutty flavor of Nasturtiums to the tart taste of the oranges. Some children find it a little on the spicy side. On one hand this is good. When children are among your guests, be sure you are seated where you can see their faces when they taste this marmalade. Some stick out their tongues. Others wrinkle their noses. Don't sit too near the children as the little ones tend to spit out the marmalade, and some can spit far. I think they must practice this at home. At any rate it is amusing to watch their reactions.

A disadvantage: It takes three consecutive days to make this marmalade. No, you don't have to stir continually for all three days.

Ingredients:

For every 6 pints of marmalade you need:

4 oranges

2 lemons

water and sugar handy to measure later.

2 cups loose flower petals of nasturtiums.

Procedure:

Slice the oranges and lemons very thin. Do not peel but remove all seeds. Measure and add 3 cups cold water for every cup of fruit.

Let this mixture stand for 24 hours.

Day 2. Bring mixture that has been standing to a boil and boil for 20 mins. Let stand another 24 hours.

Day 3. Measure 3 cups of boiled mixture into smaller saucepan, adding equal amount of sugar.

Be modern today. Use a candy thermometer. Boil until this marvelous device reads 'jelly' remove from heat, skim and stir. Repeat with another 3 cup batch for a delicate marmalade. Place in jars with 2 or 3 flower petals.

Ruby

Chapter Seven

Needles and Threads

"Now that you've looked at all of the quilts, house by house, are you ready to join us?" asked Crystal.

"Oh, yes!" Amber chimed in. "We'll officially crown you a Queen Bee."

"I'll plan the ceremony," offered Gilda.

"Why aren't you a Queen Bee?" Asked Crystal.

"Yes," said Jade. "Why aren't you two with the program? Why are you holding out?"

"We just have other fish to fry," said Lisa. "We would have to miss every other meeting, or else stop playing bridge! Bridge is where we find out all the info of things going on around Fox Hollow. We are thinking of forming our own Bee. We could be called the Busybody Bees."

The women all laughed.

"Two bees in town -- pretty soon we'll have enough to qualify as a Guild."

"Why Busybody Bee, please?" Crystal asked.

Everyone looked at someone else. Finally, Lisa spoke.

Behind our backs that's what people call us. We're always going around town minding everyone else's business."

"To the betterment of the community, I might add." Pearl said. "Just as soon as someone is sick, for example, they pass the word around. The drugstores say these two keep them solvent in the get well card business alone."

"Yes," laughed Ruby. "Even a cold or a bit of indigestion qualifies."

"With those ailments people pick funny cards. A bunch of laughs can keep indigestion from becoming heart problems," argued Gilda. "Besides, that's not the only service we do. We ought to charge for our grapevine system."

"Oh, and how does that work?" Asked Crystal.

"Go ahead," said Opal. "Tell about the time you and went to Myrtle Thompson's for tea. Myrtle complained about her next neighbor's son, Little Tommy. She said he was practicing his violin every day during her nap time."

"Lisa marched right over and asked him if he could practice in his basement." Amber was laughing as she continued the story.

"Yes, and I got in trouble with Tommy's father," Lisa chimed in. "He said he basement was damp and reminded me that Tommy has asthma. I really felt lousy. "

"That's when Tommy suggested that he only had after school to practice, especially on the nights he had Scouts." Gilda added. "So the ever resourceful Lisa marched right back over to Myrtle's. Lisa strongly suggested that Myrtle did not need a nap that late in the afternoon. Myrtle was indignant!"

"Well, the outcome wasn't so bad. When the word got around, every bridge club in town was asking Myrtle to substitute. They especially called if they played in the afternoon during Tommy's practice time. Pretty soon Myrtle didn't want to nap at all, she was having so much fun!"

Crystal was delighted to be asked to join the Queen Bees

officially. She had been all thumbs when she first started quilting. Thankfully Gilda had taken her under her wing. When Gilda explained that you use certain kind of needles for quilting, Crystal was all ears. She had never heard of a between needle before, nor of the straw needle used for applique.

"Quilting is a rocking motion," Gilda explained. "If you don't rock the needle you'll never get all the little stitches close together. The more you can rock the better."

"Why such small needles?" Crystal asked.

"Most think it's about control. If you have too large a needle it might be unwieldy or be too thick to pick up small stitches."

Crystal picked up two of the needles.

"The long thin one is for needle turn applique." Gilda explained. "For quilting, use one of the larger betweens to start."

"Threads are just as important," Gilda continued. " It will be hard to thread your small needle if you use many of these threads. Most of these are used in sewing machines when piecing. Notice the hand quilting thread is a little thicker, and a little stiffer. Not only will it go through the eye of the needle easier, it is much better for quilting three layers, because of the strength."

Once the needle was threaded, Gilda taught Crystal how to make what she called a quilter's knot. This would be easy to pull through the two layers of the quilt and not show on top or bottom of the quilt.

By the second week Crystal got the idea.

"Look at me, I'm rocking!"

"It's the sugar in that blackberry jam! Gives you that added burst to rock away." Jade laughed.

"She was learning to quilt to a rock 'n roll song." Ruby burst out in her best Lily voice. "Let's put on some music for a while."

Later, over tea, someone mentioned the fox sculptures.

"I still would like to hear their story," Crystal said.

"Amber tells it best," came a chorus of replies. Amber went to a lounge chair and leaned back.

"Shall I start with once upon a time?" Amber teased. "Very well then.

"Fox Hollow was scarcely a town as of yet. Oh there were a few houses here and there and two or three stores. On the other hand, Jefferson City was thriving. Just a few miles away was a vacation Mecca. The lake near here meanders. We local folks call it the lake, but it is truly a river which widens between Jeff city and here. Some fishing cottages, rather nice for their time, were built along the lake. These were popular rentals every summer. Some even rented them in the winter for ice fishing. So Jefferson City had tourists, and even as early as the mid-eighteen hundreds.

One very rich man had learned to fish as a boy with his father and was determined that his sons would learn also. The man had three sons, ranging from age 3 to 12. The three year old was especially his joy. He rented the largest of the cottages and convinced his wife to come with him so he could take even the youngest child. The first two days they enjoyed going out on the fishing boats. The two oldest boys took one boat, and he and the youngest took the other. They didn't have much luck catching fish, but they enjoyed the pleasant weather and each other.

That second night the man and his wife sat up late telling the two older boys stories of when they were young. About dawn, they did not hear when the little one got out of bed. Later, some said it was fortunate the water was cold, and they had not been swimming. Otherwise, the child might have gone for a swim that morning. Instead he chose the activity that he'd been enjoying with his family. He got in a boat and had fun holding on to the side to making it rock. As the boat rocked more and more the rope attaching it to the pier loosened.

The boy was delighted when the boat began moving out into the lake. The current caught the boat, along with the warm summer wind. By the time the family arose from their late sleep, the boat with the boy was nowhere in sight. The boy floated all morning long. He reached Fox Hollow, about 1 p.m. There the boat floated into some debris, mostly Fox willow branches. This stalled its trip down the waterway. The boat slowly floated to the edge of the river, shielded from easy view by the hovering willows.

The search went on for the boy for hours. Around sunset, a boy and a girl -- high school sweethearts -- went for a walk down by the river. They just wanted to get a little time to talk and a little shade to walk in. Seeing the edge of the boat, they scraped away some of the over hung branches and found the boy sound asleep and safe in the boat.

In his gratitude, the father sent the sculptures to Fox Willow. He said one sculpture would not do. He wanted one that represented the uncertainty and danger of life. He wanted another that represented the happiness in life is shared for families. Thus, we have two beautiful sculptures to adorn our park.

Chapter Eight
All That Glitters
The Carolinas, 1951- 1976

Jill hated her name! She hated the chants of the other children, "Jill came tumbling, Jill came tumbling."

It was bad enough when she was seven and eight. Now the word 'tumbling' had a new significance! Boys especially like to tease.

"Jill is tumbling, Jill will tumble down," they sang as they made lurid gestures.

The only place that Jill felt comfortable was a place where she did not belong. She lived in a resort area, and loved to sneak into the beautiful grounds of a villa filled with vacationers and well-dressed waiters. This was a place where handsome young college students server as waiters. They did not tease her. Of course they did not really know her name.

Instead of scurrying the little girl away, they brought her treats from the trays left half full by the tourists. The young men who were hired to serve the guests, were suntanned and muscular. They were fascinated by the lovely little girl who sneaked in from the beach and spent hours roaming the grounds.

True, Jill had been beautiful since birth. Her lush brown hair and emerald green eyes alone would have made her a beauty. Her features were soft, her coloring a pinkish peach, her complexion clear and shining. It was her smile, though, which was incredibly alluring.

When she smiled it was like a beam of sunlight suddenly revealing dimples in both cheeks. Jill won the heart of all observers not only with her smile but with the sparkle emanating from her hazel eyes.

Yes, Jill had been missed named. Jill sounded like a girl good in sports. At least to Jill it did. If they had called her Jillian she might have been happier. Jill liked to pretend she had a different name. When any of the young waiters asked her, Jill made up a name. Sometimes she picked a dramatic name, such as Melissa or Ophelia. Sometimes she took a name from a comic book like Veronica or Candy. Other times, she went for cutesy, such as Dolly or Ginny Sue. Whatever name she picked it had to be different from the one she picked last. And it could never be Jill.

Instead of sneaking into a resort once a week, she began to go every day. She was careful not to go to the same resort, day in and day out. This was no trouble, because there were dozens of the resorts. If she waited a week to go back to the one she had visited previously, most likely the guests would be entirely different. Only the waiters would be the same. She realized this was a risk, but she took it anyway.

She began to notice that a lot of guests left their jewelry and other valuables in their cabanas or on their lounge chairs when they played tennis or swam. She loved the glitter of the jewelry. She didn't care if they were diamonds or rhinestones or just glass. If it glittered she wanted it! And sometimes she took it. Jill was careful. She never took more than one item left in a careless pile. She hoped it would not be missed. Or if the it was missed she hoped they would not be sure if they had it with them. Or perhaps they would think it was lost. Jill had sometimes watched as a woman would search in the sand beneath her lounge chair for a jewel safely in the Jill's pocket. Sometimes if jewelry seemed valuable Jill would hurry away, glad to make a quick exit.

On long afternoons in the off-seasons when few tourists were lingering on the grounds of resorts, Jill began going to malls. She had become addicted to the excitement, the risk of grabbing a bracelet and a money clip or some other bobble. Jill was always careful to slip a couple of bills out of the money clip and to place it back exactly where it had been. She never took it all. She always took money from the innermost bills, as she had discovered soon enough that the larger bills would be there.

The mall proved Jill's undoing. The watchful eyes of the security guards were not fooled by Jill's beauty. They marveled at her sleight-of-hand. However, they caught her red-handed time after time. Most let her go the first time they caught her, beguiled by her smile and her proclamation of regret. Soon, however, Jill became so addicted to the rush that she took things even though she recognized a security guard as someone who had caught her before. At two of Jill's favorite stores she was met at the door and told that she was not welcome. She could show them money, but that did not interest them .

"Don't come in here ever again!" She was ordered. "If you do, you will be arrested. We don't allow shoplifters."

In two other stores she was followed step for step. At first she thought this was fun -- like a game. However, it was a game she soon regretted.

To Jill, her loot was really not loot at all. It was hugs; it was pats on the back; it was love. In all the times she had sneaked into resorts she had been warmed by the tenderness shown by the tourists to one another. Sweethearts and lovers, fathers and sons, mothers and daughters -- all tourists seemed to come in pairs. They all had smiles and laughter, hugs and praise. None of the bickering and yelling she found at home was evident there. These people who gave each other gifts that sparkled in the sunlight were the kind of people she wanted to be. The people kept her coming back. Not the jewelry.

At last, the tourists season returned in full array. Jill had reached her 16th birthday. She was more beautiful than ever, and attracted attention of not only the waiters, but also of the guests, especially the men. Some of the women noticed that their husbands and escorts were spending more time ogling Jill than attending them. Talk began to spread, and soon management came involved.

Jill's childhood pastime was suddenly identified as a crime. She was sent to a juvenile Center on the island. Here was the opposite of loving, caring relationships. Here Jill had the dubious advantage of contact with professionally trained thieves. When she was discharged at the age of 17, Jill had many contacts with the criminal world. Some of the young people she had met at the Center asked her to work with them on a planned bank robbery.

"That's just stealing money," Jill replied. "When you get ready to go for jewelry I'm your man."

****

Jen and Mark were childhood sweethearts. Together they had done more petty thievery by the time they were summoned to juvenile detention than most 30-year adults locked up for grand theft. They were released exactly three months after Jill. Mark had reached the age of 18, thus any more arrests and he could be tried as an adult. Mark pondered this situation carefully. Jen needed a partner to pull off a heist. Maybe she needed a new partner. One no older than her 17 years. Mark immediately thought of Jill. So, jewelry it will be!

All the leg work was done by Mark. He visited every jewelry store within 20 miles. Mostly he chose establishments safely tucked in large malls, but one or two were isolated in a small strip mall. He picked the perfect place, watched the traffic patterns over a three week period, drew maps, and obtained bus schedules.

Then he had Jen contact Jill! This was the hardest. Neither had any idea where to start. Finally Jen remembered that Jill had been in a beautician's training course at the detention center. She opened the yellow pages and began calling, asking for an appointment with Jill Baker. On the tenth call the receptionist responded positively.

"Jill doesn't come in again until Friday. She is part-time. I could schedule you for Friday at seven. You would be her last appointment."

"I'll take it. I only want a wash and blow dry".

Jill at first refused to go along with the theft. Mark changed her role, something against his better judgement.

"We really need your help. See, this is a distraction. The two of you go in, dressed real nice, and ask to see some diamond rings. Then you want to see necklaces to go with them. They never have more than one clerk between 12 and 1:30. When she has all the trays out to show you, just take the velvet pads they're fastened to and put them in your large bag and run. Once you are around the corner, get on the bus. Jen will be right behind you."

"Where will you be?" Jill wanted to know.

"By the time the jewelry dame gets her signal going, I'll be filling out some stubs in the bank. When I hear the sirens responding to her I'll make my move on the cash on hand. I'll take the get-away car and meet you two four bus stops away. That will be the corner of

Lincoln and Grant. We'll divide the cash. You can keep the jewelry unless Jen wants a couple of pieces. It will be too hard to fence. You're the one crazy about the rocks, aren't you?"

"And no weapons! I won't do it if we have weapons."

"I'll have a gun but if it'll make you feel better I won't load it. You and Jen won't need one. If I get caught I'll catch up with you two at your apartment as soon as I can. Wait 30 minutes in the diner on the corner of Grant and Lincoln. If I don't show up, take another bus and go to your place - both of you. If I don't come it will mean I had to spend the night in the cooler. I'll get in touch as soon as it's safe."

It had been a long time since Jill had diamonds in her grasp. This plan sounded irresistible. She assumed she would have no connection with the bank robbery. The jewelry story gig sounded a lot like shoplifting.

Events went as Jill expected. She and Jen had bought second hand custom made outfits at a slightly used shop in a plush suburb several miles away. Jill gave them both fabulously stylish hairdos, using the kind of color that will wash out. No need of being remembered as two brown-haired women.

The business here must be very slow. The clerk was the talkative type. She was happy to take out a white velvet-covered display pad filled with rings. Only a little hesitantly, she agreed when they asked to see necklaces on another large display board.

"I love these two," Jen purred. "Which necklace looks best to go with it? That third one might be even better. Can't we look at them side by side?"

Interestingly, the clerk continued to grasp both pads, raising them slightly as if to give them a better perspective.

Suddenly, Jen became sullen. "Put your hands behind your head," Jen demanded. She was holding a gun, pointing it straight at the woman.

"Partner, you, take those and run. NOW! Get out of here."

Jill did so, quick as lightning. She hopped on the bus just before the doors closed! She heard sirens as the bus drove away.

Jill was distraught. The frightened girl was shaking when she got off the bus. She did not go to her apartment, as Mark had ordered. Instead she made an anonymous call to 911. Jill informed the operator that two shoplifters were at the jewelry store, giving the operator the address.

"I think things went wrong," Jill reported frantically. " One women looked frightened and surprised when the other one had a gun. There wasn't suppose to be a weapon!"

The operator was impatient.

"How do you know all this? Is this a joke? ".

" You have to believe me! I was there, I saw it all. The woman who ran outside shouted that there was not supposed to be a gun."

"If the woman who ran out was you, go to the nearest police station immediately. Better still, tell me where you are and I'll send a car to pick you up. You are in big trouble, but it will be better for you if you turn yourself in."

"Yes, Maam. I have this jewelry. If I don't come in I'll call you back and tell you where to find it."

"Just come in!" The operator's voice was firm, yet warm.

Jill knew she had handled this dreadfully. She had not completely trusted the assurances of her two prison acquaintances. She had secretly taken the gun earlier that day and wiped off her fingerprints but only after unloading it and throwing away the bullets. Jen probably didn't know it wasn't loaded. Mark could have a loaded weapon. Jill had not seen a second gun. Maybe he had the unloaded gun? Should she call back and tell about the bank robbery? Would she be charged with both?

Mark's success at the bank was doomed from the start. Smart aleck that he was, he decided to get everyone's attention by firing a warning shot in the air. Yes, he had the unloaded gun! He was caught red-handed when the gun didn't fire and the security officer jumped him.

Jill had turned 18 the day before the robbery. Three months later Jill came to trial. The clerk testified in Jill's behalf, saying that Jill appeared frightened and under obvious duress. Jill had returned all the jewelry when she turned herself into the local police. The 911 operator also confirmed that Jill had called her promptly. Jill was given three years and ended up serving two with time off for good behavior. Thanks to the jewelry clerk's testimony and her phone call, otherwise it could have been much longer. No one could find Jen. She had dropped the gun on the floor and run after Jill, just missing the bus herself. Her gun, of all things, proved to be a water pistol!

Chapter Nine

Into A World of Woe

Hometown, USA, 1971

What a party! Rachel was amazed! She had never dreamed that so many people would come to her celebration. There must be a hundred people here.

Rachel had just completed her training for a position in a near-by police department. She had planned this career since early childhood. It was virtually ordained that she should go into law enforcement. Generations of family members had been associated with law enforcement of one type or another. Rachel's father, Mike O'Reilly, was a captain in the precinct nearest their home. Her mother was a clerk in the local sheriff's department. She had seven cousins, three aunts, and two uncles in various fields of law enforcement.

When Rachel was four she proudly wore her father's police hat. She especially liked to pretend that she was a school traffic police woman. As she grew older, the positions she coveted in law enforcement grew in importance. One of her most treasured she kept secret from her family - a plan to go into undercover work. Little did she know that this would happen. Also, little did she dream that this type of work would come to her so early in her career. Nor did she believe it would so drastically end her career by the time she was 20.

The Police Academy where Rachel trained required six months of intense training. Before she even began Rachel was given what she merrily called "one hundred tests analyzing my intelligence, strength, motivation and soul". Before entering the Academy her long, curly hair had to be either cut or worn in a tight bun or other serviceable up do. She practiced the latter for two days, finally reaching a point that she could make a long braid and pin it up in two minutes flat.

Anyone with test phobias would never make it through the Academy. After each lecture covering basic laws - local, state and federal, a test was given. The students had three chances to pass the tests with all the answers correct. If after three chances they missed even one answer they were OUT. Not out as for one inning - out period. No training, no recourse, no job!

The field training was as intense as the classroom instruction. Repetition, repetition, repetition was the rule here. Exercises in self-defense, take-downs, disarming the suspect were repeated until they became second nature. These were not fun when it was one's turn to play the suspect.

Mock trials were held to provide experience in testifying in court. Driving practice took place off public roadways - in abandoned industrial areas or unused runways. With helmets and seat belts the recruits learned to spin a car out of control so they could practice regaining mastery of the vehicle. Shooting with a number of fire arms was another emphasis. Rachel scored high in each phase of the training and graduated with honors. Today she was celebrating. Monday she would get her assignment, which might include additional training.

"Well, if you aren't the cat's meow!" Rachel's cousin Ned walked up from behind her and slapped her hard on the back!

"If I have one more slap on the back tonight, or one more handshake, I won't be in condition for duty come Monday." Rachel glared at him.

"Well, now didn't mean to get your dander up," Ned replied. "We're all so proud of you! If you were still 10 years old, I'd pick you up and swing you through the air."

"Sorry to be so ornery." Rachel gave him one of her million-dollar smiles. "This party is just overwhelming! I feel like I need to sleep for two days."

"Well, you'd best sleep tomorrow, then, because I understand they have quite a reception waiting for you at work come Monday."

"Can't do that either," Rachel replied.

"I'm in the choir at church, you know. I have a solo tomorrow."

"I'm coming to church then," Ned replied. "I never could miss an opportunity to hear your beautiful voice."

"Who is that guy in the fancy suit and dark red tie?" Rachel's older brother, Walt, appeared with the question.

"I was wondering that myself," said Rachel. "He's no one I've ever seen before. Whoever he is, he's about a ten on the good looks scale."

"There were some feds around at the station yesterday afternoon." Ned supplied. "He looks like one of them. I can't imagine what he's doing here, though."

The party was beginning to wind down. About two thirds of the people had left. Rachel's new supervisor walked over to say his goodbyes.

"There was someone here a while ago that I wanted you to meet. You were so busy with your guests that I didn't get a chance to bring him over. He must've left already. Oh well, he'll be at the station come Monday."

"Who was he, anyway," Rachel asked. "I saw him standing

around talking to no one. I can't imagine who invited him even."

"Well, I guess I did. I mentioned that we'd be here today. He didn't want to hang around until Monday. Name's Rex Larson. He wants to talk to you."

"Now I am really curious," Rachel exclaimed. "Who is he and what does he want to talk to me about?"

"I've already said too much," her new boss said. "He has an offer to make to you. He wants you on loan for a while to his department . He is one of the feds - a Narc to the bad guys."

Rachel slept restlessly. She knew it was an honor as a new recruit just out of training to be considered for a position with the feds, even though it was a temporary one. It had to be undercover work. She couldn't imagine any other possibility. She would be a new face in the federal building at the Capitol a few miles from here. She would be able to go places and talk to snitches maybe that other operatives would be too well-known to be trusted.

Church the next morning was filled. Rachel took her place in the choir. As she looked out toward the congregation she could see in the very back row. The stranger was seated there.

Rachel was nervous though she had never been nervous before in a church service. The organist played an Interlude. It was Rachel's cue to stand up for her solo. As she began to sing the entire congregation hushed. The only sounds were that of the organist and Rachel.

"Out of the ivory palaces..."

Rachel almost stumbled over the next words.

"Into a world of woe,"...

"Is this where I'm going," Rachel wondered as she sang. "Is

this why he's here; the stranger, who wants my life!"

Rachel felt a lilt in her voice and sang louder. A skip of her heart gave her an adrenaline rush. She **would** get through the next verse!

As Rachel reached the final chorus, her voice rang out as if from the heavens. Congregations do not give applause, but this one came close. Instead, when Rachel reached the final chorus they bowed their heads in prayer. "Only his great eternal love ..."

They didn't hear that Rachel inadvertently changed the last line of the song: "made me agree to go."

The city where Rachel had grown up had several slum areas and teenage gangs. A significant drug problem had increased due to the activities of a drug cartel, which had infiltrated the city.

Monday morning came all too early for Rachel. Her supervisor was waiting, along with the strange man. The precinct captain was there also.

After introductions were made the captain invited all into his office.

The captain began, "You know all about the crystal meth that is on the street right now, don't you Rachel?"

"Dad said three died last weekend from overdoses." Rachel answered. "It's getting worse by the day from what I hear."

"That's why I'm here." The stranger said, looking straight at Rachel. "The drug cartel has gone mad. The junk they're putting out on the streets is cut with something lethal. These suppliers don't seem to care. We think the nuclear gang works out of the State Capitol. We have little information though about who's running the show. The low life we pick up don't seem to even know who they're working for. They have pickup spots where they get the meth and others where they leave the money they collect."

"We need someone to go undercover. You fit the bill perfectly. We have a lead on a nightclub that needs a singer. We'd like to put you in there and let you see what you can pick up. You would have backup at the nightclub with a bartender. Stanley would be there every night you are except for just one time a week. That night would be covered by a regular customer, who is actually one of our operatives. We've had him in place for a couple of months now, but he hasn't had any luck. We will get you a small room nearby and have operatives watch over you as you walk to and from work.

"This will mean no contact with your family for six to eight months. It will take at least two months before people will talk more freely around you. Once we have you set up in undercover, we need to leave you there for a while. I'm told your family has a lot of law enforcement officers. We thought you would understand procedure better than most. Also, you're attractive, young and have a face that is not known around the Capital. Better still, you have a voice like a torch singer. We hate to ask such a young recruit, but frankly we don't have anyone else that wouldn't be suspect. Kids are passing out like flies, many of them dying. Will you help us?"

Rachel took a deep breath.

"I don't see how I can turn you down," Rachel said thoughtfully. "On the other hand, I can't just say yes, on the spur of the moment like this. The only time I've ever sang in front of a group is at church. You're talking about a totally different kind of the singing. I would need a totally different wardrobe than the one I have now."

"You've forgotten about your high school musical. We managed to get a tape of your performance from a year ago. You will do great as a night club singer. Our whole plan depends on it. Believe me, we have thought about all of the angles." Rachel laughed. "I had forgotten about <u>South Pacific!</u> I'd really like to talk to my Dad about this before I decide," Rachel continued. "Could I have a few days?"

"Every day we wait, is another day that kids are dying. Can't we get your Dad over here to talk now?"

"I have a better idea," Rachel's supervisor intervened. "We'll call his precinct and have him released for the day. We'll have him call here and Rachel and he will decide where they want to meet. We can all come back here at 2 p.m. and see what they've decided."

"I'd rather meet before lunch," Larson said. "But I can live with 2 p.m. Meanwhile I'll get my operative over here to take Rachel shopping. Assuming she says yes, she'll have her new wardrobe by six."

"You're talking about right away," Rachel moaned. "I thought I'd have at least a week to get ready." "If your father wasn't in law enforcement, I wouldn't even want him to know," Larson said. "The sooner we leave here, the fewer people you will talk to about this assignment. It's for their safety and yours. If you don't understand that, your father will. Where do you keep the coffee around here? I'll need coffee and a telephone."

Rachel asked her father to meet her at their home. She said,

"Bring Mother, If you can." She did not want to meet in some diner. She could be saying her last goodbyes before taking such an assignment and committing to at least six months.

Her family offered love and encouragement. She could tell that Mike had misgivings. On the one hand, he knew the problems that surrounding communities were having with street drugs. He was proud of his daughter. Proud of the skill and courage she had displayed during training. On the other hand, he wished someone else had done a little bit better. As a father he worried. Despite all the Fed's precautions, he knew that such arrangements were never perfect. Never the less, he had no choice but to congratulate her and support her as best he could. Such was his internalized loyalty to the cause of the proud citizens who worked for safety of all.

Chapter Ten

See No Evil

Drug City, 1971-73

So Rachel O'Leary became Lily Mandike over night! By Wednesday, Lily was established in her new studio apartment. The apartment was in a fairly decent neighborhood. Many elderly people lived here and had made their homes here for many years. The apartment houses were mostly three-story, made of brick and shaped like blocks. Lily was pleased with her quarters, considering. An older female operative had come with her to house hunt, posing as her aunt. Together they had looked at several options. This was by far the best, both in respect of proximity to the night club and the cleanliness of the space. The apartment was furnished except for towels, sheets and such things as dishes and cooking implements. They made quick work of filling in the items needed. They went to Smart-Mart and came out with three bags, which included two plates, 2 cups, enough table ware for one person, a tea kettle, a soup bowl, and a few pots. In the linen department they only got one set of sheets. Lily wanted two. She liked to change the sheets often, but her companion indicated there would be a storage problem. There was no Laundromat in the apartment building. Ruby would have to take her sheets to the neighborhood Laundromat. She might not want to wash the sheets so often. She probably would take everything at once and make the bed when she returned home with clean sheets.

Lily insisted on three bath towels. Sometimes she liked to take three showers a day. She topped this off with a bath mat and shower curtain plus soap dish, waste can and wash cloths. She forgot a lot of things such as tea towels and dishwasher soap. No matter, she would make another run soon. Usually her mother had done this type of shopping for her. Lily felt she would need a list.

Thankfully the shopping was done on Monday and Tuesday. Lily tried on her new wardrobe and decided she needed a floor length mirror. This would be the first thing on her list! Auditions were scheduled for early Wednesday morning at the Starlight Night Club. When Lily arrived there were only two other people to audition. Both ladies would qualify as seniors. Only one of them could sing at all. Neither could play the piano and sing at the same time. Unless more aspiring torch singers arrived, Lily was a shoe-in. The other two went first and were told to wait in the back of the room. When Lily sat at the piano and touched the ivory keys she felt inspired. She decided to open with "All of Me". Appropriate enough considering the real reason she was here! Lily used her deepest voice and let the song ring out, vibrating up to the ceiling.

The manager, Nils Simpson, clapped loudly. He was joined by the bartender and the two ladies who had also auditioned.

"Can you start on Friday night." Nils asked Lily. "Let's say 7:30 for the first set; another set at 9:00 and the last one about 11:15. Each set should last between 30 and 45 minutes. Is that too much?"

"Let me try it for a while," Lily mused. "If I find it is too hard on my voice, maybe you could call one of these of the ladies to fill in the middle set for me."

"Oh no!" One of the ladies came forward to shake Lily's hand.

"I'm Mabel and this is my sister, Gracie. We just came for fun. We like to sing at open mike night. I guess we won't see much of you because open mike night will be your night off -- Wednesday's! Maybe you could stop at our house for dinner one night. We just live up the street."

"But that won't work either," Lily said, pretending dismay. "I can't have dinner with you Wednesday nights, because you'll be here. Every other night I'll be working."

"Mabel wasn't thinking," said a blushing Gracie. "We will just have to make a point of coming here to hear you sing. Your voice will be well worth coming out another night. We can come to the early show, and still get to bed at a reasonable time. It is a good thing we did not get this job. I didn't realize it would keep us up past our bedtime."

They all had a good laugh. Lily was beginning to really enjoy this new life.

The first week of Lily's emergence was uneventful. The nightclub scarcely had any customers except for the seven o'clock group. A lot of elderly citizens who lived nearby came in, usually for one drink and the light repast served by the bar. Lily found this to be a decent supper for herself also. She typically arrived at six and ordered either a burger or the soup for the day. She had not yet dared to try the more exotic dishes, such as fried frog legs and raw oysters.

Soon business increased for the second and third sets. As more and more people came in Lily had to work hard. Many songs she could call to memory, but many others she had to relearn the words, especially those old songs so often requested. She had been fine with the 40's music as well as the 50's. As a child she and her grandmother shared a love of the 40's and 50's - from swing to ballads and especially show tunes. However, she had had to relearn a lot of the songs from the 60's.

Lily especially liked the audience for the early sets. She liked the warmth between the elderly couples who quietly held hands under the table. Several clasped hands right up on top of the table for everyone to see. Lily felt their warm in the nightclub; something she had not expected in a situation such as this. Some of their requests were for really old tunes. Fortunately the night club had kept boxes of old sheet music. 'That Old Sweetheart of Mine' was one Lily hadn't even heard before. Some of the older requests were barely familiar, like 'I'll Take You Home Again Kathleen' and 'The Girl That I'll Marry'. Lily could play by ear, but she had to come in a couple of mornings and tap out the sheet music notes for songs she had not heard. It was worth it though for the pleasure these melodies obviously brought the clients.

It was about two and a half weeks before a new clientele started arriving. They came in expensive suits and diamond studded tie clips, sporting huge diamond rings. There was a hush and whisper as these men arrived, usually in groups of three. Lily noticed that the nights that Stanley was not at the bar, the man designated as her back-up sat near these men - in eavesdropping range. So it seemed the undercover gig was beginning to pay off. Between sets Lily tried to take a chair near them also. She usually joined elderly couples who had been there before. Even when she found a couple near the newcomers, she could never hear anything the well-dressed men were saying in their hoarse, self-assured voices.

Gradually the crowds increased - especially the late-night crowd. Lily went home tired and slept well into the morning. It was a good four weeks before Mason Peters arrived. He became a regular on Thursday and Saturday nights. He always got a table by himself near her piano. He would have two martinis and listen to her sing the second and third sets. He never left until the club closed. Several times he approached her and asked for a favorite song. He confided that his wife had died a couple of years before and that Lily was singing the songs that had been his wife's favorites. Gradually he began to linger at the piano as she sang a tune he had requested. All of his requests were ballads about loneliness – "My Heart Cries for You," "Cry Me a River", "O Lonesome Me", "Tennessee Waltz", "Are You Lonesome Tonight".

Lily did not associate him with the well-dressed men who so often arrived in groups of three. Even when four or five groups came they all seemed to know one another. Mason Peters wore nothing flashy. He was dressed in expensive looking sports clothes but had no diamond rings or other memorable attire.

By the fifth week she knew his name and that he was in the business of importing fine art and other antiquities from Europe. These he grouped in lots for the wholesale market. When she got a chance she reported this to Stan, the bartender, just as she did anything else that she picked up throughout the night. However she was pretty deep in thought these past two weeks. She did not see that this job was paying off at all. She might as well just be a nightclub singer. There was no undercover work for her here with all of these elderly citizens and their songs of yesteryear. The night club offered little more than a nice cocktail to help them sleep better. She missed her family and wanted to go home.

Then one night it happened. It was a windy night and slightly raining when Lily left the club. She knew that her backup was just a few steps behind her, as always. When a car pulled over and the driver leaned out to offer her a ride she was not alarmed. She refused of course. The back door opened and Mason Peters leaned out.

"You're getting all wet, Lily. Please let us take you home."

When she refused again, two men came from out of nowhere, walking toward her at a fast pace. They came from the direction she needed to go, grabbed her and ushered her unceremoniously into the back seat next to Mason. One got in the vehicle next to the driver. The other followed them in a dark sedan.

Lily was on alert! Where was her backup? Surely they had not taken him out. They could not know that she was undercover and that she was being followed by a person who was sworn to protect her.

True, Mason did not know that the man that followed her was anything more than a lovesick cur who liked to stalk Lily. Mason understood that as he also wanted Lily. Mason was a man who got what he wanted, one way or another. He did not intend any harm to Lily. To the contrary, he planned to treat her like a queen. Soon she would come to love him and give herself freely. It was a challenge he anticipated with great pleasure.

Mason had planted a young woman in the club that night. Her task was to delay the lowlife that so regularly followed Mason's precious Lily.

"Stop him just as he gets out the door," Mason's henchman had instructed. "Ask for directions. Be the damsel in distress. Say your date never met you in spite of your plans. Ask where you can get a cab; have him light your cigarette. Do whatever you can think of to hold him up for five minutes."

This plan had succeeded! By the time the body guard stepped out of the shelter of the doorway, Lily had been whisked away. No amount of running or searching for her en route to her apartment nor inside it gave him any clue as to Lily's whereabouts.

Mason insisted that Lily should not be afraid.

"It is not my intention for you to be upset. For just once won't you please sing for just me alone? It would mean the world to me."

Lily knew that he was lying. She had three capsules filled with a tasteless powder that would make a man impotent for several hours. She wasn't, therefore, afraid of being raped. She was afraid of dying.

"Take me straight home if you mean that. Then we'll set up an appointment to open the club an extra hour one night soon. You can be the only patron. Surely, you don't expect me to sing for you in circumstances such as this!"

"I had to take these extreme means or you wouldn't have come. My wife's grand piano is in my penthouse parlor. I want to hear it's lovely tones once again! I want to hear you play and sing as she once did."

They pulled in a gated parking lot next to a tall apartment building, stopping next to the dark sedan. The two strange men each took one of Lily's elbows and whispered she should co-operate if she was wise. They entered through a backdoor, taking an elevator straight up to the penthouse.

When Mason unlocked the door, they went into a large, windowless room with soft couches, huge TV, and a bar. The henchmen stopped here and Mason ushered the reluctant Lily into the adjoining parlor.

It was furnished impeccably, all in white leather upholstered furniture. Dark walnut wood paneling with walnut desk and cabinets were reflected in a mirrored ceiling. The room was lit by multifaceted chandeliers. Huge windows overlooked the city. To the right the beautiful lights from the bridge that spanned the river promised a breathtaking view come morning. To the left the tallest buildings forming the city's sky line stood like thousands of lighthouses from the brightness that made each window sparkle.

The carpet was a deep gold and in the very center of the Goliath sized room stood the grandest of grand pianos. Lily had never seen such a piano; certainly she had never played one.

Mason was speaking, his voice pleading and at the same time hoarse, seductive, and demanding. Lily heard the tone of command, of expectancy that his every wish would be honored speedily.

"This piano will be a much better compliment for your lovely voice than the old piano in the nightclub. I have been wanting to ask you up here before. Please try out the piano."

"I just want to go home. I've been singing for hours and I'm tired, " complained Lily. "This is not fair. You have forced me to visit you . You should have asked me and made an appointment. You could have had a few other people, like a small party. That would have been much more proper."

"My dear, then I, alone, would not have been your audience. Well, if you are too tired to sing tonight you can stay in the guest room. Tomorrow is another day. It is the room on the right. You will find robes and everything you need either in the bedroom closet or the private bath." Mason was polite, but persistent.

"This is blackmail!" Lily fought back angry tears. "At least find me something to drink. My throat is dry. I saw a bar in the room where your, ah, friends remained. I prefer something like club soda or lemonade. Nothing alcoholic or I'll probably fall asleep on the piano bench."

"Of course! I should have offered already!" Mason smiled,

patiently. He was in no hurry to win her over completely tonight. The 'courtship' would be fun. He would eventually have her asking to come to his bed!

Mason pressed a button and an elaborate bar appeared as the walnut paneling opened. He made himself two martinis which he mixed together in a large glass and poured her a club soda as she had requested. When he brought them to her she was sitting at the piano. As he began to set the drinks down near the music stand, she stopped him.

" I know you have a coaster somewhere. Surely you don't want to mar this beautiful wood."

Mason set the drinks on a glass coffee table and went back to retrieve two coasters, clearly amused. Earlier he had noticed when this ingenious woman took a small capsule from her purse. As he expected, she was taking the capsule from her pocket and emptying it into his drink.

Fortunately, he had seen, and planned the large drink to dilute whatever powder she carried. Just in case he would sip slowly. It was probably a mickey they used at the nightclub to quiet unruly customers by lacing their drinks - a sleeping pill of sorts. A good night's sleep would be good. He had important business tomorrow. She was proving a worthy challenge. Better than a wild animal hunt; even better than safaris which he loved.

When Lily played the first chords she was mesmerized. The sound was delightful and the acoustics in the high-ceilinged room perfect. She played and sang willingly, enchanted by the piano. She was sure that Mason would be too tired to make sexual advances. Surely he would take her home tomorrow. If not, her operatives would find her by noon.

Mason was pretending to be dozing when Lily at last rose from the piano.

"Dear Lily," he said sleepily, "You don't know how thankful I am. You have just given me a pleasure to exceed any that I've ever known. You must understand. I'm just too tired to see you home tonight and I think the boys have had their fill of beer since we got here. I would not want to risk your safety by having someone driving under the influence to take you back to your dwellings. Please be my guest tonight. I promise you will not be disturbed."

Saying this he went quickly into his bedroom and closed the door.

Lily walked into the other bedroom Mason had indicated earlier and found it beautifully adorned. Lilies had been painted all over the ceiling. The wallpaper teemed with lilies; the bed spread featured lilies all over. This man was obsessed with her! She was in deep trouble and he wasn't even a gangster! At least he didn't know she was undercover.

Just as Lily feared, the next morning Mason again made excuses not to take her home. He offered her triple what she made in the nightclub to sing just for him. He wanted her to stay in his penthouse and order her meals from the restaurant on the ground floor of the apartment building. She could have anything she wanted from sheet music to CD's. But she was to stay here with him indefinitely and sing to him. He claimed that the only decent nights sleep he had since his wife died was last night when Lily sang to him.

Clearly Mason was not giving Lily a choice. She was worried about this arrangement. She had to trust her friends and the agency to find her and get her out of this mess. Then maybe they would abandon the whole undercover gig. She wasn't doing any good spying on obsessive men and friendly senior citizens.

Mason served an elaborate breakfast ordered from downstairs. Afterward he had given his ultimatum about how she was staying there.

"Try it for a week, Lily. If you are uncomfortable still after that we'll look at other options. He had dressed in a dark business suit with white shirt and deep maroon tie. He looked much like the gangsters that patronized the nightclub after all.

"I have some business meetings this morning that I must attend. I will have Deuce bring you some magazines and books to read. You can make a list for him of your preferences. Or better still, you can play the piano, or perhaps watch television."

Walking across the room, Mason pushed another button next to the one that opened the bar. In seconds another section of the walnut paneling rolled away, revealing a huge entertainment center with a TV set bigger than most screens in movie theaters.

As Mason went out the door he called back over his shoulder.

"By the way if you need anything else at all just knock on the door here. Deuce and Guy will take care of you."

Lily paced up and down. She had determined that Mason was not going to push a sexual relationship with her. He was obviously trying to woo her; to bring her around to feeling deeply about him. She could see from the flash of anger that was in his eyes from time to time that he may not be so patient if the Feds took too long to find her.

She tried exercise; she tried to do nothing and relax. Finally she napped. Two hours later the telephone rang. Lily did not answer: the answering machine picked up. Mason's voice was clear."

"Pick up, Lily. There's been a change of plans. I'm going to have to hurry to get through this meeting, I'm expecting business associates from Las Vegas at the penthouse about 2:00 p.m. I fear it would be best if you stay in your room and were quiet. Has Deuce brought you something to read yet?"

"No, I haven't seen either of your, er, employees."

"Well, he probably left them just inside the door . Why don't you open it and look. Then you'll have something to do while I'm having the business meeting. It might not be good for your reputation if the others knew that you were actually living here. They would make erroneous assumptions. Or I could introduce you to them if you would rather. I want to do what makes you the most comfortable. I would meet with them elsewhere, but the only safe place to discuss our affairs is the Penthouse, unfortunately. "

"I'll stay in the bedroom. But I would really rather go home. I need to change clothes; you know I can't wear the same clothes for a week."

"Don't worry about that," Mason assured her. "Guy is taking care of that this morning."

At 1 p.m. promptly Guy and Deuce arrived and knocked loudly on the door. When Lily opened they wheeled in a cart with a tray of luncheon treats. Several packages were piled on a lower shelf of the cart. Lily was doubly annoyed to see her suitcase from her lodging. All her personal belongings that she had kept in the boarding house were stuffed in the suitcase.

Lilly was suddenly delighted. Her undercover contacts knew the whereabouts of her room. They would get descriptions of these goons who were guarding her. Perhaps they had already followed them here. Meanwhile, she had some most useful gizmos in her suitcase.

Objects that were not at all what they seem to be.

The captive nightclub singer, Lily, suddenly became Rachel, Ace detective; alert undercover agent! She set her pen that was actually a voice recorder to voice activate mode. She carefully lay it on the desk, casually positioned. Adding paper, no, too obvious! She took the paper away. Without it, the pen was scarcely noticeable. Instead, she fished out blank stationary from the desk drawer and scribbled some words to a song she had started to write a few days before. If Mason opened the drawer to tidy up by putting the pen inside, he would see the stanzas. He would not suspect the pen had other purposes.

Lily enjoyed her lunch; then opened the anti-room door and pushed the tray through it nonchalantly.

"Thanks for the lunch," she told the man seated there. "Are you Deuce or Guy?"

Guy answered grudgedly. "Guy! Anything else you need?"

"I made a list; here."

Lily handed him a small spiral bound notebook opened to a page with her list. He tore the page out and put it in his pocket, grimacing. Lily had asked for sanitary napkins, Midol, deodorant, Nair and coral nail polish.

"I'll send Deuce!" he decided. "He'll be right back." He sank back into his overstuffed chair and picked up his drink, sloshing a little over the side.

Ruby whisked a tissue from her pocket, "I'll get that," she offered. Deuce didn't notice that she slid the notebook he had returned to her under a table in the anteroom as she blotted the drops of beer. If he had examined it closely he might have noticed that the spirals were quite unique. Even so, he would not have imagined that they could

-104-

record his voice.

Four hours later, the meeting over and Mason out again for dinner with his associates, Lily listened to the recordings made by the pen. This was indeed a part of the drug cartel! She had names and places and plans. She knew when numerous shipments would arrive, at what dock and in what city. She knew what price would be paid for the shipment coming next and for three more thereafter. Now if she could just get this to the feds.

"I think this information could lead to the biggest drug bust to ever come into the US," Lily hoped.

Meanwhile the Feds were very concerned. They questioned patrons of the nightclub who came regularly. They had to find out what happened to Lily and find out fast. No one ever saw again the woman who had delayed Lily's bodyguard at the door. They suspected she was a plant but couldn't be certain. Both Stanley and the man she had duped looked through hundreds of mug shots, with no luck.

Stanley gave them information on all of the regular people that he knew. Those who used credit cards were the easiest. He had addresses and phone numbers for each of those. Follow- through teams sought these people out and questioned them much to the nightclub owner's dismay.

"These customers will never come back," he complained. But he had been fond of Lilly and he was also worried about her. So he did not complain too loudly.

The people who came through with the best information were Mabel and Gracie. They had been regular customers on Thursday and Saturday nights and had noticed the fashionable gentlemen with the manicured nails who liked to sit at a table near the piano.

"He always sits alone," explained Gracie. "Mabel and I tried to talk with him several times but he just ignored us. It was as if I was talking to someone who wasn't there. He only had eyes for Lily. He stared at her for her entire set."

"Yes," added Mabel. "He did talk to Lily; between every set he went over to her - to make requests, we both guessed. I overheard one night when I was standing next to Lilly. He claimed that his deceased wife had loved the song she did last."

"Just last week I saw him tip Lily with a $100 bill. He put it right in the little basket on the piano," Gracie continued.

No one knew this man or his name. Stanley confirmed that he always paid cash. The owner said he had never seen him before hiring Lily. He had become a regular, but only on Thursday and Saturday nights.

Finally Mabel came up with a possible name.

"It was at least four weeks ago, and I don't remember so well as I once did! I think he was the one I saw drop a piece of paper on the floor. He had just paid for his drink and was coming back from the bar, just passing our table. As he put his money clip back in his pocket, I saw something white flutter out! I picked it up and glanced at it briefly. It was a receipt for dry cleaning at that new One-Hour place. The last name wasn't clear at all. It was blurry. If I'm not mistaken the first name on the slip was Mason or maybe Masoniel."

" Come to this address tomorrow morning," the Fed advised Mabel. "Bring your Sister, also. We'll set up a sketch artist to work with you. Hopefully we can come up with a face."

Armed with this information and drawings, the Feds set out in teams of two. Through records at the dry cleaners they got a last name, although they expected it was an alias. There was no such name in the yellow pages or listed by the local phone company. Fortunately, information came back fairly quickly from police stoolies.

"Mason Peters," three stoolies reported independently. "He's the big shot that goes around with two henchmen. They aren't thugs to reckon with, either. They would as soon rough up a guy as look at him, make that 'rather'. Only one stoolie knew that the perp lived in the tallest building in that part of town.

Over the next three days, Lily devised ways to leave her recording devices in the large room when Mason had guests. On the third afternoon new guests arrived. Mason said they were flying in on their company jet.

"I hate to ask you this, but I need you to take a sleeping pill before they come. My colleague always has his sidekick check out the penthouse. He's a paranoid nut! He's bound to spot you. If you're passed out, you'll be safe and they won't even get a good look at you tucked under the covers."

"Why can't I just take a nap," Lily protested.

"Because you could wake up at anytime. They'll never go for that. Vincent uses the sleeping pill technique himself. He always has a woman or two in his hideaways. His purposes are less platonic than mine."

"So, you want me to agree to be drugged?" Lily asked in disbelief.

"We really have no choice, Lily. I can't let you leave the apartment before the meeting. Unless you are completely naive or a moron, you have already guessed that this meeting is with a person who operates outside the law. Either you read these directions with me so you'll sleep deeply but wake up none the worse in 3 or 4 hours. Or, Deuce will have to give you a shot!"

"Can you give me thirty minutes, then? I'm on a roll putting words to this song I'm writing. If I wait hours to get back to it, I'll lose my train of thought."

"Twenty minutes, then. Any more than that and the jet will arrive before I will. I'll take a quick shower while you work on your music. Be sipping this stuff, OK. I'll see you tucked in before I leave."

Ten minutes later, Lily was feeling groggy. She reset her recorder pen and slipped it under the edge of the sofa, where she had settled with her writing in her lap. Even if Mason spotted the pen, which was unlikely, he would not know it's purpose.

****

It had been almost a week since Lily disappeared when the Feds finally got a judge to issue a search warrant. When they burst into the penthouse Mason was not there. Lily was delighted to see them. She gave them the tapes of all the conversations she had recorded.

She had been ever observant and Mason had made the mistake of believing he could detain her until he could earn her unwavering loyalty. Lily showed her colleagues how to use the magic buttons to move parts of the wall paneling. She'd often played with the buttons when Mason was gone. Behind one section, between the bar and the entertainment center, she had discovered a large walk-in safe. Larson sent for a safe opener to break the code. When they did get it open it paid off in spades.

Fifteen arrests were made within the next two days. Unfortunately one was not Mason. He must have been alerted by someone because he never came back to the penthouse after the raid.

They could not find him anywhere.

At the time of the raid, Mason was sitting on a private plane on his way out of the country. Regarding the man who leased the penthouse, he did not exist. When Mason's stoolie in the local police department had sent word of the subpoena and search, Mason had ordered Deuce and Guy to take Lily to his hide-away on the coast. Deuce was to set a timer to blow up the safe before leaving. Fortunately for the Feds, Deuce was the greedy sort. He had no intention of blowing up close to a million dollars in the currency of various countries. Deuce was waiting for Guy to watch Lily as he opened the safe using his former well-tooled skills from his days as a thief.

Guy never made the penthouse. He was arrested entering the door to the private elevator in back of the building.

Since the Feds could not find Mason, they quickly whisked Lily to a safe house. The federal agent masterminding Rachel's recruitment reappeared. He insisted that she stay hidden in case she was a target.

"We'll find him," Rex Larson insisted. "He was using an alias when he leased the Penthouse. But his fingerprints were everywhere. It's just a matter of time before he is behind bars."

As the weeks went by it was discovered that indeed she was a target. Not only was the man called Mason searching for her, so was the father of Vincent Lopez. Vincent was headed for a life prison term based on the recordings Ruby had made, her testimony, and documents found in the safe. The senior Lopez had hit men out to shoot Lily on sight. He was out for blood.

"Kill her before Vince goes on trial and I'll double your usual fee," he ordered.

Mason had private detectives looking everywhere for Lily. He wanted to take her away to his own private island where she could not be found by Lopez's snipers. According to one source Mason was so besotted with Lily he could think of nothing else. He wanted to make her his own personal property and would do so at any cost.

When Guy turned state's evidence and confirmed the danger to Lily, the feds decided she would have to go into the witness protection program.

"How long for this?" Ruby was against the idea. She knew though that if she went back to her family her life as Rachel O'Leary would be connected with Lily. This Lopez was a Godfather type with a huge criminal network. He would stop at nothing to find her whereabouts. Better he never connect the O'Leary's with Lily Mandike.

The Feds gave Rachel a new identity. She was no longer either Rachel or Lilly. Her recruiter visited her at the safe house.

"Rachel, I'm sorry you have to sacrifice your family and career for this. I hope you take consolation in the service you have done! Many in law enforcement for 20 years never make the contribution you have made." Rex was truly sorry about the isolation this meant for Rachel. In truth his admiration for her had become something more. He had never known a more lovely, feisty woman!

"What's done is done," Rachel sighed. What happens now?"

"I'm going to be your contact from here out. That is often the plan - the recruiter is the contact person. You only know me as Larson, but I'd like you to call me Rex from here on out."

"Rex it is then," Rachel agreed. "And what is my name? I assume you chose it for me." Rachel could not stop a little sarcasm creeping into her voice.

As she expected, Rex's team had chosen her new name - Ruby Fentasia. There was a real birth certificate for an infant with that name who would have been Ruby's age had she lived. It was easy to make the death certificate disappear. The child's father was unknown and her Mother died, under-nourished and weak, in the charity ward where the real Ruby was born. Both were cremated at the expense of the state.

"We found a perfect fit. Almost the same birthday as yours." Rex explained about the original Ruby.

"The history we have created for her is in this folder. Memorize it and burn it except for the records. Your credit card expenditures as Ruby are there. Also, the record showing that you won the lottery a year ago. That will explain where you get the money to buy and renovate a house or start a business. Pick a small town! Any state but this one! There are some suggestions in the folder. We're all set to open a bank account for you with a check from lottery headquarters as soon as you know where you want to live."

"I'd like to stay in the safe house until after the trial," she answered. I want to be Rachel - Lt. O'Leary when I testify."

"Not a good idea. Lily won't expose the other O'Leary's to any revenge crazy crooks. The trial has been given a top priority. Should all be over in a few weeks. Be studying your new identity and thinking about what kind of work you want to do.

Ruby was relocated in the small town of Fox Willow. She was given a choice of houses that were currently on sale. When Ruby saw the huge Victorian house she decided that she would like to open a bed and breakfast. She knew she had to do some kind of work. She had never imagined doing anything outside of law enforcement . Her long dreamed of career had ended abruptly. Thankfully, her mother had taught her to cook. Certainly she could bake muffins and fry eggs. She would start out small. But then she realized how much money the Feds were giving her to renovate and furnish the huge old mansion.

"Maybe I won't be starting so small after all." Ruby opened the new page of her life with enthusiastic optimism. "I'll bake my own muffins and make jams like no one has ever tasted before.

Ruby's Jam of the Day

Dandy Apple

Hints for Picking Dandelions:

Buds are sweeter than blossoms. Pick early when very close to the ground.

Wear knee pads to crawl around on the ground. Do not try to pick enough by bending. You will be too achy to stir! Consider bribing very young children to gather buds. Watch out for insect wings, worm segments and rocks when washing blossoms.

If someone has picked leaves, save them for salads or a cooked vegetable. They will taste funny in jam. Remember - the younger the sweeter. As they age they get bitter; it happens to dandelions; don't let it happen to you.

Ingredients:

9 cups sugar

1 cup water

6 cups peeled and finely chopped tart apples

6 cups peeled and finely chopped sweet apples

40 Dandelion buds, quartered (some flowers may be substituted for buds)

Procedure:

Boil sugar and water until mixture spins a succulent thread

Stir in apples and buds. Boil about 20 mins. until apples are translucent and begin to all mesh together. Test by putting about a half teaspoon mixture on saucer and stir until cool. Taste and spread on bread. If not the consistency you prefer, return to heat, repeating test when mixture becomes noticeably harder to spread.

Don't forget to prepare you jars and process your jam.

Chapter Eleven

Every Quilt Has a Secret

Carolina's, 1974-77

Jill was angry with herself for listening to Jen and Mark. She was even more angry for not turning herself in immediately. She should have taken the jewelry directly to the police station. Of course her fingerprints were all over it. Her prints were on file due to her time in juvenile detention.

Well, what happened, happened! Now that she was in prison she wasn't going to cry about it. She knew that what she had done was outside of the law.

Jill had a thoughtful cell mate who felt anger could get one extended sentences. She suggested that Jill see the prison shrink.

" You know, lifting stuff in stores is an illness. A psychiatrist comes to the prison once per week. I see him because I am an obsessive gambler. Neither of us should really be here. We should be in a treatment center for our illnesses.".

Jill was skeptical. She felt that Gertrude, her cell mate, mostly saw a psychiatrist to avoid working in the dining hall. As the days went by Jill began to see a difference in her roommate. She was much calmer after her sessions with a psychiatrist.

Jill decided that instead of signing up requesting same that she would read about obsessions in the prison library. She found that she loved reading. She learned more reading about other women with psychiatric illnesses. However, she did not limit herself to the study of illnesses.   She loved stories of the pioneer women who traveled across country in covered wagons. They were strong and resourceful. Jill became determined that she was going to replace her need to steal shining things with more creative endeavors.

By the time she left prison she had graduated from high school through the High School Equivalency program.   Jill had long forgotten that her grandmother quilted and made brooches. The brooches were made of old buttons. broken jewelry and other 'found' pieces of shiny junk.

Jill announced she was starting a women's crafts group when she left prison.   She had learned a lot about quilting and had taken sewing lessons in the prison shop. With six months left to serve, Jill was moved to a halfway house.   There, she made   good on her declaration to begin a crafts group.   Gathering scraps left over from a church bazaar, Jill organized the others in the halfway house. They cut squares and triangles from the old clothing. They sewed these back together in varied patterns.   After backing these with old sheets they embroidered words to nursery rhymes in the centers.   When finished, these small quilts were sent to a home for abused women with small children.

This activity and Jill's role in developing it, possibly influenced the choice of her probation officer.   Doris was a jewelry maker. She got Jill started with inexpensive beadwork .   Jill caught on very quickly. Her creations were not only beautiful but they were very original.

Jill finished her probationary period while working at a fast food joint. In her spare time she made jewelry and took it to open markets and craft shows . She saved enough money to move away from the place where she was known as Jill Baker, the ex-convict. She took the new name of Opal because of her love of jewelry and her belief that the name Opal Baker would increase the selling value of her jewelry.

Opal met Jake the week after she moved to a city in a neighboring state. She had set up her tables up at an open-air market Jake had tables next to her. He was selling wood carvings. They immediately formed a bond. Even though Jake and Opal were soulmates in the deepest sense of the word , Opal did not share with him her past life as a convict. She wanted to keep that to herself, secret and in the past. Opal did not think of this as disloyal. She simply thought of it as something that she did not even want to think about in anyway or form.

Jake and Opal moved to Fox Willow three years after their marriage. He inherited some property from his spinster uncle which included a lovely old house very near Ruby's Victorian house. By the time they moved there Sylvia was one year old and Olivia was on the way. Opal had made a new life for herself. Because of the inheritance she and Jake were able to spend most of their time on their artistic creations. Their hobbies became more and more lucrative; their original works of art more and more in demand.

Opal became very skilled at making quilts. She had become interested in this activity while in prison. She had studied quilts made by pioneer women crossing the plains on their way to California. She read books about this and about women quilting while on the Oregon Trail. She also had studied the underground railroad quilts. It was fascinating to learn about the signals that these quilts provided to those escaping from slavery.

Although her interest was in traditional quilt patterns, Opal preferred stunning jewel tones rather than browns and neutrals which the plain women were so likely to choose. Irish Chain, Crown of Thorns, and Churn Dash proved dramatic in the bright colors that Opal chose. She had begun to cut squares and triangles from colored paper to experiment with secondary patterns . These secondary patterns were created when two or three different squares were combined. The intersections turned up a pattern quite unlike the original quilts. Therefore, even though Opal's squares were usually traditional, her quilts turned out unique. Opal began to sell her quilts as well as the jewelry. Jake began refinishing furniture as well as taking orders for new pieces . His hand work became popular for miles around. They took many of their creations to major art shows within a five hundred mile radius. There was no show where their work was not prized by buyers. From their cottage industry within 2 years they were shipping all across the United States and Canada.

It was Opal's interest in quilts that brought about the creation of the Fox Willow Quilters. She made a masterpiece for the 'Gems & Jams ' bed and breakfast. Ruby felt that having quilts on the beds of her rooms added a neat dimension. However soon afterward she decided the quilts were too valuable to be exposed to the public. Some guests took great care of the quilts. Some did not. Ruby hated to go into a room in the mornings and find an antique quilt on the floor. Sometimes they sported shoe prints. Other times they were covered with crumbs. It was obvious that people had picnics on top of them. A distraught Ruby came to the decision that she would use comforters in guestrooms and keep the quilts for herself. In her own suite she had accumulated a huge collection of quilts by the time Crystal arrived.

Crystal was amazed at the beauty and the variations of the patterns. Many of these had been made by the Fox Willow quilters even though they mainly made small quilts for hospitalized children. From time to time they took turns making quilts for one another. In addition, Ruby collected quilts from neighboring towns. Ruby remembered many aunts and a grandmother making quilts. As a child she played on the floor under the quilting frame as the ladies of her family worked away.

As they quilted, Ruby's relatives exchanged stories of the past and hopes for the future. The lights and darks of the sunshine and shadows setting reminded her especially of that other life so long ago. Her memories were so happy and so full of sunshine and yet they were shadowed by the fact that her life had to be separate from her family for both her safety and theirs.

Crystal was delighted to see the quilts that Ruby showed her with tears moistening her eyes.

"I heard a speaker once, long ago, when I was still teaching school." Crystal had not realized that she was giving away a part of her secret. "This woman said that quilts are like people. Every quilt has a secret to tell. The older the quilt, the more secrets they've heard.

"Every quilt could have a secret meaning that comes from deep inside the person who made it. What did the quilter think of during all those hours as she quilted?   Was she tired as she pondered over the stitches? Was she remembering things or dreaming of what she still wanted to do in life? Or perhaps she thought of things that are lost to her now that she once felt important. Is she quilting for the joy of creation? Or does she feel quilting is yet another chore so their family can keep warmer?"

Ruby laughed. "What do you see as some of the secrets, then? Tell me. For example, what kind of secrets she would Pearl pour into a quilt".

" Pearl doesn't appear on the surface to have ever had a deep dark secret,." Crystal dared to reply. "Her favorites are landscapes, but all of us know that she only does winter scenes. Why not Summer, Spring or Autumn? All are beautiful. What does Pearl think of as she designs those lovely tributes to the dark months?"

" I don't know why," Ruby reflected, "but she makes beautiful wall hangings and also huge quilts with snowy colors or medallion centers featuring snowflakes or snowmen."

"She is forever looking for fabric with snow as a part of the printed design. She shops through catalogs and goes to stores whenever she can." Crystal observed.

Ruby was growing somewhat uncomfortable. She changed the subject. "Twice a year we have kind of a pilgrimage where we lease a large van and go to quilt shops all around the county. You can come with us the next time if you like. It's lots of fun. We're usually gone for four days and three nights."

"That might be scary," Crystal observed. " Especially if we started telling our secrets that we only tell our quilts. But I think you're right. That was just something the speaker made up to get our attention. It is more like quilts reflect one's interests, rather than their secrets. Don't you think? Amber for example. She is in real estate and she quilts houses and houses and more houses. She showed me her house patterns, one day. I can't believe the variety. Sometimes she even creates her own."

Ruby laughed.

"Perhaps I should make quilts with Muffins and jars of jam, do you think? Plum Jumping Johnnys would make a hilarious quilt!"

"Well if you could find fabric with food already printed on, you could feature food in the center of your log cabins. You know, instead of the red square in the center of each block. Jade said it represents the hearth with the welcoming fire burning when the wayward family member finally comes in from the cold ."

"Perhaps all of us miss the homes we had as children," Ruby answered more sharply than she had intended. " Perhaps you should not come with us on our overnight trips after all. I think it is perhaps you and I who have secrets we keep dear. Do you really want to go there. "

" I don't know what's gotten into me. I would never say this to any of the others. I've just had such a bad feeling lately. I've wanted to tell you, in case I have to leave quickly. You have made my life special. More than that! You've given me my life back. Whatever the future holds, my decision to come here has brought me great joy and wonderful friends. It was you who made it possible for me to stay. Thank you from the bottom of my heart."

" If there is something I can do, so that you can stay longer, just say the word," Ruby answered. " Does your bad feeling have a real basis?"

"No! Maybe it is just because I feel so lucky for this delightful life to have lasted this long. Maybe this uneasy feeling started yesterday when Amber showed me some quilts from an old cedar chest. A photograph fell out of the folds of one of the quilts. Amber seemed surprised as though she had forgotten it was there. She didn't try to hide it, rather she let me hold it. She said the photograph had been in her family for a long time. If she knew where it was taken she didn't say. Neither did I ask. I felt as if I had walked in on her bath or in some way violated her personal space. I had seen the photograph before, but not in that form. I had seen it in many of her quilts."

"You mean the farmhouse, those special quilts that she's made over the years that she hesitates to part with for my collection or any other? The architecture is French, or perhaps Austrian? Perhaps she bought the photograph somewhere or the property was once in her family. She has used it for a pattern over the years."

" You are probably right. It just seemed that she cherished the photograph - not just the photograph. It was as if she cherished the house."

Long after Crystal left, Ruby was still thinking about what she'd said. Certainly, Crystal was right on track so far as Ruby herself was concerned. She had never thought of it that way before. But every time she made a log cabin quilt, she made numerous hearths, usually with fireplaces aglow, welcoming her back to the home she no longer dared to even visit .

If all this was true, Opal was a bright ray of sunshine. She liked and created sparkly jewelry and used brilliant jewel tones as her colors of choice, both in her clothing and her quilts. She brightens up our lives, thought Ruby. Why then was Opal the most driven? Jake Jenkins had inherited a fortune. Neither of them needed to work. Yet they both seemed to have a need to prove something to the world.

Crystal had come over to borrow books about quilting from Ruby. Once she had learned the basics, Crystal had become an avid lover of art quilts. She liked the concept of thinking outside the box. The boundaries that had limited her before, especially during her marriage were gone to the wind, just like Crystal. No squares and rectangles for her. The artist within carried Crystal beyond the boundaries of traditional quilt borders. Often Crystal's quilts ended in points or in butterfly- like wing effects. Crystal also like to make quilts in panels, usually with contrasting sections connected with woven braids and ribbons. She called her quilts "gentle art".

Ruby mused over the conversation she had with Crystal. Could it be true? Were Jade's lighthouses, for example, representative of her need to watchful? Does she do so many of the difficult Mariner's Compasses because of wanderlust? The need to find her way in life? Does she have a secret that involves water or the ocean? Maybe she has a secret desire to travel the world.

"I know I have a secret that I can never tell. Crystal has a secret also. We are both hiding. I wouldn't know that, except I guessed when Crystal first arrived. Thanks to Rex Larson, I was able to get her a Social Security card and a new identity."

Ruby was not going to pry. By helping Crystal, Ruby had given Crystal a clue about her own secret.

Do any of the others suspect, she wondered. Do we quilters have a secret, unwritten pact not to ask questions about the past of any one of us? I never hear a story of childhood or about a Mother or Father who is coming for a visit. We are indeed an unique group. More like the Queen bees of Nature than I had realized.

Ruby's Jam of the Day

Plum Jumping Johnny Jam

Ingredients:

4 lbs. Plums	1 lb box seeded raisins
1 lb. Chopped walnuts	25 Johnny Jump-Up Blossoms
Sugar	2 Oranges

Procedure:

Gather and wash the Blossoms when fresh in Spring. Freeze.

Wash plums and remove stones. Chop walnuts and set aside out of reach. If you forget and nibble you will have to chop more later.

Add blossoms and raisins to plums. Peel and Slice oranges; grate rind of one orange.

Add to plum mixture. Measure.

For each cup of fruit add 1 cup of sugar; vary if you want tarter or sweeter.

Cook over slow heat until so thick it's hard to stir. Of course you are stirring. Otherwise you have scorched your jam.

Cool and do the jar thing! Don't cut corners here or jam will be yuk!

Spread on toast and enjoy the hint of wintergreen brought by the flowers.

Part II

The Hunters

Chapter Twelve

The Vengeful Scout.

Bogota, Columbia, 1989

Amber married in New Orleans and moved with her family to Fox Willow in the late 60's. She and her husband, John Dumonti, had four children and eventually six grandchildren.

She was surrounded by love from her new family. She still felt a deep sorrow, however, as she had never heard from her brothers and father. She worried over a grandson now, who was determined to join the Marines. Any day now he could be involved in a war somewhere in the world. These people born in America did not know what it was like to live in a war-torn country. Amber adored her grandson and longed to tell him of the sorrow of her heart -- the bitter sorrow of losing her beloved brothers and father. Did she dare share her story -- at last?

Little did Amber know. The man she had actually saved that fateful day still lived. Herman Geits still had hatred in his heart toward the young girl who had left him so cruelly to die. He did not know she had saved his life. He had been unconscious still, when her brother wanted to throw him into the unused privy.

The first year of Geits' search he had a lead that she had been taken to a seaport in Australia. The captive, who had shared this information under great duress, was truthful! His Gestapo friends were so sure of it that they had finished the boy off before bothering to check. The imbeciles! The trail ended there and he had come to doubt that she had ever been in Australia.

Over the decades he had private detectives searching for her, using her photograph and artistically aged drawings. Choosing South America as his new home, he had spent a fortune looking there. Next he had begun to look in Canada and now in the United States. His one true wish before he died was to find the girl and make sure she had a long and painful death.

His dreams were so full of her he could not be with any other woman. He always thought of her as a girl just coming of age and coming to him naked as a frightened and unwilling virgin. No amount of reason persuaded him to forget this and few people were close enough to him to try.

With the help of his uncle, a General in the German Army, he had stolen a fortune from Jewish families who were sent on the trains. Most of it was gone now -- spent on his search for the girl whose name he did not even know. He called her "Daisy" from a comic strip he had once seen that featured hillbillies and jugs of "White lightning". So fixated was he on that one eventful day of his life, he even took a new name modified from the same comic. He needed a new identity to escape the Nuremberg trials. Abbot Young was in his mid-70s, sound of body and living for one purpose and one purpose only!

Abbot had toyed with the name. He wanted to sound very English! He had done nothing wrong in the war - just followed orders. Well, maybe the loot! All soldiers took loot, though. He had to admit his uncle made sure he and his got the best to pick from.

Abbot's mistake was that he had taken small, easy to pack treasures. Those huge paintings intimidated him! Where could he hide them? He should have found a way. But then, who knew he would live so long?

"I chose all that jewelry and half of it was paste!" Abbot spoke out loud, stomping his feet as he paced in his den. "That brat! That cunning child! I'll never get her off my mind until I have her! That's why I live! I'm too hungry for her to die. If I had not been wounded and so tired I would have taken her then and had a decent life. If not wives, at least a string of women! Now, nothing but dreams!"

Abbot looked through his dwindling supply of stolen goods. He had a few trinkets - a very old gold watch that he liked to wear. If he had to sell that he really would be desperate. There were some coins he had never been able to identify in books. Taking them to a specialist was not an option, nor was selling them. Until he knew if they could blow his cover he had to keep them out of sight. He understood that coins had alerted the Israelis to find at least three German generals in Argentina. Those were old coins that could only have come from a synagogue and he suspected his were the same.

A few pieces of jewelry - either rubies or glass. He'd have to risk having them pawned. Also, a couple of old books. He'd looked around old book stores for something similar, to no avail. From what he had learned from his library searches one was written in Hebrew. The other seemed to be Gaelic or some form thereof. They were in a sealed box he had stolen without opening. A pretty good haul - the solid gold candlesticks and crosses found inside the sealed box had reimbursed him well.

Abbot found his hat. He started to take off the gold watch to pawn but changed his mind and wore it instead. He took a matched set of bracelet, earrings and necklace from the box of 'rubies' and headed to a nearby cabaret. There he ordered his favorite among their regular dishes - a seafood paella.

Abbot ate heartily, referring to his watch several times. He needed to leave for the pawn shop. If he lingered for his after dinner drink, the shop would probably be closed. The old Scout was not as vigilant as even a couple of years ago. He did not notice the woman at the next table squeeze her companions hand and point to her own watch. He did not even notice that they lingered after paying their bill, sipping from empty coffee cups. He was not aware that she stealthily followed him, watching as he went into the pawn shop.

Sarah and Ari were gleeful as they examined the rubies. Sarah had purchased them minutes after Abbot left the pawn shop. She had paid almost twice what the man Abbot had received for them. Still, neither sum was anywhere near their worth. These would go in a museum in Israel. They were a part of a famous collection lost during the war.

Ari had trailed Sarah at a safe distance, and picked up Abbot's trail when she went into the pawn shop. He now knew where the Nazi lived! Sarah had teased his name from the pawn shop keeper, saying she needed information to validate the jewelry. When this ploy didn't work, a small bribe proved irresistible to the clerk.

Their supervisors were not quite so exuberant. They needed more proof to expedite Abbot and put him on trial. There was always the option of a quick kill. The trials got more publicity and more donations to this covert operation, so they were preferred. Sarah and Ari were ordered to stay in contact with Abbot.

"Go where he goes. If he begins to notice you strike up a conversation. Be tourists in need of a local to help them to find the less trumpeted aspects of Bogota. Pay the dinner bills when you run into him at a restaurant.

"If he's who I think he is, he is a loner. It'll be difficult to trap him through an offer of friendship. You'll need to make him think he is pulling one over on you. Taking advantage of your naivete."

Meanwhile, the 'young girl' Abbot longed for was no longer so young. Amber had worked as a real estate agent during all of her adult life. She had met John Dumonti when he was a student planning a summer trip abroad. Their attraction for one another was instantaneous and mutual. He canceled his plans for travel, taking summer classes instead. The sooner he finished law school, the sooner he could support a wife.

After marriage, Amber continued her work on a part-time basis, so she could spend most of her time with their rapidly arriving children. And a few years, John became tired of the limited role he had in the large law partnership in New Orleans. He wanted his own practice back in the town where he grew up and had friends and contacts. The only one disappointed by this decision was Amber's mother, Alexia. She had thrived in the city environment and was the chief cook in a popular French restaurant. Also, she had a close relationship with the owner of a small, picturesque inn in the French quarter. She had refused his marriage offers, wondering if she was a widow, but not knowing. With Amber's new family moving, Alexia left the Dumonti household and moved into her lover's posh apartment in the inn.

John's connections in Fox Willow proved helpful not only in starting his law firm, but for Pearl's chosen career also. So, it happened that it was Amber who welcomed Ruby to Fox Willow. It was Amber who helped Ruby find the lovely Victorian home.

Amber had always wondered how such a young woman was so well-heeled. True, it was easy to understand how Ruby could afford to buy the old Victorian house. The house was run down and was priced very low even for a low market. What Amber did not understand was how a woman with no family had the funds to make major repairs and modernizations. The renovations alone cost a fortune. The lovely Victorian furnishings with which Ruby filled the house were fabulous.

It was when Ruby began to plan so that she could accommodate more people, that Amber's curiosity became unbearable. She asked Ruby to share with her the reason for such a gamble.

"If this were a tropical island or a beautiful plantation or near a ski resort, I wouldn't ask. But, we are in the middle of nowhere. Why should people come here to our little town? We don't have enough guests here in a year to make it worth spending this much on the house."

"Well, just think of the business I will create for you," Ruby teased. "I plan to have most of the house converted to small studio apartments that are handicapped accessible. I can name at least three elderly people who hobble into a restaurant at least three or four times a week. When they leave they go to their homes with steep steps, outside and inside. They heat homes almost as large as mine, yet they live alone.

"When my renovations are complete, if I'll invite them for tea and show them the apartments. Then they can call you. You can sell their homes to couples with three or four children crowded into those wartime two-bedroom cottages. Then you'll have houses to offer all the first time homeowners. Don't you think Alice and Jim Davis would love to get out of his mother's house before their baby is born? Also, there's Joan and Fred Thompson. They don't have a baby on the way. But everyone in Fox Willow knows that Joan's mother has trouble hiding how she feels about Fred. Or how about the Moore's? They have three teenage daughters to share one bathroom. It must be a difficult situation.

"Fred and Joan are praying for the promotion at the bank. If Fred doesn't get it, they're thinking of looking for jobs out of town. Think of it this way," Ruby continued. "What do you have on the market right now, that might be affordable for the Davis's or the Thompson's?"

"To be honest? Absolutely nothing!" Amber replied, shaking her head. "You are absolutely unbelievable! How many studio apartments did you say?"

Ruby smiled. "Most of the furniture I purchased is from secondhand stores. I've had fun searching for it within a 200 mile radius."

"Nevertheless, Ruby," Amber advised, "you could put the money you're spending into some kind of growth fund. That would probably garner you as much as you will make on the B & B. You wouldn't have to work so hard."

"Well I guess you won't give up until I tell you my real reasons. I'm trying to create an instant family. I want to have all the people that come to my house to be a family to me, whether they stay one night or several years. Imagine how good it would be for Lisa Reynolds to have some place to live that serves a fine breakfast every morning. No need to even mention the small refrigerator in her room and the elevator and handicapped accessible bathroom. Also do you know a woman who is more fun? "

Ruby did not add that she hoped her own mother could find such a place. Ruby had always thought she would be the one to never leave home. She had not imagined marriage. She always thought of taking care of her mother or dad in their darkest years. The hardest part of the witness protection program was leaving her family behind. She continued to explain to her new friend.

"I'm not really looking to make money. A place of peace where I can make friends with my customers is my plan. Hopefully some will come back year after year and vacation here. It is truly beautiful in the fall when the leaves are in the height of their colors. I've heard the lilacs are glorious come Spring. I'll plant lilies and roses and all sorts of cut flowers so that there will be blooms all year. I'll make the house so beautiful that just to see it will make it worth the trip to Fox Willow."

And that is as far as Amber ever got in terms of finding out the source of Ruby's finances. Thinking back, she decided it was just as well not asking more questions lest Ruby start asking questions of her.

Chapter Thirteen

Dreams and Realities

That night Ruby woke up from a deep sleep – one of her most restful sleeps for a long time. She had been dreaming about Jack, her childhood boyfriend. What a sweet dream!

Ruby lay back on the pillows and let the dream embrace her. She wanted to linger with it just a little longer. In the dream she and Jack were on the back seat of his sedan. Jack was mumbling about how sweet she tasted. Ruby was breathless! She had her hands under his shirt, caressing his back. Jack was nibbling a little now, teasing her with his tongue.

Ruby sighed. It wasn't working? She couldn't get the feeling that had been so real in her dream. Well, that was the trouble. For Ruby, eroticism was for dreams; not for reality. She wondered where Jack was and who he was dating. Probably Margie. Margie was two years younger than Jack and Ruby. Even so, she had made no effort to hide her attraction to Jack.

"And why do I care now?" Ruby asked herself. "I should be hoping that Jack finds someone to care for him. All I have left of my old life are dreams and memories. The sooner I accept that, the happier I'll be."

Miles away, a young man awoke from the same dream. Jack stretched sleepily in the bed, turned over, and cuddled the woman next to him.

"Rachel, sweet Rachel," Jack muttered, nestling closer. The

woman sat up in bed, abruptly. She slapped his face hard.

"Get dressed!" She demanded. "Get out of this house! Go and find her – your precious Rachel! She's the one who left. She obviously never wants to see you again. But she's under your skin and you will never be happy with another woman until you find her. I don't want to ever see you again!"

Margie shouted. She did not mean what she said. She knew she would regret saying it, even as the words came out. She could not hold them back. She with aching with anger, and with love that would never be returned in full portion to hers.

Jack dressed in the clothes that he had worn the day before. He would shower and change at his mother's house. Then he'd asked for a leave of absence from the police force. He was a good detective; he should be able to find Rachel. Except for one reason, he would have searched already. Mike, Rachel's father, had discouraged him from trying.

"Rachel's made her own way. Let her be." Mike had been adamant. Jack couldn't shake the feeling that something was dreadfully wrong. True, he and Rachel had never talked about a serious relationship. At least they had not talked about marriage and children. What they had done in the back seat of his sedan had been pretty serious. It'd been a commitment to him. It had been a way of pledging his troth to his childhood sweetheart.

Jack had never imagined a life without Rachel in it. What if he found her, and she told him to get lost to his face? Well, if she was convincing he could accept it. Somehow, he didn't think she would be convincing at all. If Rachel was in trouble, and he didn't even look, he'd never forgive himself. He'd already waited way too long.

"Mike, I need to talk to you," Margie whimpered into the telephone. "Jack is going off to look for Rachel. At least I think he is. I thought you should know before he left. He told me that you didn't want him to go several months ago. I'm afraid, well to be honest he talks about Rachel in his sleep. I got my dander up and told him he should go and find her. For some reason, I just thought you should know."

"Thanks for the call Margie. I'll talk to him. Rachel doesn't want us to come looking for her. She's not coming back. Jack needs you. Dreams are one thing, and reality another. If he decides to stay, be good to him."

Jack was signing the paperwork for his leave of absence when Mike walked into the precinct.

"Let's go have a cup of coffee and talk about this."

"Rachel's in trouble. I can feel it. It's just not right. I don't understand why you aren't looking for her, too."

"Not here!" Mike's voice was stern. His tone said more than his words. Jack reluctantly followed him. They went not to a diner, but to Mike's house. There they had the house all to themselves and Mike put on coffee before they sat down to talk.

"You're a bright boy, Jack. You tell me what happened to Rachel. You tell me why she just disappeared. Remember it was a day or two after she got through her training program. You know how long she had planned her career. You played cops and robbers with her when you were kids. Now you tell me where she is. You tell me why she doesn't want us to look for her."

Jack thought he spotted a tear in Mike's eye. He couldn't be sure, as Mike turned quickly and got up to pour the coffee.

The light went on in Jack's head.

"Undercover! You're telling me she went undercover?"

"I'm telling you nothing!" Mike blurted as he handed Jack a hot mug of coffee. "Do you drink it black? I'm asking you to think."

"Okay. Can I think out loud?" Jack answered thoughtfully. "It's been too many months, Mike. Unless things went wrong; I mean dreadfully wrong. No one is undercover for this long unless it's a huge operation. No, I don't want to think what I'm thinking."

"You didn't answer about the coffee - is black okay?" Mike slowly sipped his steaming drink. Jack nodded, indicating the coffee.

"Whatever you're thinking, Jack, we are out of the loop. You, Me, the Mrs.! Get a grip! Live your life! We think about Rachel everyday. We miss her! We're damn proud of her! We don't expect her back! Not that we know. We just figure the time is right for the next step to happen. We have to trust our colleagues. We have to believe they will take care of her."

"How did you know I was going to look for her?" Jack asked after a thoughtful interlude. "Did Margie call you?"

"That woman is crazy about you." Mike advised. "Count your blessings and let sleeping dogs lie!"

Jack ripped up the papers requesting a leave of absence. That night he went back to Margie's apartment.

"I can't promise I won't dream, Margie. When I'm awake I'm with you. If that's not enough, then so be it."

"I love you Jack. I need a lifetime guarantee. I need children and grandchildren someday. I can't wait forever for Rachel to step out of your dreams and knock on your door. But I'm not ready to give up. If it's okay with you I'll give you until a year from today. If you aren't ready to commit to me by then, I'm going to look for someone else."

Jack couldn't answer. He took Margie in his arms and cried like a cop never cries. Finally, he controlled himself.

"I just hope she hasn't knocked on death's door. Whether or not that's happened, she's just a dream now. A kid I played cops with from age four.

"You're my reality. You're the one I'll have kids with when the time comes. I'll get you a ring if you'll still have it. We'll make this legal so long as you promise not to kick me out over a stupid dream."

Devlin O'Leary had long ago arrived at the same conclusion that Jack was just now trying to accept. Rachel's younger brother was intrigued by his Sister's sudden disappearance. A stout and athletic twelve at the time, the feeling he got from his parents was his clue. They seemed anxious when anyone asked about Rachel. Jack and three or four of her girlfriends kept calling for her address. At first his Mom would say Rachel was traveling. After a few weeks she would say that Rachel was trying to decide where to settle down - she didn't have an address. Yes, Rachel was fine. She just called yesterday.

"Mom, next time Rachel calls, can I talk to her?" Devlin asked at the dinner table.

"Rachel hasn't called, Son." Dad's voice was questioning. It also had that strange mixture of pride and anxiety that accompanied any mention of his Sister.

Devlin looked at his Mom.

"Well, what am I suppose to say when people ask for her address? Should I say that as soon as she finished her training she up and joined the circus? Ran away with a clown?" Kathleen dashed from the table, knocking over her chair.

Mike looked at his son.

"We all miss Rachel. She misses us, too, but we have to think of her as doing what she chose, whatever that is."

"Yeah, and you wouldn't be bursting with pride if that didn't have something to do with police work," Devlin thought.

By the time he was sixteen, Devlin had a plan. He took extra courses and completed high school in three years. After two years at the local community college he had saved enough from his part-time jobs to go to the state university. At twenty-one his resumes and references from various law-enforcement cousins and college teachers brought the letter he awaited. Devlin was accepted by the FBI as a New Agent Trainee or NAT.

Jack was the first person Devlin called. They had first become close when Rachel and Jack were dating. Even though Devlin was a pest at times, Jack thought of him as his little brother. Since Jack had made detective in the local police force, the two had renewed their friendship.

Devlin had a long road of evaluations and training ahead of him. The NATS were trained at the U.S. Marine Corps Base in Quantico, Virginia. Devlin would be there for over four months. The physical training alone culled many of the NATS. By the second week Devlin was convinced that he had not started out in the outstanding physical shape he had thought. By the third he began to enjoy the exercises to increase strength and endurance. In fact, there were many things about the training he enjoyed.

His favorite days were the role plays set up in Hogan's Alley. This was a little town set up within the Marine Base for hands-on simulations of actual crimes. The trainees and faculty were divided into good guys and bad guys as various scenarios were acted out.

"Just like us kids use to do in the back yard," Devlin thought.

"Well, a little like that," he admitted when it was his turn to play 'robber'. Experiencing the 'takedown' from the criminal's end of things was no fun.

Chapter Fourteen

Thirst for Power

Greg threw his glass into the mirror, smattering it. Another bill from a stupid private eye! He had private eyes in 30 cities, and none of them could find Amelia. It had been ten years, and he had paid out thousands of dollars for nothing! Absolutely nothing! Perhaps she really had met with foul play. Surely they would have found a body by now, though. Greg was furious. Could she really have tricked him and gotten away. In addition to all these private eye bills, housing prices had gone down - down - down. None of his investments were doing well. The locals were on his back to do something about the junkie places he was renting to a bunch of stupid tenants. Even the newspaper was carrying articles with pictures of the busted plumbing and the holes in the sheet rock. He needed a plan.

The phone was ringing. It'd been ringing for an hour. Finally he picked it up.

"What is it?" He demanded.

"Mr. Brason? I'm so glad I reached you! The press called! Channel Two. They're coming here early tomorrow morning to interview you about the apartments."

"The hell they are! Don't open the office, Mildred. Report for duty here at my house, 9 a.m. Make sure you're here sharply at nine and don't tell a soul that we're closing the office."

Greg slammed down the phone. He had to think! Now, he would be annoyed by that stupid secretary! Why had he asked her to come? He should call her up right now tell her not to come.

"On the other hand, maybe he could use her." Greg let his imagination soar. "Yes! Maybe he could use Mildred. The woman had a crush on him. For the ten years she had worked for him she practically fawned over him. Once or twice he had taken advantage of her obvious amorous feelings.

He had kept her working there because of her skills. She was one of the most efficient secretaries he had ever had. Mildred wasn't beautiful, or even pretty. However, in a certain way, she was attractive. She took care of herself, groomed herself well, and stayed on the skinny side. He liked his women lean and passive. Mildred was anything but passive. Well, maybe tomorrow he would try again. Anything to take his mind off these wretched bills.

By the time Greg woke up the next morning he had devised a new plan. Mildred was easy prey. He would whisk her off her feet and marry her by the end of the week. They would go on a quick honeymoon, while he bought insurance on her life. Too bad she couldn't live much longer! Depending on the terms of the insurance policy, perhaps she was going to be suicidal. Maybe she was prone to accidents. He'd figure it out on the honeymoon. This was going to be almost as much fun as living with Amelia. He would never forget the rush he would get from the power he had over Amelia. Yes, she must have run into foul play. She would never have run away from him; she wouldn't have dared. Greg called and fired all the private detectives he currently had looking.

That morning Greg took extra time in the shower and groomed carefully. He started dressing in his business clothes, then changed his mind. From the back of his closet Greg pulled out his silk lounging pajamas. Amelia had given him these on their first anniversary. He had only worn them one time. The silk felt sensuous against his body. He had punished Amelia for spending so much. It had been her first severe punishment. Always before she had thought he was playing. Even so she would get angry. He'd loved to see her angry. Too bad it didn't last longer. Greg had loved to see the fear even more than anger.

When Greg opened the door to admit Mildred, he had his old swagger back. Yes, Mildred was the perfect patsy. She had no family to ask stupid questions. Her mother and father had died in an automobile accident some years back. He knew this from the investigative report he had done before he hired her. She also had no sisters or brothers. Usually loved ones were an advantage in Greg's scheme of things. They could be used to intimidate. He had used this technique often, especially with Amelia. But he did not want to kill Amelia. He had not needed to kill anyone at that point. Yes, no family was definitely an advantage in this case.   Greeting Mildred, Greg was nothing if not charming. He dictated two or three letters of minor importance. When she tried to talk about the phone calls and messages he hushed her. He stared at her as if he had never looked at a woman before.

"Mildred, I hope you don't mind that I call you Mildred."

"Oh, no sir, I prefer that!"

"There is something we seriously need to talk about. All these messages will have to take a back seat. I want you to start training your replacement. Should I dictate an advertisement, or would you prefer to write it? You certainly know what the job entails."

"But Sir? Why? Is it money? My salary? I would much rather take a pay cut than to lose my job." Mildred was desperate.

Greg faked a deep sigh.

"Don't pretend, Mildred, that you don't know how I feel about you. You could have filed a harassment charge against me long ago. It has come to a point that I just can't work with you day in and day out without touching you. Without wanting you."

Greg rose and started pacing the floor.

"You cannot know how much this pains me. This kind of burning desire and to know the woman is totally untouchable. Because of all things - the law dictating zero fraternization. I'm your employer. I cannot touch you without it being illegal. I fight every day to keep my hands off you.

"Right now I want to take you in my arms - darn, why am I saying this? I cannot think of my business when you're around, and as you well know, it's going downhill."

Greg turned so that he wasn't facing Mildred. The mixed look of joy and fear on her face was overwhelming. If he laughed he would give it all away. He'd better not add the part about his dreams. That would be overkill.

" Good thing I rehearsed this in the mirror," Greg thought. "Otherwise I know I couldn't keep a straight face."

When he turned back to face Mildred, she handed him a sheet of paper. Greg looked down at the neat handwriting, and almost felt ashamed.

"I, Mildred Moore, hereby do submit my resignation, effective the date noted above. I volunteer my services to find and train a replacement. In no way will I hold my employer accountable for any future, present or past actions of an intimate nature. These were sought by me, and enjoyed by me. Clearly the pleasure was mutual." Signed and dated by Mildred Moore.

Greg set the paper on his desk and took Mildred in his arms. He started with gentle, tender caresses, hoping his anatomy would not betray him. Mildred became impatient and stripped open her blouse. Greg reached to help her, purposely ripping the blouse.

Throwing his silk robe to the floor, Greg lifted and Mildred and carried her to the bedroom. She was tearing at his buttons, anxious, excited. Greg felt the power – his power! Women found him irresistible! Why had he been sitting around waiting for Amelia. He could've had any woman he wanted.

Greg entered her too soon. Not that she wasn't ready. He just would have preferred to make her wait; to keep her on edge, wanting him. Before they rose from the bed, Greg proposed. They ate a hearty lunch on their way to the town hall. There they discovered that there would be a waiting period of a few days. They took an afternoon flight to Las Vegas and were married in the first chapel they found.

By the next morning they were back in the office. Mildred set up appointments for her replacement to be interviewed by a private employment service. Greg was equally busy. He had insurance papers made out for 2 million each for himself and for Mildred. He made Mildred his beneficiary, explaining he always wanted to take care of her.

When he took the papers to her to sign she did not notice that they were not all alike. In front of the insurance salesman as witness, Greg laid out the papers so that only the signature line was evident. Mildred was signing a document which she had not been told about as well as the one she knew about. The second set of papers purchased insurance on Mildred's life. This document made Greg the sole recipient of her estate and life insurance.

Greg had forgotten just one small detail. He had no death

certificate for Amelia. He had no record that they had ever divorced. Greg's marriage to Mildred was illegal.

****

All went well at first, or so Greg thought until the insurance company and the cops began an investigation. Would it never end? Mildred had been dead for six months. Still, the inquiry was continuing. Greg couldn't have been more furious. The nerve of the law enforcement people hounding him like this. Mildred's death was clearly accidental. He wasn't even there when she fell down the stairs. They couldn't prove that he was anywhere near.

As Greg's plan had evolved in his mind, he was sure he needed stairs. It would not work very well to have her fall from the stairs in the apartment building. Not with all the elevators around. Greg wanted the joy of watching her as he killed her. He wanted to beat her, and only steep stairs that he could throw her down later would suffice to cover his actions.

One week after they were married they left for an extended honeymoon in Bermuda. Silently, he cursed her efficiency. She made reservations ahead of time. Greg insisted on looking for a better condo for the second week.

"This is beautiful," Mildred had protested. "How could we want anything lovelier?"

"It's moldy. Don't you smell it? It stinks!" Greg complained.

He would not let her call agencies no matter how much she pleaded. Instead they took trips every afternoon looking over condos. They only had one day left in the pleasant cottage before Greg finally found what he was looking for. One good thing had come about during this wait for the insurance to come through. Amelia's little sister,

-145-

Bess, had grown into a beautiful young woman. As a child she had never seen anything but Greg's charming side. Recently she had come to his law office and offered to testify in his behalf if he decided to sue the insurance company. She would tell the court of the loving marriage that he had with her sister.

"We haven't been in touch at all, regretfully," Greg mentioned casually. "How did you know about my disagreement with the insurance company?"

"Why, it's made the national news. Some guy with a byline picked up the sad story of a woman dying on her honeymoon. A human interest story it was called to begin with. I guess some people read it who are uptight about your apartment houses. Last night an 'investigative reporter' was on the late news saying he believed you would either sue or be sued."

The information annoyed Greg, but right now his attention was on the girl. She resembled Amelia in every way, except she was younger, fresher. What could be better! Give it a few months and he would be courting Bess. Since he couldn't find Amelia, Bess would be his next, well -- he wouldn't say victim. He wouldn't go that far.

Chapter Fifteen

Bread, Jam and Friendship

Early May, 1989

The Queen's were taking advantage of the glorious Spring day, gathering for their tea at the Gazebo. A couple had checked in earlier appeared, each armed with cameras. Ruby had approached them immediately.

"I'm sorry," Ruby said to them. "Please put your cameras away. When you signed in you agreed to no pictures of any guest or employee without their written, signed and witnessed permission. If you want pictures of the gazebo you'll have to wait until no one's here. Unfortunately, now I'll need to take your film."

"We'll just have everyone here sign their permission," the woman responded. "We're freelance photographers and we have an assignment from one of the television networks. I'm sure all these ladies would love to be on TV."

"You're assumption is dead wrong," Ruby answered. "I, for one, do not give permission to have my picture taken. Please take your film out and place it on the table. If you refuse I'll call the local police station."

The woman complied with a snarl; the man without comment. Ruby pulled the streamer of film from it's casing, destroying the film placed on the table. She was not aware of the earlier footage the male photographer had taken with an optical video camera. The small patios that led from the bedrooms had been perfect for his purposes. He would have liked to keep the stills on the film Ruby demolished but he didn't need it. Thankfully, Ruby had not noticed the tripod he had set up on the patio. His state-of-the-art video camera with vroom zoom lens brought the ladies at the gazebo into full focus. If there had been a real bee sitting on this innkeeper's nose, the optical camera would have picked it up. Almost as good, he had a great shot of a sparrow eating crumbs on the table.

The Queen Bees were close to abandoning their tea after this unwelcomed interruption. However, Gilda and Lisa had seen the encounter from the window and came out with questions. The conversation soon turned to the quilts the Queens made for the hospitalized children. The past week had proved a challenge keeping up with admissions in the pediatric section of the hospital.

"We couldn't have covered all the children this month without your help," Amber praised the two women. "It is rare that our small hospital has over 2 children admitted in a week and some weeks absolutely none."

"It is this dreadful flu going around. It's a wonder more don't have problems. Four of the children Opal and I saw last week were asthmatic with flu on top," Pearl shook her head. "Little Jerry Owens could hardly breathe when we were there."

"You know we love doing this!" Gilda said. "Lisa and I are forming our own Bee, did we tell you? When we aren't working with you we're going to make a quilt on the side."

"We may have to ask one or two of you some questions. We want to make the New York Beauty.

"Now that is a tall order," Jade answered. "If you'll pass that Rosy Raspberry Jam over this way, I'll consider helping you."

Mel Owens walked out to the gazebo where the ladies were sipping the last of their tea.

"I guess I'm going to have to learn to quilt, so I can get invited to your teas," Mel teased.

"Whatever gave you the idea you needed an invitation?" Ruby asked, fondly.

"Actually, I was in the middle of a who-dun-it or I would have come out before. You're message machine has been singing a tune in there. Rang at least seven times in the last 15 minutes."

"Probably Mathilda from the Church. She wants me to join the choir and has threatened to pester me until I say 'Yes'," Ruby fretted.

Lisa stamped her foot! She was very protective of Ruby.

"I told her Sunday morning was often your busiest time. Late brunch instead of breakfast, locals begging to be invited, guests of the Inn asking to have their families included."

"It's because I often make it to the early services. She understands I can't be in the later choir. I'd best go check the message machine. Do I need to bring more jam when I return?"

Three of Ruby's calls were from the same person - Rex Larson, her contact! He sat up a meeting with her for the following week, but not in Fox Willow. Oddly, he asked her to drive to the nearby village of East Elmville. A couple of the calls were for reservations and one from Mathilda. Ruby agreed to one hymn as a guest soloist, but not to a long commitment.

Deciding that Ruby was tied up with phone calls, the Queen Bee's loaded the trays with the remains of the tea. Amber turned to Lisa and Gilda.

"Crystal and I are going on a day tour next week - an antique search, just for fun. Would you like to come."

"I'd love it," said Lisa. "I've been searching for something special for my granddaughter's birthday."

"Can we stop at a couple of fabric shops?" Gilda asked. "There are several things we still need for our quilt."

"Don't forget to look for my treasures," Opal interjected.

"We know," Crystal answered. "Any time a Queen Bee worth her salt crosses the threshold of a flee market or antique shop, look for old silver coins, broaches or anything small that looks like Opal!"

"Who else is going?" asked Pearl.

"We're hoping Ruby, but we haven't asked her yet. If you want to come, we can skip her this trip."

"No, too many recitals, scout meetings and softball games for my crew next week. I just like to hear all the juicy details!" Pearl confessed.

"You know I'll swap vehicles with you for the day," Opal offered.. "Minnie the mini van at your service. That way if you find anything made of teak you can call Jake with the price and have room to transport it! He's getting desperate to get started on that special order."

"I don't know teak from oak," Amber laughed.

"Got you covered there," Lisa spoke proudly. "I didn't spend 20 years dealing in antiques without learning something."

"If you're taking the van, could I ride along?" They all turned to look at Mel. It was rare for him to leave Fox Willow. He usually stuck close to the Inn.

"Why, just what we need!" exclaimed Amber. "Our very own handsome escort."

No one, not even Ruby, knew that Mel had been an officer in

the Secret Service before retiring. Nor did they know that Rex had been the one to tell Mel about the Gems and Jam. This place was a perfect retirement solution for Mel. With no family, he had soon adopted Lisa and Gilda. Mel had never married as his assignments meant he had no place to call home. He wouldn't submit a wife and children to that kind of life. He had almost married once, but she had wanted him to change careers.

Always a man to enjoy female company, Mel was delighted to have the daily contact with the other permanent residents. He and Lisa shared an interest in professional baseball, and loved to argue over who might win. All three enjoyed gin rummy. Mel was writing his childhood memoirs and Gilda was an eager typist. Doggone efficient, too, but then she had done it for 20 years. All this and a consultant salary to compliment his retirement check and for nothing except keeping a watchful eye over Ruby. If she decided not to take the trip with the others, his arthritis was sure to flare up again!

Ruby's Jam of the Day

Rosy Raspberry Jam

Ingredients:

5 cups sugar

1 stalk rhubarb

6 roses - use petals only

1 qt. raspberries or enough to make 2 cups when crushed.

Procedure:

It would be nice if we could just save any flower petals that were falling from a bouquet of roses that came from a florist shop. However, we do not know what has been sprayed on these roses. Likely it is something we don't want to eat. Also, if they were a present from your lover to atone for jerk-like behavior, they would probably be bitter.

Growing your own roses or getting them from an organic gardener assures your guests have no stomach aches following consumption. Of course, overeating can cause stomach aches. Perhaps I should prepare a note for all to sign when they sit down to eat. How does this sound?

This establishment bears no responsibility for physical pain or ailments caused from overeating. Likewise, for injuries from food fights occurring when all want the rest of the jam! Sit down at my table at your own risk!

Rose petals are pretty placed in the jelly whole or chopped up in the jar of jam to add color. I particular like white rose petals cut up like confetti and sprinkled throughout my deep red raspberry jam - like little stars in a cerise sky.

Wash your petals and dry between 2 layers of paper toweling. Wash raspberries and crush until you have 2 cups crushed red raspberries. I like to add rhubarb to my raspberry jam. Slice one stalk rhubarb into circular coins and cook until soft coins blend together.

Add half of the sugar to boiled rhubarb and stir in raspberries. Cook until the mixture is well-blended and all one color. Remove from the heat and add the remaining sugar. Cook until candy thermometer indicates jelly/jam. Or cook until mixture is at a spreadable point when tested on a spoon that has been kept on ice for this purpose. Don't forget to stir in chopped roses petals before you put jam in hot sterile jars prior for processing and sealing.

Serve in small old-fashioned salt cellers placed beside each breakfast plate. Provide salt spoons and a choice of yeast breads such as Parker rolls, Angel biscuits, or French Twist Roll-ups.

Chapter Sixteen

Crossfire

Mason had not lost his obsessive desire to have Lily completely enmeshed in his own world – for him alone. Even so, he had almost abandoned his search for Lily. He had discovered that the father of his partner, Vincent Lopez, had sworn to shoot Lily before the trial of his son. He hired hit men , mostly snipers, to find her with orders to shoot on sight.

One of the hit men had a reputation of being merciless. It was this man, Elroy, who argued with Lopez.

"What do you mean you have more than one hit man?" Elroy said angrily. "The others will just get in my way."

"This has to be resolved immediately," Lopez yelled into the phone! "There can be no room for error. This woman cannot testify against my son!"

Elroy slammed down the phone, steaming!

By that night he found a woman singing in a night club in Chicago. One of his cohorts had described her. She had the same coloring and was about the size of Lily. She even went by the name of Lillian. Lopez and all of the other hit men were working without a photograph of Lily. They were going on what information they had managed to elicit from some of the gangsters who had been customers at the Starlight nightclub.

Elroy took the next plane to Chicago. He found a roof across from the singer's apartment. From there he watched until he had a clear shot. He reported to Lopez that the job was done.

The murdered woman was identified as Lillian Green. Her

family in the Chicago area claimed her body and gave her a burial service.

You fool! You killed the wrong woman!" Lopez yelled at Elroy.

"How was I to know? You don't even have a picture of the Broad. I want my money!"

"I'll have you shot first!" Lopez yelled back at the hit man.

Elroy was furious. He decided it was time to look up Mason Peters. The information that Elroy furnished Mason was devastating. Mason was really worried. So worried that he hired Elroy to eliminate Lopez. At the same time he doubled his efforts to find Lily. He was determined to go about this carefully. He did not know how many hits Lopez had out on Lily. Mason realized if he found her too quickly, Lopez or one of his thugs would be right behind him. They might shoot Lily before Mason could stop them.

Mason did have a photograph of Lily. He had taken it discreetly one night in the nightclub. He treasured it and kept it with him at all times. He refused to even give it to the men he had searching for Lily. He was fearful if he did, that a copy of it would get back to Lopez. His orders were "Find her; Immediately call me. Keep an eye on her until I arrive to identify her.

So far there had been 32 women he had been called to observe. None of them were Lily. However, the lackey Mason had watching his back confirmed Mason's suspicions. Lopez did have people shadowing Mason. He would be thankful when the hit could be made on Lopez.

Mason's major concern was the size of Lopez's operation. Lopez had a huge family. He had three other sons besides Vincent. Lopez was known as the Godfather with a territory larger than Mason's.

Mason would have to work carefully. He refused to believe that Lily was any kind of spy or undercover cop. Someone else had leaked information about Mason. Probably even Lopez himself. Lopez had not liked the fact that he and Vincent were doing business together. Lopez had long wanted Mason to join his operation. Mason had refused each time approached. Mason was a loner. He preferred to run his own show, with no boss to tell him what to do and what not to do.

Yes, Ruby had not one but two entrenched gangsters searching for her. One wanted to keep her in a cage all to himself; the other wanted to kill her on the spot.

"Would they find her? Would she get caught in the crossfire?"

Lopez wasn't used to delays. He hated incompetence. He set up a meeting with his son, Zeke.

"Any organization worth its salt would have found that Broad before Vincent's trial, " Lopez complained. "Now he's in prison for years! Someone's got to take the blame for this. Who did you have in charge of the search?"

"That would be 'the knifer' - Kiefer!" Zeke replied anxiously. They both knew that Zeke had taken personal charge of the operation.

"We need to show the others that we don't tolerate incompetence. Choose three you can trust to give him a lesson. I don't want to see him in the hospital. I want to see him back at work in a week. No broken bones."

"I'll just have them slap him around a bit. It will just give him more incentive to look harder." Lopez was ashamed that his son was not taking responsibility for his incompetence. All the men would know that he was giving the knifer the beating that he, Zeke, deserved.

After the meeting Lopez paced the floor. He had four sons.

Now the brightest one was in prison.

One was still a kid, just turning 14. Another, Steven, wanted nothing to do with the business. The best Lopez could hope from him was that he would become a lawyer and advise Lopez from a legal perspective. And then there was Zeke. Lopez had high hopes for Zeke. Now his dishonesty among the faithful was going to get him killed.

"Probably by the knifer!" Lopez worried. "Well so be it!"

At least Vincent's sentence gave him someone he could trust behind the bars. Lots of information went through federal prisons. Lots of action, too. What do they say, "No ill wind doesn't blow somebody good."

Another old saying is that all good things come in threes! Or is it all bad things? Either way, there were three men determined that Ruby's future was in their hands. In addition to the one who wanted to cage her and the one who wanted to kill her there was another. Yes, another man was enchanted by Ruby.

"Ruby the beautiful! Ruby the endangered! Ruby who had been Rachel - a small-town kid who wanted to grow up and be a cop." Rex Larson first met the multifaceted young woman as the new recruit, Rachel. He had quietly followed her training, sometimes through one-way mirrors; sometimes through paper review.

Rachel was one of four recruits across the state who were being considered for the undercover job. In the end Rachel was the unlucky one - the winner! Rex would be in love with Rachel except for his fatherly feelings toward her. His own daughters were older by just two and three years.

Lily was a different story. She was nothing like his daughters! Oh, what a torch singer Lily had become! One day she stepped out of her jeans and sweats into slinky dresses, bolero jackets for chilly nights, and spike-heeled shoes. On that day Rachel became Lily. 'The perfect undercover agent. 'A chamaeleon'! Rex accepted that he responded on a different level to Lily. A much more physical one. Rex was a professional. He had full control of his feelings. It was his job to keep this woman safe. He could best do that if he stayed professional and objective.

Now Lily, once Rachel, had become the business woman, Ruby. As much as Rex had admired the other two personalities, he admired Ruby the most. What Ruby had done within her budget was deserving of respect.

"True, she's taken a home improvement loan. That's not usually allowed. But this seems like a great investment." Rex scratched his chin. "Not so much as a bed and breakfast. The real value in Ruby's investment lies in the apartments for the elderly. Those lucky people who get to live there would have most of the advantages of one of those step type homes for the elderly. However, they would not have to sign their life away. They keep the money from the sale of their homes, and control it themselves. Ruby offered a six-month lease, or one year if the renter preferred. She was providing a healthy breakfast, but the "guest" did not have long corridors to walk down to get to the dining room. Rents were reasonable. So much so that Ruby did not have to worry about vacancies. She already had a waiting list.

"I should go ahead and sign up," laughed Rex, who was near retirement. "That way I won't need to worry about how committed the next agent assigned as her contact will prove to be. Also, I love her jams, especially the blueberry. What did she call it? Blueberry Florets, because of the borage blossoms that added the great flavor."

Rex began thinking this in jest, but it dawned on him that this was really a great idea. None of his kids would want to take him into their homes. Not that they didn't love each other. They had their own lives scattered all over the States. Also once he was out of the loop regarding Ruby, he'd have ants in his pants worrying about her.

Rex's worry about Ruby was well founded. Sooner or later, either Lopez or Mason would figure out what had happened to Ruby. Whoever found her first, the other would be close on his heels. Even if Rex or his successor was there in time, Ruby might get caught in the crossfire. Rex needed to set up a backup identity for Ruby. He just couldn't get the go ahead on funding. No one else in the agency shared his concern.

Ruby's Jam of the Day

Blueberry Florets

Preparations:

Gather borage blossoms when the little blue flowers are smiling up at you. These will be a lot easier to pick than Dandelion buds. The blossoms freeze beautifully and will add a great deal of cool, sweet richness to your blueberry jam. Try to collect 40 to 50 blossoms for this recipe.

You need six pints of blueberries. A pint less would be okay but any less hardly makes enough jam to last until it's cool.

The berries do not have to be all completely ripe. A few not quite ready to nibble will add tartness. Did you know that women through the ages who did not have oranges or lemons to add tartness simply used partly unripe berries?

Crush the berries. Hopefully you have 4 cups crushed berries.

If you have a lot left over just call me. I love crushed

blueberries even if a few less ripe ones make my tongue tingle. If I am too far away, make a pie. Call a kid. Add milk and sugar and eat them yourself. Put them in muffins. Put them in nut breads. I could go on and on. There's a song about lots of ways to leave your lover. Believe me! There are even more ways to use extra blueberries.

If you don't have quite enough you can add water or minced apple to make 4 cups. I suggest you go out and get more blueberries. If you don't eat them soon, the birds will.

Add 7 cups of sugar for your 4 cups of very crushed berries. Be sure you have measured your crushed berries rather than your whole berries. The crushed ones compact.

You measured the whole? Oh, No! Have you already eaten the extra ? Oh, well you could just eat the berries and save calories from all that sugar. Or, go to your blueberry bush - send someone to the store.

Meanwhile boil the little blue borage blossoms in a quarter cup of water. Once you bring to a boil, turn down heat and simmer for about 10 to 15 minutes. Strain, removing flowers. Boil liquid down to about 1/8 cup of rich borage juice.

Mix sugar, berries and borage liquid. Bring to a full rolling boil, so high that you can hardly stir it down. Boil hard like this for one minute, but don't forget, you must be stirring all this minute; stirring fast and stirring constantly.

Remove from the heat and stir in a bottle of liquid fruit pectin. Ladle these into your hot jars and follow the usual procedure, you know the drill by now. You will have 10 half pint jars, and you can decorate as you please. I like to tie little sayings printed on strips of heavy paper around each jar that I will put on my 'for sale' shelf. Those that will be used on my breakfast tables will simply have tightfitting lids to keep them from any harm.

Of course, I know how to remove the lids quickly, so the jam is endangered any time I need a midnight snack!

Hint: If you enjoy ice tea in hot weather, freeze borage blossoms in ice and use in the tea. They are lovely!

Chapter Seventeen

Ghosts of the Past

Ruby was well aware that more than one person was looking for her. Rex kept her fully informed in their quarterly contacts. Others were traveling in a path of inquiry that, if followed successfully, would lead to Fox Willow.

Unknown to Pearl, someone was searching for her also. Pearl's life had been a happy one until Brad appeared on the scene. Her once loving and adoring mother shifted her attention from Pearl to this stranger. From the time Brad moved in, Pearl was left pretty much on her own.

After Brad's death the chasm widened between Pearl and her mother, Patricia. Once Brad's body was found, Patricia was inconsolable. She had truly adored Brad and had been blind to his faults. Pearl was disgusted that her mom was acting this way. She also was guilt ridden. She wanted to run away. Pearl and her mother talked about nothing important anymore. A little small talk or maybe what they were having for dinner.

Over the months that followed Patricia became more and more depressed. When summer break came, Pearl suggested that her mother go a trip.

"You need to get away for a while. I can stay with aunt Marie. That way you can go on a cruise or something. Something you really enjoy."

"Honey, would you mind? I think that is really what I need,"

Patricia agreed.

Once Pearl was out of the house, Patricia's first action was to seek a meeting with Brad's family. She drove the hundred and twenty miles to their home, anticipating a warm reception. Instead she got a cold shoulder. Brad's mother and father wanted nothing to do with her. They disapproved of the live-in arrangement that Brad and Patricia had preferred.

Only Brad's little brother seemed interested in Patricia. He was three years old and quite the charmer.

Little Bobby did not understand why his mother and father did not want to talk to Patricia. She seemed nice enough to him. When she came back a second time in the hope of making friends, Bobby met her at the door.

"My mom is sleeping. Dad isn't at home. Will you play with me?"

"That would be fun," Patricia told the boy. "Your Mom seems to have fallen asleep on the sofa. Do you have a room we can play in?" Patricia whispered.

Large sized lego blocks covered the floor in the room they entered. Patricia and Bobby sat on the floor and built a 'city'. Patricia noticed a lot of Brad's stuff. A large shelf dominated one wall of Bobby's room. The shelf was filled with trophies with Brad's name. Patricia had never realized that Brad had won so many ski awards. He was a Slalom champion and was a member of the local ski team.

Tiring of the blocks, Bobby showed Patricia his collection of stuffed monkeys. She asked about the trophies.

"A big brother won these. I'm going to win more when I get big," the child replied.

Patricia's visit with Bobby was short lived. His mother woke and ordered her out of the home.

"I never want to see you darken our door again," Brad's mother shouted. "Brad was no longer our son since he moved in with you. You're nothing but a whore."

The trophies Brad won skiing made Patricia even more thoughtful. The more she tried to forget about Brad, the more he was on her mind. She began her cruise and tried to party the night away. It seemed the more she tried to forget the more she thought about the ski accident that cost Brad his life.

Brad had been skiing since he was three years old or so it appeared when she was in Bobby's room. He had won kiddie trophies at five. Patricia never understood how the ski accident had happened. Why was Brad so foolhardy as to go on a trail not approved by the ski area? Why had he, an experienced skier, fallen off a cliff? She just couldn't understand it. She believed that Pearl knew more about it than she had ever told. Pearl had been skiing with Brad at the time. She had said they got separated earlier in the morning. Pearl said that Brad was just too good a skier for her and she couldn't keep up.

Over the years Patricia had sent presents to Bobby, Brad's brother. She always sent them on Brad's birthday. She had no idea when Bobby's birthday was. With the present she sent a message that said she knew that Brad would like to share birthdays.

"Unfortunately I don't even know when your birthday is, but I know when Brad's was and I know he would've liked to send you a gift on yours." Bobby always looked forward to the present that came gaily wrapped, and always holding something popular with kids at the time. The gifts had stopped abruptly. Unknown to Bobby, Patricia had contracted early Alzheimer's disease. She was placed in a nursing home to live out her days.

Bobby, too, fell into unfortunate circumstances. He and his father were on a fishing trip when they got a phone call to rush home. Bobby's mother had suffered a heart attack and was in intensive care. Speeding home in the late evening, their vehicle skidded off the road, hitting a tree. Bobby was thrown clear, suffering a few bruises. His father never woke up from the head injury which occurred on impact.

When Bobby finally reached his Mother, she was barely able to talk.

"Find Patricia, Bobby. She will help you. She's probably your real Mom."

"You are my real Mom," Bobby signed.

"Actually, your Grandma!" came the whispered response. "We adopted Brad's baby. He took you from your Mom when you were a newborn and told us if we didn't want to raise you he'd get rid of you. You're Grandfather didn't want you to know, but now you have no one except Patricia. Maybe not even her."

Bobby was beyond surprise. In her last breathes the woman who had been so dear to him tried to say that she really didn't know if Patricia was his Mom. She only knew that Brad lived with Patricia most of the time the year he was conceived. Bobby did not hear or did not understand. As he tearfully said good-bye to one Mother, he pledged to find another.

Pearl had lost contact over the years with Marie, her mother's sister. She felt that both Marie and Patricia had abandoned her. Aunt Marie had been nice enough the first summer that Pearl came to stay with her. However, once Fall came, Marie made it clear that she was not a boarding house to keep Patricia for her last year of high school.

Patricia had given up the house where they had lived with Brad. Instead of going back to her hometown, Pearl took a high school equivalency course. She passed with flying colors and got a job at a local department store. Pearl shortly found out that she enjoyed helping women who came in to choose dresses. Pearl did not flatter the women, whatever they put on , going for the quick sale. Instead, she honestly helped them to find clothes that they truly looked great in when wearing. Pearl's approach paid off. She had more and more returning customers asking particularly for her as a clerk.

After working two or three years in the department store, Pearl married. The floor supervisor in the luggage and home store department turned out to be a close confidant. Also, he was the man who stole her heart. They moved to Fox Willow when he was promoted to manager of a large hardware store. There she opened her boutique.

Pearl and Paul had four children: Jacqueline and Judith arrived first. Jacob and Jerome were the youngest. Both sets of twins were adorable. Pearl delighted in reading stories to them when they were little. They especially loved stories about twins. The Bobbsey Twins were almost a nightly ritual. Now that they were in their teens, Pearl loved watching their games, helping them with homework and with planning sleepovers.

Pearl had never told anyone about Brad. She almost never mentioned her family. When asked, she only said that she was on her own from about the age of 16. At times she added that her aunt had helped her get a high school education. This was not entirely true, but Maria had been more motherly toward her than her own mother. From the time Brad appeared as one of the housemates, Pearl had been all but forgotten.

Paul had opportunities to move to larger cities to manage even larger chain stores. The couple had decided to stay in Fox Willow. They liked the atmosphere of the small town for their children. The schools were good and Pearl enjoyed her relationship with the other women in their little quilting bee.

It never occurred to Pearl that someone in her past was looking for her. Brad's brother Bobby finally located Patricia. By then Patricia was in a nursing home. Her memory was so bad that she could not even tell him her name. She did have several pictures showing her family. One showed Brad and Patricia with a younger girl standing to the far side of Patricia.

"Who is this girl?" Bobby asked. Patricia replied, "Shirley Temple." Patricia smiled. "Shirley Temple with the dimples," she chanted.

Bobby decided this could possibly be a child of Brad's. He would find her and maybe she could tell him more. He so much wanted to know about his biological father. This woman could help him learn more about the subject which his grandparents would not approach, except at death. Actually, this girl was probably his half Sister.

"The only family I have," he thought. "I must find her! She may need me!"

The dynamic of brothers protecting sisters is strong. Over many years and many miles this bond can continue. Distance sometimes strengthens the bond. Seldom does it weaken. Bobby, for example, wasn't even sure he had a sister. It was at best a guess. Maybe she was an adopted sister at least. But if he could find her, he could learn more about his biological father.

Chapter Eighteen
The Photograph

Meanwhile, far away across the ocean, another brother was thinking of his sister. Jules had a multitude of memories of his sister, Suzette. Suzette had been the Apple of the family eye. From the day she was born, she was full of smiling enthusiasm. She blew funny bubbles and waved her hands around like they were dancing.

Of the four boys, Jules was the only survivor.

"I'm the only one left now."

Jules was staring at the single, lonely picture of his family standing in front of their farmhouse. Jules had found this after the War when he was in contact with a cousin. This cousin had some of his grandmother's belongings and offered this picture to Jules.

"It has been long enough." Jules decided on the spot and took the photograph offered him. He remembered clearly the day it was given to him. Though he had never met this particular cousin before, he felt blessed to be with family again.

As soon as he was alone, Jules sat down and studied the photograph. It all came back to him as though it was yesterday.

"It's all over now," Jules had murmured consolingly. It had been a hard birth and the mare was still agitated. "You have a lovely little colt. Just lie down and rest. Your little guy will wake soon and he will want to eat."

Crooning to comfort the mare, Jules felt drowsy himself. He must've fallen asleep, because the next thing he knew Suzette was screaming. She was so frantic and he was so sleepy! It took a few minutes for him to understand what she was saying. Suddenly he was wide awake!

If this was the scout for the German army he was way ahead of his schedule. Jules' family had been advised just yesterday that one would be coming dressed in civilian clothes. Jule's brother, Pierre had elaborated.

"He was spotted by a runner. The man is of medium height with light coloring. He is dressed like a mountain climber – like Swiss, perhaps. They must think we are fools. No one dressed to go mountain climbing would be running around our farmlands." Jules brother Calvin came close to laughing about the absurdity of the disguise.

"We have at least two days," Pierre suggested. "Father wants two of us to hide up in the ravine by the creek. He says four able-bodied men, working one farm, will arouse suspicion."

"At any rate, the man is on foot. He'll have to stop at night. Our information says he doesn't seem to know the roads here. He stops to consult a map often." Pierre was sharing this information with Mother, Jules and Suzette.

"I want to take Suzette with me when we hide. You, too, Mom, if you want to go. I don't trust any of this occupation force. There are dreadful rumors about what happens to the women they find in their searches."

"Your father and I have a run tonight. He doesn't know it yet. I just received the message."

Communication equipment was hidden in the privy, just under the seat to the left of the hole. A box had been concealed here, bracketed skillfully and lined with sheet metal to keep it's contents as dry as possible. Hopefully no one lurking around would look in an outhouse. Yvette, Suzette's Mother, had just returned from a trip there, where she had purposely gone as it was a designated time for contact by the wireless messenger.

She continued,

"Calvin go and get your father. He is in the north pasture. Suzette help me get some food ready. We need to plan to feed six newcomers, but just for tonight."

When Calvin had come back with Father, Father took charge.

"We'll leave at dusk. Make sure there's plenty of straw in the back of the wagon. Calvin I'll need you to take the stallion and go on ahead. Take some of this food and leave now. Make sure the path is clear to our destination. Jules, about noon tomorrow we'll need a lookout posted up on Tug Hill. Make a newspaper kite. Do your best to get the kite in the air if we need to avoid the farmhouse. Pierre, you stay here with Suzette."

"Father, the mare is about to deliver. She won't let anyone near her except me. Pierre flies a better kite than I do anyway." Jules knew his father's plan would have been best had the mare not been involved.

"Very well," father advised. "If you have the least suspicion of anything going wrong, Jules, get Suzette to the cave down by the ravine near the creek. Keep her there until I send for you. Yvette, you come with Claude and me. It'll look better if there is a woman in the wagon. You said we're picking up six women. If you're along they won't make a fuss about coming with us."

As Jules thought back he dwelt on how sure they were of their plan. It was based on faulty information about when the Scout would arrive. Pierre had been so sure that he had a couple of days. He had left early in the morning to clean out the cave and leave fresh supplies there. He would go straight from the cave to Tug Hill to serve as lookout.

Jules tried to think what he could have done differently. When Suzette had run into the barn, Jules had been calm. They could deal with the Scout coming early. He must have stolen a horse or mule after the lookout spotted him. Jules was not worried. He had been told that Scouts were usually three to six days ahead of the armies. He had hidden the Scout well considering he only had Suzette to help. Jules was an expert at tying knots. There was no way the Scout could have loosened his own hands and feet.

Jules had never killed a man. To do so for the first time right in front of his little sister was despicable. He had no way of knowing that the Scout was truly a spy. When father came back without the escapees, the information he brought could not have been guessed by Jules. The entire family had to leave right away. There was no time to go back to kill the intruder.

Yet, what a mistake that had been! It had come back to haunt them, twenty times over. There was some consolation. Jules and Claude had been able to abort at least three efforts of the scout to find Suzette and Yvette. That his search continued, assured them that their mother and sister were still alive. They had gotten away and were safe somewhere. Now Claude was gone to another dimension. Mourning Claude and burying him in a lonely graveyard with no other family grieved Jules deeply. The grief had given him the incentive to think about cousins. Now he had this precious photograph. One photograph for a lifetime of sorrow.

Jules felt he had been in Australia long enough. If his sister and mother were here, they were certainly well hidden. The paperwork had come through for his visit to Canada. He would give notice at work and leave in two weeks.

Chapter Nineteen

Blackmail

Jade was completely in the dark. She had no idea that anyone was looking for her. She had felt guilt about never telling her husband anything about her past as a prostitute. This was before the birth of her son. Joseph was so proud of their son. Ritchie had brought a new dimension to their lives. She wasn't about to bring up any past history that might reflect on Ritchie as he made his way through the growing up years. Jade's guilt was alleviated by the wonderful family bond that was sealed by the birth of their son.   Duke Daniels looked at his dirty nails. He needed a manicure and a massage. Forget that; he needed a hot meal! Duke longed for the days when he could travel to the Caribbean and pick up new broads. He needed to be running three or four at a time to meet his basic needs. He had never even driven a car. Until about a year ago a strong armed chauffeur was at his beck and call. Now Duke was unable to use his charm and his easy swagger to attract women. It had been three years since he had seduced a woman and sold her into a life of prostitution.

The Madams in the finer houses had given him the Bum's Rush for at least five years. He had done well enough with the lower establishments, and with running street girls. Even now, he still had a couple out there.

He really needed a steady income. It never worked to be sentimental in this line of work. Duke's mistake had been promising marriage. Sure, that snagged the most beautiful. But four pretty prostitutes could bring him a lot more than one beautiful one. He could have lived high on the hog and still have saved money.

He could've had the women too - sooner or later. Take the gorgeous Jade for example. There was no one who would argue that Jade was the most beautiful of all the prostitutes that he had once controlled. Hell, that didn't go just for him. You could make a case for her being the most beautiful ever in the city.

Duke figured that Jade owed him big-time! He would collect too! It was a matter of survival. If she didn't have the money he'd take it out in her hide. He'd keep her to cook for him and clean up after him. He'd make her go on the street and promise kinky sex. She would work for him until she could get enough money to take them both to the island where she used to live. She must have a dozen little cousins running around reaching a stage where every woman is beautiful, especially if she doesn't have clothes on. She would tell them what great jobs they will have if they come back with us.

First though he had to find Jade. The problem was Duke couldn't even think of her last name. But it would come to him. Oh, he would find her all right. He wasn't about to be one of those guys homeless, out on the street. Now when someone owed him big-time.

Duke counted his pile of dwindling cash. He kept it in a metal box under his mattress. Barely $1000! At one point he considered that loose change. Things were worse than he realized. He would have to get a cheaper room at the end of the month when his paid time ran out on this one. The old biddy who ran this fine establishment had better give him his deposit back. The last Dude who tried to cheat him on the deposit ended up with a broken arm.

Suddenly it dawned on him. Chicago! That is where he ran

her. That is where he'd find her! By the next day he had increased his funds by subletting his room to an unsuspecting chump. The fool actually believed that six months were left on the lease and three of them prepaid! With over $1500 in his pocket and a hot meal in his belly, Duke took to the highway - hitching to Chicago. A trucker gave him the longest ride, stopping for gas along the way. When Duke saw the wad of bills the guy used to pay for the fuel, he salivated. At the next intersection Duke claimed stomach problems and left the truck, doubled over. The trucker helped him walk to the restroom.

"I can't wait for you long; I'm on a tight schedule," the trucker explained.

"You go ahead. I need to sit in a dark corner for awhile. Looks like a café by that gas station. I'll get another ride when I feel better. Oh, and thanks a million."

When the semi drove off, the wad of bills was in Duke's pocket.

"I should have been an actor!" Duke thought. "Was I a "cool hand Luke' or was I not? My luck's turned for sure.!"

Just in case the trucker missed his money clip and doubled back soon, Duke didn't go to the café. Instead he caught a ride heading East rather than the Northern route the truck took. It was out of the way, but who knows. Maybe he'd find another patsy on the road!

Duke was traveling with no extra clothes and no baggage of any kind unless you count cash. By the time he reached Chicago he was pretty ripe. He got a room in a dive and washed up at the rusting sink in one corner. The cheap stakes didn't even furnish a towel so he dried off with the bed sheet.

"There was a Goodwill near here," Duke thought. "I'll find

something clean there and throw these duds away. It'll be cheaper than getting these clean."

Dressed in jeans and striped T, Duke tossed his filthy socks in the trash with his other clothes. He'd just wear his old shoes without socks. The ones at Goodwill were kid's socks or threadbare. Duke hung around the old place where he had been thrown out seven years before. Apparently, it was still used for the same purpose, but it had a seedy look about it now. The Madam he had known was getting long in the tooth when he last saw her. He needed some eyes inside the house.

Duke decided to take drastic action. He found a suit that fit pretty well at a Goodwill. He could get by without a tie, but he needed a decent shirt. Taking a bus out to the suburbs he jogged through a middle-class suburb until he found what he was looking for. He watched from a vacant lot while a woman hung out her laundry. Now if she would just leave.

Duke was in luck! He woke up from his nap under a big willow tree and saw that the car was gone and that the clothes were still on the line. Duke took a couple of pin stripe shirts, one solid white, and all the socks and underwear he could grab. He cursed that he had not brought a sack or bag. Well, he'd just have to improvise. Back under the willow tree he added the look of about thirty pounds as he put on layers of shirts and socks. He rolled the underwear up in a bundle and stuck it under his waist band. When the woman returned and found her clothesline robbed, her helpful neighbor reported seeing the culprit.

"He'll be easy to spot," she told the officer sent to the scene of the crime. "He is as wide as he is tall - I'd guess he weighs about 400 lbs. and he waddles when he walks."

Dressed more like a regular John, Duke went back to the

establishment of ill-repute. He did not recognize the new madam, nor she he. Duke asked to talk to some of the girls before choosing. Describing Jade, he soon found out that he wasn't the only one asking about her.

"I only know him by Sean," one of the oldest 'girls' told Duke, eyeing the ten he was holding with greed in her eyes. "He use to come and see this Jade quite often. It was my first few months here and I envied this girl. She was so beautiful and had this exclusive clientele. She didn't have to take just anyone!"

"What else do you remember?" Duke asked.

The blonde took the ten from his hand and slipped it under her blouse's low neckline.

"What else do you have in your pocket," she replied.

Duke left minus a twenty, but with enough information to find Sean. The blonde didn't know much else but she sneaked records out of the office and shared them with Duke.

"Why are you looking for Jade," Sean wanted to know.

"She owes me money," Duke blurted out, not thinking.

"How much money?" Sean was insistent. They struck a deal. Sean would pay Jade's supposed debt and Duke would give up his search for Jade. Sean had some clues he wasn't sharing. Now that his children had left the nest and his wife deceased, Sean was free to marry his heart's desire. He didn't want any pimp around messing things up. Maybe he was acting hastily, Sean thought as Duke was leaving his office.

"One more thing. If you should hear anything about her whereabouts, I'll pay well for the information," he announced loudly.

"Another stupe!" thought Duke. "I'll be watching you. You've got it bad and you've probably got a battalion of detectives searching night and day. This one-time pay off is nice for now, but I need to eat for a few more years!"

Yes, this was pay dirt!

Chapter Twenty
Thick as Thieves

"What time is it?" Jake asked.

Opal stretched comfortably in the bed and snuggled up to Jake.

"That was really great! Why does it just keep getting better as we age?" Opal asked Jake, ignoring his question about the time.

"I feel like a million dollars!"

Jake and Opal had taken advantage of their freedom from 9-to-5 jobs. Often after the kids had left for school they went back to bed and made leisurely love. Today it seemed especially great. At time of tenderness and passionate caresses. "If we don't get up soon I'm going to be ready for a second course," Jake joked.

"Well, maybe I'd better just hold you in bed for a while," Opal murmured. As she spoke she threw her leg across Jake and straddled him.

"Oh baby, you don't have to ask me twice."

Jake was scrambling eggs when Opal came into the kitchen. She wrapped her arms around his waist nuzzling up to his back.

"That coffee smells wonderful," Opal purred. "But not so wonderful as earlier."

Opal had to thank Jake 1000 times over. With his inheritance they could afford to live the life that she is so admired as a youth. When they went on cruises or to vacation resorts she remembered those days of her youth. How could she forget? One thing for sure! She never left jewelry or money lying around.

She had plenty of money -- more than she could have dreamed of as a child. It wasn't just inheritance either. Opal and Jake had both made names for themselves with their craftsmanship. Opal's jewelry had taken off like a skyrocket. She couldn't make enough to satisfy her distributors. Jewelry she had sold a year or two ago, was not going for three times as much at some shops that still had pieces left to sale.

Jake's contribution to the income also went well beyond his inheritance. They would be able to send Sylvia and Olivia to the finest schools should they so desire. Olivia was already showing that the apple does not fall far from the tree. She was interested in art made with found objects. She could do wonders with junk, ranging from partly broken coffee cups to ceramic vases. Olivia wanted to study at the San Francisco University For the Creative Arts.

Sylvia was another question altogether. She flitted from one interest to another. Just like a butterfly, who can't find enough nectar without bounding all over the garden. Sylvia had always been a happy-go-lucky child. Now that she had reached her teens, her current interest was boys! boys! boys!

"Well, you might expect that!" Jake had answered when Opal mentioned this to him. "She has your beauty and your great, great smile and winsome personality! It's not as if the boys aren't interested in her also."

"Beauty of that sort can get you in trouble," Opal had replied.

"And when were you ever in any trouble?" Jake responded.

"If you only knew," Opal had a twinkle in her eye, or so Jake thought. Opal turned so that he could not see the tear that caused the sudden glistening of her eye.

Opal loved being a wife! Especially being a wife to Jake!

Motherhood with even greater. This beautiful woman had blossomed and thrived. On the rare occasion that they visited her childhood home, she came away feeling totally blessed. None of the happiness that she shared with Jake and her girls seem to have ever penetrated the walls of her parents' house. Opal had begun to think that she had gotten her role models from watching the families at the resorts. Maybe the childhood that brought her to prison, was the childhood that made this life possible. If that was even partially true, prison was worth it. Well, almost!

Jen got out of the shower and dried, then dressed in her outfit. This uniform was required at the short order place where she worked. She liked to call it her outfit, because it really filled her out. She had been well endowed since about 13. If there was a God around passing out body parts, she had overlooked her until he got to the breasts and then tried to make up for it all at once. As a result, Jen preferred oversize shirts, T-shirts, and sweatshirts. This button down the front uniform looked absolutely trashy. Even Jen recognized that.

Oh well. It helped Jen pay her bills. She had so many mouths to fill. Over the years Jen had three children by three different fathers. The first one was Mark's. She was sure of that; he had been the only one who touched her. Gabe was born when she was 15. The next two she wasn't so sure about the fathers. She hated herself for doing it, but she had sold the third baby to a couple who dearly wanted a child. Mark was coming out of prison soon, and she just did not know what she would do with another baby. It would be hard enough to explain the second one to him.

Jen knew she should get over Mark. He was bad news! It was like he had some kind of hold over her. No matter how he treated her, Jen just didn't have the strength to oppose him. What he said was what she did, whether she wanted to or not. His son, Gabe, was just like him. He had his mother twisted around his little finger; at nine years old! If truth be known this was just as true at age 2, as at age 9. She feared Gabe would be the death of his little brother, Sami. But she did know what she could do about it. In their household, Gabe ruled the roost.

Maybe her mom would take Sami. That would solve a lot of problems! Sure mom was old, but Sami was seven now. She wouldn't have to lift him. He'd be happy if she just cooked for him and kept him away from his brother. Yes, that was a plan and a good one. The next day she had off, she'd just drive the 40 miles to her moms and leaves Sami. Gabe could fend for himself while she was gone. She might even stay a couple of days to give Sami a chance to get better acclimated with her mom. Also, it would give her a break from her older son, who could be a menace. It must be something in the genes.

"We'll bless my soul," explained Gladys, delighted with the rare visit from her daughter and grandson. "Where is Gabe?"

"I'll tell you about that later! I think we best go to the bathroom and get something to drink first."

Sami had the first turn while Jen backed the car into the driveway and Gladys fixed lemonade. Sammy washed his hands and ran into his grandmothers kitchen.

"I've come to live with you Grandma. Please say I can stay."

Gladys hugged the little boy.

"Of course you can stay, honey, if it's okay with your mom. Wouldn't you miss her?"

"I don't like Gabe. He's mean! I don't want to live where he lives!"

Jen came in just in time to hear this last statement.

"I hear Sami has already told you why we're here," Jen said sadly. "We'd both like to stay a couple of nights, so you can get used to the idea. And we really want you to decide. No pressure. If you decide to try it and it's too much for you, I'll come and get him."

Gladys felt her heart tighten. She would love to have little Sami. He'd be a delight! No matter how hard she tried to deny it, she was delighted that Gabe was not with them. At the same time, she felt heartsick for Jen. It must be time for that devil of a man, Mark, to get out of prison. They should've locked him up for life.

While it was hard enough for a family to live with Gabe , it'd be a lot worse if Mark was thrown into the mix. Mark would know that Sami could not possibly be his son and could not be happy about it!

"Let's just go ahead and bring everything inside," Gladys said. "Sami and I've always been best buddies, haven't we Sami? Not only would I love for him to live with me, I really get lonesome around here by myself. If you can spare him that will just fill the bill for me!"

"I knew it! I knew it!" Sami said. "Grandma loves me! I will be so good, grandma! Can I go to school here too?"

"Of course, you can. Soon as it starts again in September. We can go to Sunday school too, if you like. And we can watch Scooby Doo twice a week!"

Gladys remembered how much Sami enjoyed watching the dog help solve mysteries the few times he had visited her before.

With relief in her heart, Jen left her mother's house two days later. She was surprised at the emotion she felt with leaving Sami. He was a little joy. Jen wished she knew who Sami's father was. He must be quite a guy! Well forget how she felt! It was more important to keep Sami safe than for her to see him day in and day out!

Three weeks later Jen picked up Mark and introduced him to his son. They eyed each other like the two alpha dogs they were; each taking measure of the other. Jen wondered what would happen. Either they would be like two peas in a pod and get along exceptionally well. Or, more likely, they would be sworn enemies, each determined to win the upper hand.

Mark decided not to move in with Jen and the boy. He had a strange reluctance to living with the boy. Instead he took a room in a flea bitten motel! He is much as ordered Jen to join him there, at least for the early part of the night!

"Why don't I come about midnight, after Mark is asleep?" Jen suggested. "He needs supervision during the evenings. No telling what he will get into!"

"Let him grow up! Do you think I was tied to my mom's apron strings at his age? Give the boy room to breathe! Besides he's had you for years! It's my turn now!"

Within a week Mark was planning to hit another bank. He laughed at Jen's weak protest.

"How do you think were going to eat? We all three can't live on your salary at the hamburger joint. What do you have in your savings account? And don't act like that; I know you have one."

Indeed she did. The last night at her Mom's she had waited until Sami was asleep. Then she had approached the very difficult subject of Mark. As Gladys feared, she found that Mark would be out on probation very soon.

"I don't really have the choice, Mom. Don't you understand? If I don't play along with him and keep him happy he could hurt you or Sami or even his clone, Gabe. I hate saying that about someone I care about. I do love both my sons. But Gabe is just like Mark for the world. I just need you to keep it quiet about the baby I gave up for adoption. I know it was a dreadful thing to do but the couple wanted a baby so much. The regular adoption routes are so encumbered. If Mark finds out about the money it will be spent in a month, maybe less.

Gladys and Jen had made an agreement. The money had been transferred into an account that could only be accessed by Gladys and Sami. That is, all of the money except a couple of thousand. This was just a little more than the amount that Mark and Jen had together, before he went to prison. Both women believed that Mark would expect that Jen would have kept the money safe for him. He would have no thought that Jen needed it when Gabe was born. The account was interest-bearing and Jen suggested that her Mom use the interest for the extra expenses she would incur because of Sami.

"Don't worry about that, honey. We'll be just fine without that money. There might be an emergency some time. If not he can use it to go to college or to start a business. It's best to use it as a security blanket for you both."

"That's great Mom, but don't hesitate to use any of if you need it. Even the principal!"

The next week Gladys made a phone call to a close friend from long ago. A friend so close that they been lovers before she married. Just before and just nine months before the birth of Jen.

"He's getting out. Thankfully she's left Sammy with me."

"Can I see him? We can say a cousin or uncle or something."

"I don't see why not. Victor and Alice are long gone now. Maybe it's our time together! I feel safer living with you if you're willing?"

"That's music to my ears! Your place or mine? While you're deciding I'll put out the word to watch out for Mark. We'll have him back behind bars before Fall. The guy can't resist hitting another bank."

With Sami as a witness, along with a few neighbors, Gladys and Jerry were married quietly on the same day that Mark was released. Gladys didn't bother to call Jen. She well knew her daughter's priority.

Mark was happy living off the savings for a few weeks. Then one morning he dropped in at the hamburger joint.

"Take a break." he commanded. "It's time we found Jill!"

"Jill? Who? What does she have to do with us? You don't mean???

"The Jill who jilted us is who! If I'd had bullets in that gun we'd been living like royalty all these years. It's time for her to pay!"

Mark was pumping Jen for information regarding the whereabouts of Jill every time he stopped by. Jill didn't have any information, but Mark wouldn't believe her. Jill was almost frantic every time Mark showed up. Gabe and Mark were beginning to click. "Thick as Thieves" they were. Thankfully she had gotten Sami away from here.

"I just hope they don't go stirring around Mother's," Jen thought . She'd like to see Mark right back in prison. It would be the safest place for Gabe, too. At the age of twelve he had the build and height of the average sixteen year old; maybe older. He bullied everyone around him. Jen felt responsible for any problem that Gabe caused others. After all, she was his Mom.

Jen turned on the television. This was her only escape. She wanted to think about people other than herself. People with another kind of life. People without a 'Mark' in their lives. People without a son who had turned out like Gabe.

Jen flipped through the channels, looking for a happy story or movie. Her mind was half on her problems and half on the TV. Suddenly, she saw Jill! Jill! Yes, that was her or her twin!

Unbelievable, Jill was right there holding a tea cup with several other women!

Jen knew it was an unlikely coincidence. At the same time she was certain it was Jill. No one else had that mixture of curls and dimples. No one else had that smile that lit up the sky - the smile that woman was smiling now as someone turned to her.

Jen jumped up, excited. The image was gone. Too bad her VCR wasn't running. Checking the station, Jen was relieved. It was a local station. She called immediately.

Oh, I don't think it will be aired again," Jen was told. "It's a filler; a public interest story about some great places to stay. This one was in a place with a weird name. Fox Hollow; no, a tree - Fox Willow! I don't recall the state, but there can't be many towns with that name."

"YaHoo!" Jen danced around the room! She picked up the phone to call Mark. Just as quickly, she put the phone down.

"I'd best go to the library first and get an atlas. I need to find out the state and how to get there. If I tell Mark he'll go there without thinking and either hurt Jill or cook up some plan for us to break the law again."

By the time Jen had reached the library she knew what she wanted to do. She had to warn Jill. Maybe together they could find a way to stop Mark. At any rate she had to see Jill before she saw Mark. He'd see she was keeping something back with one look at her face.

When Jen saw the distance she would need to travel, she took a portion of the money she had left in the bank, packed lightly and took a cab to the airport. She'd leave her old Chevy or Gabe would have a fit. That he wasn't old enough to drive it gave her fits. He was so large, no one noticed. At least he had sense enough to obey the traffic law. The old heep was in no shape for a trip anyway.

"Yes, I'll warn Jill and see if she'll team up with me. Maybe we'll both have to hide out awhile. I don't think it'll take long for Mark to blow his probation."

Chapter Twenty-One

The Clue in the Quilt

Jules hardly had time to mope around. He had a job to do! Jules got in his semi and headed for Iowa. He had worked for a trucking company since coming to the States. It paid well and kept him on the road. Every place he stopped, he looked in phone books. He put ads in newspapers asking about horses and donkeys for sale. Jules tried to think what does Suzette look like now that she is all grown up! Grown up, heck! By now, she would be in her 50s. Jules was and he felt it! Some day he'd have to give up these truck routes! Just kept him sitting for too long.

Four hours later Jules pulled off the interstate. He just had to take a break. He didn't see any of the usual chain diners around. They had all come to taste alike anyway. Maybe something different would be good. He had seen the sign down the road for a restaurant called Grandma's. That must be it over to the left!

Grandma's was something else. Something more like the Cracker Barrel's! Half gift shop and half diner. It was a popular place alright! Twenty minute wait! Jules thought maybe he could spare the time, especially if he ate fast. Jules conferred with his watch. The food sure smelled good. He gave the receptionist has name.

Jules headed for the door for a ten minute walk. Before he got there, he heard the rain. A sudden downpour curbed his desire for walking outside. Frustrated, Jules strolled around the gift shop. Hanging on a far wall, something caught his eye! Something about home! He went closer and looked up at the quilt hanging from the ceiling. There right in the middle of the quilt was his home! His house! His house in France!

Jules stared at the picture of the house which dominated the quilt. He pulled out his picture from his wallet. It was pretty roughed up from all the years he'd carried it. In the lone picture he had of his family they were standing in front of their farmhouse. He had long lost touch with the cousin who had, thankfully, parted with it. Otherwise, Jules would never have had the picture. He could never have been sure.

"Suzette! It had to be Suzette!"

Jules went directly to the checkout lady.

"I'm very interested in that quilt. The one on the wall! How much is it?"

"Oh, it's not for sale! Grandma wouldn't part with it for the world! But you can buy a kit that has something very similar. It's back there on the wall. $129 each if you get the fabric with the pattern."

"Can you tell me who made it?"

The young clerk almost said no, but something about the man gave her pause.

"Look, the checkout line is getting long. If you're eating here, I'll come and find you. I get a break in about ten minutes."

Almost immediately Jules' name was called to be seated.

"Order me a hot chocolate and say you're my uncle if anyone asks. OK?"

"OK, Marion." Jules agreed, glancing from her name tag to her eyes, which told him she would not forget.

Jules saw a table in a back corner and tipped the hostess to seat him there.

When Marion came she slipped in the booth beside him, reaching across for the hot chocolate.

"Ok, here's the story. If the waitress comes this way I'm going to switch to the weather in mid-sentence. The owner of this place buys a couple of really nice quilts a year. Then she makes up rip-off quilt kits with inferior fabric and people think their quilt will turn out like the one displayed. She doesn't want the quilt makers of the originals to find out, as they might sue her. So she rips off the name tag if there is one.

"Why are you so interested."

Jules showed her his picture.

"Sure looks similar. Could be the same house."

"Yes. It's the house I grew up in back in France!" It felt good to tell someone.

"Your kidding. How fascinating!" Marion looked again at the photograph.

"Which one is you?"

"Here, and this is my Sister. She should be over 50 now. Did a woman come here to sell the quilt. I've been looking for Suzette for over 40 years."

"The owner goes out of state to buy the quilts she copies. All I can tell you is this! There was a name on the back of this quilt when she brought it in. I helped to hang it and watched her rip the label off. The label was so pretty I looked for it in the trash basket later. I would have kept it, but she had ripped it through the middle. I'm almost sure the name wasn't Suzette. The quilter had a beautiful name though! Amber. DuMonti or maybe DiMonti or DuMont. I'm sure about the first name and the DuM. I wanted to tell my Mom about the quilt and she always is interested in the maker. "

"Look, I can't thank you enough! Can your 'uncle' give you a little cash for your next birthday."

"No, just find your Sister and send me a post card here that says, "Thanks Marion! Mission accomplished.""

Marion hopped out of her seat, leaned over and gave Jules a quick peck on the check and disappeared.

At the same moment that Jules saw the quilt with the house, Ruby saw Opal's van out the restaurant's window. Amber was having a hard time parking it. The only available spaces were small and Amber was used to a much smaller car.

"Well, I knew my friends were going antiquing today," she said to Rex. "I didn't expect them here however. Should we look for a backdoor or are you ready for introductions?" Ruby and Rex had just sat down and had no time to discuss the reasons that they were meeting, supposedly secretly. She had made strange excuses for not accompanying the Queen Bees on their antique hunt. So Ruby was doubly on the hot seat.

"I think I see a back door," grinned Rex. "Do you want to run or pretend we're having a clandestine meeting."

"Let's make a run for it!" Ruby said as she grabbed her purse and dashed out the back door. They waited until Ruby's friends were settled inside the diner before walking to the other restaurant in the small village.

"Maybe we shouldn't meet for meals. That was a close call. I lied to them about why I didn't go with them today."

"I'd like to meet them sooner or later; maybe after I retire. That's one of the things I want to talk to you about. How would you feel about putting me on your waiting list? I can't think of a better place to live for a man who never really had a steady home for over two months."

"That can be arranged. I'll just modify one of the suites especially for you. I was thinking of doing that anyway. The permanent residents get to be close friends. They understand if occasionally you don't want to make such a fancy breakfast. I 've found life is much more relaxed when I don't have any day by day guests."

"Well, would you like to order before we talk?" Rex asked. They had settled comfortably in a back booth in a bar and restaurant combination that looked a little seedy. It was dark and private, at least.

"Let's order first and get it to go, just in case we have to dash out again."

A buxomly waitress arrived with water served in fruit jars. She handed each a rather lengthy menu.

"I'm Betty and I'll be your waitress," she chanted, sing song. "We don't usually get much lunch traffic. Lucky for you though, Andy's finished the soup for tonight. I just tried some and it is delicious. It's called red pepper soup. One of our favorites. If you're not very hungry you could split a sandwich and both have a bowl of soup. We've got some really good pie back there too. I might be able to talk Andy into making you one of those big dinners listed on the menu if you don't mind waiting a while."

"Looks like we have an honest waitress here." Rex nodded toward Ruby.

"Well, we'll each have that bowl of soup," Ruby answered. "Rex, you choose the sandwich."   "If you'd like my opinion on sandwiches here, I'd say you can't go wrong with the corned beef. The turkey is pretty good too." Betty chimed.

"Corned beef sounds good to me." Rex looked at Ruby, who

nodded.

"Ok, the coast is clear. I'll put you on the waiting list and start the renovations as soon as I can arrange a contractor. You wouldn't have called me just for that, however."

"True." said Rex. "It's about that friend of yours. The one you wanted new papers for about nine years ago."

"Crystal. Is she in trouble?"

"No, but her husband may be. Apparently he remarried and his new wife is dead. They were married all of 2 ½ weeks and the insurance company is smelling fraud. They've begun an official inquiry. If they uncover data about Crystal or rather info on who Greg married first, they'll find he wasn't legally married to the second woman and can claim fraud. It's a ten million dollar policy, and neither side wants to settle. I doubt the guy's lawyers even know about Crystal. I should write a report but can wait awhile. I unearthed this on my own after hearing bits and pieces, but officially I'm not yet in the loop."

"What a mess? How did the woman die?"

"She fell down steps on their honeymoon in Bermuda. Lousy follow-up by the locals. Ruled accidental and not much forensic work at all. The guy seems to have an alibi, but the insurance company believes it is contrived. Something about renting a fishing boat so he had to be out at sea."

"This sounds serious. Should I tell Crystal?" Ruby asked.

"I brought copies of all the newspaper articles I could find. She should have a head's up, but keep it all under her hat in the hope it all blows over. If there is an official inquiry and she wants to come forward, of course I'll arrange it. If not, it'll all come to nothing and she'd be best off staying in the shadows." Rex looked pensive.

"I hope you're not in trouble for giving her identity papers."

"No, I followed procedure. Here comes our soup."

When they parted later, Rex promised to keep Ruby informed.

When Lisa and Gilda finally got back to their quarters, Lisa couldn't wait to find Mel and have a three-way tete-a-tete.

"Ruby's got a boy friend! Ruby's got a boy friend!" she exclaimed.

"Whatever makes you think that?" asked Gilda.

"Remember at the restaurant in that little village. Amber let me out by the door - because of my gimp leg - you know. Well, I saw them leave. Ruby was facing the front window and they had menus in front of them. I was hanging up my raincoat and it kind of shielded me I guess. I was going over to greet them as soon as I got situated, but Ruby looked out the window and pointed. Then all I saw was the back of them rushing out the back door.

"It probably wasn't Ruby at all." Gilda said, a little perturbed.

"Oh yes it was and she was with a handsome man, not much younger than Mel, I'd guess. In real good shape. I had a great look at his back end as they rushed out. Tightest tush you'll ever see!"

Lisa grinned and Gilda blushed. Lisa and Gilda often admired men from their backs, but never before in front of Mel.

Mel paid no attention to that part of Lisa's story.

"Rex!" thought Mel immediately. Aloud he spoke softly.

"Bad storm could be coming. Look at the sky!"

Gilda and Lisa were still giggling when they took their take home boxes to the large kitchen.

"Did you see Mel's reaction when you said the man had a tight tush?" Gilda asked just as Ruby rounded the corner with a large box of groceries.

Gilda blushed, but Lisa grinned.

"How was your *shopping* trip?" Lisa asked Ruby, winking one eye.

"Great! How was antiquing?" Ruby answered.

"Actually I wished I had gone with you," Lisa replied daringly. "I think you must attract *good finds.*"

Gilda gave Lisa her firmest stare.

"I think Lisa had a little too much wine for lunch. I didn't stop her because I was sure she had ordered ice tea. She's been tipsy all afternoon!"

"I had ginger tea. Thought maybe it would be as good as your Gingerberry Jam. Can ginger make one tipsy? Or maybe it causes one to see things that aren't there? Oh, no! That was before I drank the tea. At any rate the sight delighted me!"

Ruby had to laugh.

"I thought I heard you talking about tushes when I came in. Leave it to Lisa to observe carefully when a man is walking the other way."

"Leave it to Ruby to have that man in her wake!" Lisa continued. "Why did you pop out so quickly? Didn't want to share your date with the Queen's and us?"

Ruby decided to go along with this.

"If you were with a man with a cute back-end, would you want to share? Actually, we noticed no alcohol on the menu and we wanted to get a little tipsy. Clandestine meetings are more fun that way, don't you think?" Ruby teased.

"Ruby! Hold your tongue." Gilda burst out laughing. "Didn't your Mother ever tell you not to kiss and tell?"

"Invite him for Sunday brunch," Lisa suggested. "I want to see a little more of him!"

"Actually he may come here to live when he retires. My 'clandestine' meeting was an interview. He's signed up on the waiting list."

"For permanent residency? That will be a long time. None of the three of us plan to give up our suites! You can take that to the bank!" Gilda was adamant.

"I'm thinking of making a fourth suite - well, a fifth if you count mine. I'd convert the large quilting room into the fifth one."

"O-ooh," crooned Lisa. "A suite next to yours. The interview must have been very *impressive.*"

"Hush your mouth, Lisa," Gilda urged. "Ruby deserves a love life if she wants one! This is none of our business! I am curious though? Where would we quilt?"

"There's plenty of room in the parlor. I'll set the frame up in there and we can look directly out into the garden. It'll be a nice change. I thought about changing the rooms over yours; converting from short-term guests to permanent. It would be much less expensive but I'm booked solid through Christmas and even have some scattered reservations for next Spring. I will ask him to brunch, though, before I commit to him. I'd like him to fit into our little family."

"Lisa's already crazy about him and she's only seen his rear end," Gilda supplied.

Ruby's Jam of the Day

Ginger Berry Jam

Ingredients:

1 ½ quarts red ripe berries (strawberry or raspberry)

5 cups sugar

1/3 cup lemon juice

1/4 cup Fresh ginger cut from rhizome and cubed

Procedure: Wash and crush berries; Please use hand or electrical utensils meant for crushing.   If you try the foot stomping technique alleged to be popular in vineyards you are sure to regret it.   It may feel very sensuous at the time, but you'll never get the berry stain off your toenails!

Mix crushed berries with sugar and let stand 4 hrs. plus or minus 1 hr.

Combine ginger and lemon juice and let stand in separate container than berries and for similar length of time. Drain.

Bring berries to a boil over medium heat and boil with lots of bubbles for 1 min.   Stir frequently; and continually from the time when light bubbles begin to form. You know, very light bubbles like babies blow for fun.

Remove from heat and stir in ginger/juice mixture.   Return all to med. Heat and stir and stir and stir until mixture becomes a thick, clear red syrup.

Cover and leave to sit overnight.   Believe me; you'll be ready for a break!

Ladle into pretty jelly jars following standard procedures for sterilized jam - should be in one of your cookbooks or inserted in a package of unflavored pectin.

Chapter Twenty-Two

Crisis of Conscious

Back in her apartment, Ruby called Crystal.

"I have something I'd like you to see," she began. "I think you'll be interested."

"Can it wait until tomorrow?" Crystal asked.

"I'd really rather do it this evening. I'll come there if you like."

"Sure, come on over. Amber has company. Some woman claiming to be a professional genealogical family finder. Says she represents a cousin of Amber's deceased husband. I was sitting with them when the phone rang. Sounds to me more like she's asking questions about Amber rather than John."

"Go back in and I'll join you both in a few. I'll come in the back door!"

When Ruby arrived the woman was leaving. Amber introduced Elinor Barton and Ruby expressed regrets that she had missed chatting with Elinor.

"My visit wasn't really social," Elinor replied rather stiffly.

"Then I hope you got what you came for," Ruby said, fishing.

"Oh, yes! That and then some!"

When the woman drove off, Amber offered tea and asked for a serious chat. Ruby was anxious to talk to Crystal alone, but she was also curious about this unexpected visitor.

As Amber poured tea, she began her story. She told all; all she could remember about the War, the Occupation, the narrow escape and the Scout and his oath.

"The only other person I ever told about any of this was my husband, John. This woman knew something that even John didn't know. When Crystal was out of the room, Elinor asked if John kept any newspaper clippings from the personal ads. Or maybe from Want Ads seeking to buy a horse called 'Billy Gray'.

"What did you answer? She wasn't here long enough to hear this entire story."

"I played it cool. Asked for her card and promised to look through John's things and call her if I found any such clippings. The more I think about it, the more I want to call right now. It has to be one of my brothers. Pere would be too old. There is an outside chance that the Scout who wants to kill me was able to learn about our 'Billy Gray' if he captured one of my brothers. I believe I must take the risk! I would love to see my brothers again - even one of them. I'm thinking of calling her tomorrow and inviting her and her client to 'go through the box of interesting papers I found in John's library.' What do you think?"

"The Scout would be a good bit older than you," Crystal observed. "He's likely dead.

"Why not offer to meet at the bar-b-q place on the square. There will be lots of people around. That way you can find out if it's your brother without risking being alone with a cold-blooded killer!'

"What a great idea! I hear the tea kettle. Just a moment."

Crystal turned to Ruby.

"I confided in Amber one night. Not about the help your contact gave me, but about running away from my husband. She was very supportive. Is what you have to show me very secretive?"

Ruby handed Crystal the overstuffed manilla envelop.

"Actually they are mostly newspaper clippings. If your husband's name is 'Greg', he remarried. Someone named Mildred."

"Oh! Well, that is good news. He must think I'm dead."

"He certainly hopes you are. He took out a ten million dollar policy on Mildred and she 'fell' on the honeymoon. The insurance agency is investigating. Rex thinks they may have more luck tracking you than Greg did."

"Oh, I see!"

"Look over the clippings. Do you want me to wait?"

"Yes, please do. I might be unnerved. I always thought he would find me one day and I'd have that 'accident'. I never imagined another woman involved."

As Amber returned with more tea, Crystal was clearing the round table and was emptying the brown envelope. The information was all clipped together with large postage notes giving the dates.

"What is all this?" Amber asked, sitting the tea tray on an empty chair.

"Ruby's brought information about Greg," Crystal sighed. "I guess this is 'Secret's Disclosed Week'."

As Crystal read one article, she passed it on to Amber, who read it and handed it to Ruby.

Ruby had read three or four when Rex first brought them. About half-way through the packet,

Crystal gasped loudly.

Sobbing, she covered her face with her hands and dashed for the bathroom. Ruby and Amber stared at one another.

Amber reached for the clipping that had caused such a reaction.

"It's a photograph. Seems to have been taken in front of a Court House. I can see the Justice symbol on the building behind." Amber supplied thoughtfully.

"The man must be Greg," Ruby guessed. "The one kissing his cheek looks very young. Do you guess he already has another girl friend. She looks so familiar!"

"Why, she looks just like Crystal," Amber exclaimed.

"Bess!" Came a soft voice from the doorway. "My little Sister, Bess, all grown up and coming to his rescue!"

Crystal was shaking all over and pale as an icicle.

Amber brought blankets and wrapped Crystal and Ruby together like butterflies in a common cocoon. She reheated the tea and helped Crystal sip. Finally Crystal spoke coherently.

"Please, Amber. Read the rest to me."

While Crystal and Ruby listened from their blanketed embrace, Amber read. Greg had been called before a Grand Jury in Hilton Head. Bess had read about the death in the papers and called his lawyers. They had brought her to testify as a character witness.

In addition to the news clippings, Rex had included a couple of memos and some correspondence from the insurance company involved. One was a request for a certified proof of Amelia's death sent not to Greg, but to his lawyers.

An immediate response came from the lawyers saying Amelia had been missing over seven years so no proof was needed. A handwritten note at the bottom of this letter asked a question:

"When was Amelia reported missing and by who? In my investigation I found no such document. Legally, I believe Amelia is alive. In actuality, she may have taken a 'fall' similar to Mildred's."

"I'll have to go and get Bess out of this mess. I brought the devil into our home! On the few times he agreed to visit my family, he was Mr. Charming himself. He especially spent time playing dolls and Candy Land with Bess. I thought it was because he was ashamed to face Mom and Dad for fear they'd guess what our life was really like. They made a big fuss over him and if they ever noticed anything wrong, they pretended they were imagining the worse."

"We'll help you find the best way to do this," Ruby promised. "Let's sleep on it. Are your Mom and Dad still alive?"

"I don't even know," admitted Crystal. "It's well after midnight. We should all go to bed. Tomorrow is already here."

Alone in her room Crystal dialed Opal.

"I'm sorry to wake you, but I've had a tragedy in my family. May I rent one of your cars? A small one? I'll need it for a couple of weeks."

Jake had answered the phone and agreed at once. Surprised to hear she wanted to leave immediately he offered to bring the car over if she'd drop him back home on her way.

"Why not fly?" Jake asked. "I can get you a ticket."

"It would mean several stops and waits at each airport," Crystal answered. "If I'm driving I'll feel like I'm getting there; not just waiting for hours. Waiting gets to me still."

Next morning when Amber awoke to find Crystal gone, she immediately called Ruby. Ruby called Rex, but it was later in the day when Opal got in touch.

"I must have been sleeping like a rock," Opal grieved. "Jake just lent her the car and let her go; no questions asked! No offer to get

Gilda or someone to keep her company!"

"Don't worry, Opal. It's the way Crystal wanted to do it. Could you get me the car make and license number, though. I have a lot of law enforcement people in my family and they can find out if she has any trouble. Amber says she left her driver's license and birth certificate in their house safe, so she's not traveling as Crystal Williams."

"Don't tell me anymore, please! I'm worried sick about her as it is!"

Pearl, too, was alarmed. Pearl felt something in the air. Something foreboding.

She talked to Paul about visiting Patricia in the Nursing Home.

"If you need to go, Honey, the boys and I'll get by just fine. Why don't you fly and rent a car? What will you do about the boutique?"

I think Jade might cover for me when Richie is in school. Maybe Gilda and Lisa will help out and of course the regulars will be there. I hate to close 'for inventory' like we do when you have your vacation and we all take off for the seashore."

Paul laughed.

"Everyone in town has their own idea about what you inventory at the beach! While in the Bay Area why don't you visit a few garment stores in San Francisco. You can write off the air fare on this year's taxes. More importantly, it'll give you some fresh ideas and a more fun reason for the trip."

"With both boys planning college in the Fall we could sure use the tax write-off. I'll do just that. Do you think we can stretch the budget to get a ticket for Jaclyn to go with me? She seems at such loose ends in that little apartment alone. She misses Judith terribly."

"Another good idea. Maybe you can get her interested in the clothing industry. As beautiful as she is, I don't think a career in modeling awaits many in this part of the country. Where is Judith anyway? I can't keep up!"

"Her company sent her to Boston for more PR training. She has one more month there, then I think the next assignment is Washington, DC. At any rate it'll be a long time, if ever, before she moves back in with Jaclyn. It isn't surprising to anyone but Jaclyn. Even twins eventually go their separate ways."

"I don't think your Mother has seen Jaclyn since she was a toddler. Do you think the Alzheimer's will throw Jaclyn a curve ball?"

"I'm hoping it will help her appreciate her intelligence while she has it. Use it or lose it, people say." Pearl answered.

"They're not talking about intelligence when they say that. If you're leaving in the morning, how about a 'nap'?"

Jaclyn had balked at going with her Mom. Someone had to watch the apartment and feed the cat, she had argued.

"Judith is paying the rent; that's the least I can do!"

"The boys are picking up the cat. The super will watch the apartment. This trip is going to be emotional for me. I really need you to come."

"I'll miss my soaps!"

"I'll tape them for you on the VCR. I already bought the tickets. By acting quickly I could get companion fare for one of us," Pearl admitted.

"You're talking about tomorrow, Mom. Look at my hair!"

The bleach job was pretty bad. Also, Jaclyn had lost weight recently. Her clothes were falling off her.

"Gertie said they had some openings if we get a move on. After we have our hair done we'll open up the boutique and you can choose a couple of new outfits! On me! Then we'll meet Dad and the Boys at Pizza Place and they want even know us! We'll play twins for the week.!

Jaclyn cheered up a little. Looking at her Mom, in her early forties and at the prime of her life she thought Pearl might be taken for the younger instead of the twin.

When they walked into Pizza Place in matching turquoise pants suits all heads turned their way. Jaclyn 's hair looked it's natural chestnut brown again; just like Pearl's. Each had an up do; a kind of French twist that Gertie concocted by adding a hairpiece to Pearl's cut which was shorter than Jaclyn's. The girl had balked at having her's cut as her twin wore the longer style, but in a neat pageboy. The turquoise pants and unbuttoned jackets were set-off with lovely teal slipover sweaters. Gertie and her staff had even squeaked in make-up and manicures while they waited for the process necessary to get rid of the botched bleach attempt that Jaclyn had tried alone.

Dressed alike, the similarity in size and facial features between Mother and Daughter was more noticeable.

"If Judith or even Mom would just do this with me, we really could make it modeling," Jaclyn thought.

Early the next morning Paul waved automatically as the plane lifted off with his wife and daughter. Jaclyn had never been to San Francisco. Pearl wanted to make this trip special for both of them, so she suggested a day of sight-seeing. They picked a hotel right on Union Square and had a marvelous dinner at a Meditirrean restaurant.

The next morning they hardly had to step out of their hotel to catch a cable car and 'climb halfway to the stars,' as the song describes. They spent the day at Fisherman's Wharf, taking the boat from there to tour 'The Rock' - Alcatraz. Before returning on the cable cars they treated themselves to a delicious crab dinner.

That night they saw an offbeat musical in the theater district and had dessert back at their hotel. The following morning they visited two establishments and ordered several one of a kind outfits for the boutique. By two in the afternoon they reached the nursing home.

"There are several people in her room already. You can wait in the lobby and I will call you when some leave," a pink lady volunteer informed them.

"Our plane leaves in a few hours and we live too far away to come often. Can't you ask her other visitors to wait. I am her daughter and she doesn't have other relatives."

The volunteer looked at her sign-in sheet.

"Three of the visitors are relatives of her roommate. The young man with Patricia comes at least twice a month. He signs in as her step-son."

"Then please ask him to come out here! She has no step-son!"

The volunteer disappeared and Pearl followed her. There was more than one way to find the room number! The room the volunteer attempted to enter was crowded indeed. A man was helping Patricia's roommate into a wheelchair.

"We're taking her down to the chapel," a woman said. "If you'll give us a minute we'll make room here."

Pearl glared at the man sitting next to Patricia, an open book of poetry in his hands. His resemblance to Brad was so striking she had trouble breathing. It was like seeing a ghost!

"We were just reading," he said. "If you'd like some time alone I can come back."

"Yes, please. My daughter is waiting in the lobby. Will you please tell her how to get here?"

Bobby found Jaclyn and explained to her that he enjoyed frequent visits with Patricia.

"You see, I was adopted by my Grandparents. Patricia came to see me as a little boy of three years. After that she always sent me birthday presents. I think she may be my biological Mother. I had hoped to meet your Mom someday - I didn't know your last name, so I really didn't know where to start. How lucky that you came here. Your Mom seems a little uptight, though."

"She's really very nice," Jaclyn replied. Before he showed her to Patricia's room, she gave him her full name and their address in Fox Hollow.

"Maybe you should write my Mom and explain who you are and why you want to stay in touch. She was just surprised that you wrote step-son on the sign-in."

"Well, that much is defiantly true," he said. "My biological father was Brad; your Mom has to remember him. Patricia had lots of snapshots of the three of them - they were a family!"

"Weird," thought Jaclyn. She had never heard of any Brad.

Crystal woke from a nap stiff and needing a rest room. She took a moment to recall where she was and where she was going. The rest stop where she had parked had a coffee machine. That would do for now. She'd stop down the road and eat a good breakfast. Amelia checked her wallet. Yes, everything in it said 'Amelia'. If she or the car were searched, they would find no reference to Crystal. Jake, good ole

Jake had given her the registration to the car.

"I really need a paper saying you lent it to me," Crystal said a little panicky.

"It'll be easier if I just sign it over to you. You can sell it back to me when you return. Do you have a ten?" Jake had offered.

"Bless you, Jake. I have twenties in my pocket. If you'll just sign your name, I'll fill out the rest. If something should go wrong, I'll buy you a new car!"

"Just be safe and give Opal a call when you get a chance. For twenty dollars I'm glad to get rid of this auto. It's so low I can hardly fit my long legs in here and I have the truck anyway. My three girls are all set! Opal thought I needed this when I didn't have stuff to haul, but I hate to drive it. She says I identify the truck with my manhood."

Crystal smiled at the memory. It was her who first made that observation to Opal. Oh, what good friends they had become! What a wonderful nine years!

Before starting the motor she reached over to the glove department. She read the transfer of ownership yet again. Yes, just as she had written, the car now belonged to Amelia Branson. At breakfast she would find out if one of her old credit cards still worked. If it did she'd have breakfast and a new outfit on Greg.

Part III

House of Cards

Chapter Twenty-Three

Changing of the Guard

The renovations at the "Gems & Jam" progressed rapidly through April and early May. By June the interiors of both the new suite and Ruby's own quarters were completely revamped.

Quilting in the parlor proved a great idea, as the expansive windows provided sunlight and delightful views of colorful birds and playful squirrels.

Rex saw his renovated space for the first time on the day he arrived to stay. This was truly a luxurious suite. It had all of the amenities you could hope for - whirlpool tub, a good shower, a big comfortable bed with a hard mattress just like Rex preferred.

He had a separate dressing room with walk-in closet. Even better, there was a hidden entry between the adjoining rooms, his and Ruby's. From his dressing room he could access hers.

As Ruby gave him the tour he watched her for a sign. Ruby said the adjoining door was so they could secretly leave the Inn in the event of some unexpected trouble. She showed him how a door in the far corner of her suite led down hidden stairs. It exited outside where a grape arbor blocked the view from the street. One could leave the house in this manner without being seen. and with great ease.

"I was thinking or hoping that maybe this door to your room had another meaning." Rex ventured, knowing the waters here might spoil the entire arrangement.

Ruby blushed. Over the years they had become very close. No

one else knew about the door or the stairs except Jake who had done all the work, bless him. Rex had just opened the subject she had shied away from. This was time to make her intent clear. If she didn't, he would probably never mention this again. Hopefully he wasn't jesting, which would leave her with a double red face, as she had decided on the door without consulting Rex.

"It's been a long time for me, Rex. Only once and with my high school sweetheart. I know very little about flirting and dating and stuff like that. I put that on the back burner when I went undercover lest I endanger another person. If you don't mind a novice, I'd like to share more with you."

"It's been a long time for me too, Ruby. We'll start slow and see if you like it. I would love to visit you at night and to make things legal if you're willing to do that someday. I've wanted to ask you for a long time, but until I retired it just wasn't proper."

Ruby blushed again.

"There's something in the air," Ruby said. "Two of my best friends are either missing or on trips that are very unusual for them. Another thinks a long lost brother is coming here any day. It would be great to be your wife, but that is not something to decide right now. First, we have to survive the next few weeks. I know and you know that is reason number one that you moved in here! But that's also a reason not to go slow. Do you think we could rush things along, just in case!"

"Right now isn't too soon for me," Rex said, his heart racing overtime. He lifted Ruby in his arms.

" Let's go back in my room. Do you want to start in the shower with me? I have travel dust deluxe."

After her one experience of grasping through clothes in the

back seat of a car, the joint shower made a believer of Ruby. The hot water massaged her back and shoulders while Rex covered her face and neck with sweet kisses. He soaped her back from her neck to her ankles, removing the shower noozle to rinse her. When he handed her the soap she did the same for him. Turning off the shower Rex grabbed two towels and they energetically preceded to dry one another, back to front then front to back. As Rex held the towel with one hand at each end and whisked it lightly over her bare breasts and tummy, Ruby felt a deep shuttering throughout her body. Her breathe came in gasps and she cried out unexpectedly.

Rex lifted her and carried her to his bed. Forty-five minutes later she was spent, partly from the first fifteen minutes and partly from what Rex called, "after play."

She lay limp on the bed while he ran water in the whirlpool. Twenty minutes in the hot water and they stumbled back into the shower, which Rex set so that the water was barely warm, then a little colder. Shivering, they left the shower chasing each other with the towels, each scoring hits aimed specifically at bare butts.

"Lisa was right about your tush," Ruby laughed. "She'd flip if she could see it like this."

"When did Lisa ever see my tush?" Rex asked, grinning and shooting around Ruby quickly, landing another snap of his towel dead center.

"For that you'll be sorry!" Ruby teased, dashing behind Rex, bending and lightly biting his tush.

"Lisa and Gilda go on expeditions to look at the tushes of men! Didn't you know?" She said, hoping under the covers to pretend she was hiding from a retaliatory bite.

"Oh, do they?" Rex rejoined in his throatiest, deepest voice. "I think I'll go on my own expedition - now where could I find a tush?"

"Let's call ahead and order so we want have to wait when we get there," Ruby suggested. "The seafood place ok? I have their menu by the phone."

"Oh, and what will we do with all the time we save by not sitting around waiting for our order?" Rex asked.

By the time Ruby and Rex stopped their games and dressed, they were starved.

"Probably I'll have a headache and have to come back to my room right away. You'll probably get hot and sweaty in the restaurant and need a shower. Or maybe we'd both come in the secret door and the others won't see us." Ruby mused.

"Gilda, Lisa and Mel are planning a surprise welcoming dessert party for you. We'll have a hard time eluding them."

"Maybe we could give them a few minutes then say we need to be excused as we're going on a tush hunt?" Rex suggested.

Rex had met with Ruby's new contact, Davis Quinn. Quinn turned out to be a gung ho, excitable trooper, in Rex's opinion. Quinn had a great success record in solving cases. Rex's feelings about him were mixed, however. He felt Quinn's methods lacked sensitivity and led to unnecessary and excessive use of force.

The week that Quinn learned of his new assignment, he decided that he would go for the kill. If he could arrest Mason and Lopez he could wind up the drug cartel. With them behind bars he could end it all. He could quit this dull, routine assignment of protection of Ruby because no one would be threatening her anymore.

Quinn paid a surprise visit to the Inn a few days after Rex

retired. Ruby was pleasant enough but he wanted new cases to solve. This assignment was not much more than babysitting a woman whose biggest excitement was when her homemade jam boiled over.

Quinn laughed remembering his first, and so far only, visit.

"Great to meet you!" Ruby lied. She was dressed in jeans and knit top covered with an enormous apron.

"Same here. I'll just stop by every few months and make sure everything is OK. Also I hear a rumor that you make great jam here."

"Yes, I have a batch of Bud 'N Red Currant on the stove right .... oh, my jam!"

Ruby dashed to the kitchen with Quinn right behind her. The simmering pot failed to simmer. It was at a full rolling boil and threatening to exceed the capacity of the pot at any second. Ruby grabbed an oven mitt and moved it to a large slab of marble.

"This is so NOT good." Ruby said.

"Smells good to me." Quinn wasn't fooling either. The entire kitchen was filled with the aroma.

"I just about croaked," Quinn remembered when she handed him a pair of plastic gloves and a stick of soft butter.

"We'll make Taffy," she said, as if I was cut out to be a candy maker. "We'll have to work quickly or it'll all get too hard to use."

She turned that boiling hot mixture right out on the marble slab and flipped it over a couple of times with a wooden ladle. It was still smoking when she began to use the tips of her fingers. I thought the flimsy gloves would melt.

"Thankfully, I had the sense to not put anything about my participation in the report! I'd be a laughing stock around here if it leaked out that I spent the next half hour pulling one end of a batch of taffy while my contact pulled the other."

As they pulled they talked.

"I heard a rumor that Rex decided to retire here." Quinn hoped this wasn't true. He wanted no interference from his predecessor.

"Yes. He's already settled in. Pull a little harder. We need to make a longer rope," Ruby urged. "Over the years he's gotten to know my establishment and he feels he can make his home here. I guess it's pretty hard to get settled in one place when you're in the kind of job you two have chosen."

This was bad news to Quinn.

"He'll be sorry he missed you. Our police commissioner asked Rex to drop by and discuss part time work there."

"Is that so? Is this mess almost done? I need to get going. Any problems and you know the drill. Use the secret, special cell phone. Have it with you at all times. Do you still have it charged."

"Sure do, but don't desert me now. It takes two to pull taffy. When we get this rope about a yard long, I can handle it alone. I'll lay it on the marble and slice out bite sized pieces with a cleaver," Ruby explained. "Haven't you ever made taffy before?"

"Not in my job description! I typically work 18 hour days, so I don't have time for anything like this."

As soon as Quinn got back to his office, he sent out three men to bring in some lowlifes who had served as stoolie's before.

"I'm mainly looking for some creeps to pump who were around when the big drug cartel bust took place around 10 years ago."

Quinn requisitioned boxes and boxes of old records and he mulled over them for hours. He wasn't getting anywhere. Frustrated, he put the screws to one of the stoolies. He told the guy he was going to have him arrested for withholding evidence.

"With your record you're going to do time. Maybe we'll send you to that Federal prison down South where they still have the chain gangs. You look like you could use the exercise involved in manual labor."

The stoolie came up with a name. Unfortunately it was not the name of a gangster or anything to do with the whereabouts of Lopez and Mason Peters. It was only the name of another stoolie. It took Quinn three weeks to find this person. His name would have to be Jones! Harry Jones! If ever a person had announced he was using an alias, it was Jonesy.

Jonesy was smarter than he looked. He actually got more clues from Quinn than Quinn got from him. To begin with Quinn carelessly used the name, Ruby, instead of Lily.

"I can't tell you much about ten years ago," Jonesy said. "I was in the slammer then. Right now you probably know there are rumors on the street, especially on the Internet. The drug people have a lead on a singer named Lily. They are coming after her. The best I can tell you, you better watch out for the next two weeks. There's going to be some action."

Later, on a secure line, Jonesy called Mason Peters.

"Sure, I can describe this guy for you. Matter-of-fact I took his picture coming out of the courthouse today. He doesn't know I took it. I can fax it to you if you give me an address that is safe. If you just have someone follow him he's going to go right to Lily, alias Ruby. I set it up so that he thinks there will be some kind of action in the next two weeks. He's going to go there and alert her and you can find her if you can follow him."

"Tell you what, Jonesy," said Mason. "You seem like you can use your head. I'll give you $20,000 if you follow him for one week. Keep in touch with me."

"$20,000 above what you pay me steady to keep my eye out"?

"Of course. In fact if you come up with finding Lily for me without her having been harmed, I might make it $50,000. What about this alias? Did you get a last name."

"No, sorry. I don't know the last name, but the jerk drilling me slipped and called her Ruby two or three times."

"Good work. Thanks so much. Keep in touch. I'd like a call every evening about this time. If you can't get to a private place at that time try an hour later, then an hour later until you reach me," Mason requested.

Ruby and Rex woke up next to each other, smiling. Their night together had given them a kind of release of emotional tension, a mind-clearing epiphany.

"What a night!" Ruby said, snuggling up to Rex.

"The best thing is that many nights like that lie ahead of us," Rex replied.

"I've got to get up. I'll never get breakfast together in time. When the others see my joyous face and find there's no breakfast served, wonder what they'll guess."

"There have already been enough secrets around here. Maybe we should just announce that we spent a marvelous night in bed together," Rex teased.

"Now if you want to be completely honest, you would have to add, 'In the shower, in the jacuzzi, on the floor, against the wall!" Ruby laughed as she teased back.

"Let's sée. Did I sleep through the wall part?"

Ruby hopped out of bed. As she came out of the shower, Rex dried her before taking his own shower.

Ruby, dressed for the day, watched Rex dry his magnificent body.

"Let's not tell yet," she decided. "There's been enough excitement around Fox Willow lately for twenty-five people."

"That's all too true. I've been thinking. Would you consider closing the B&B for a few weeks? Until we get a feel for how Quinn's going to handle his job. I don't like the idea of complete strangers staying here overnight right now. People who've been here several times would be OK."

"The free lance couple who were here in the Spring really annoyed me. Jade said she saw a clip on TV. With pictures! I'd like to sue them but that would only attract more attention. You can't imagine what it's like to have you right here to discuss this kind of thing, face to face."

"You'll think about my idea?" Rex asked.

"I'll put a message on the answering machine this morning. 'Inn closed for renovations until further notice'. I'll have to cancel some people, but I'll ask Gilda to help with the calls. She'll put her foot down if they argue. I'll ask the two motels out by the interstate if they can honor my reservations.

Ruby's Jam of the Day

Bud an' Red Currant Jam

Don't ask me why my recipes seem to have very early spring flowers and mid-to-late summer fruit. I think it's because I love my freezer. I particularly like opening it and looking at all the good stuff. It just makes me feel wonderful and blessed. I do have a tomorrow here; and a tomorrow and a tomorrow. Why else would I have all this lovely food and all these beautiful flowers gracing my shelves and crowding them until they're about to burst?

Needless to say; you will once again need to go out in the Spring. However, red bud trees are easy to spot. Usually the trees are pretty short and most cooks can reach the blossoms. If you are 5"2 or under and don't have excessively long arms, play it safe. Take a tall friend or a step ladder with you.

Pick all the blossoms you can reach, wash carefully - they are tender. Place on tray covered with wax paper. Freeze. Store in pint freezer bags.

When your currants are ripe, gather, wash and pick off stems of enough berries for 2 cups uncrushed. Set aside 4 cups of sugar. Combine currants and 1 bag frozen blossoms. Have a cup of water handy, adding a little at a time to mixture on stove if it looks like it's in trouble if you don't. Double this recipe if you have enough good blossoms and enough currants.

Bring quickly to a boil over high heat. Stir & stir. Reduce heat and simmer for 10 minutes. Let the mixture drip through cheesecloth; then measure your juice; add the sugar that you measured earlier. You can modify the sugar at this point, if you have more juice. In other words, mix juice and sugar in equal parts.

Return it to the stove. Cook to desired consistency using one of the following methods to determine same.

1) thermometer

2) stir on saucer and taste test on toast

3)place on spoon you have had in ice

4)use the spin a thread method

5)use the eyeball method and if that doesn't work serve as syrup or candy.

Enjoy!

Chapter Twenty-Four
Frantic Preparations

Crystal's plans did not go quite as she had thought. She went straight to her parents' home but they were no longer there. Since there was no forwarding address and someone else owned the house, Crystal looked in the cemetery. The overseer looked through his records. The plots her parents had purchased when she was in her teens were still vacant. Exasperated she began to talk to people who she remembered and people she didn't know. She went from one name in the phone book to another cursing herself that she did not have a better memory. If she could think of her sister's childhood friends, they would be younger than those she had questioned so far. Surely some of them stayed here. If she could find even one of them she could possibly find her sister.

Finally it dawned on her that she should go to the high school. Why hadn't she thought of that before? The school librarian there was young, but friendly. She provided Crystal with several annuals and a private alcove.

The most recent annual had Bess' picture with the Senior class and in the Beauty section. Bess and her class had graduated just the past year - 1989. Crystal copied the names of several people who were in the Senior class photographs, cross referencing with a local phone book. She made appointments by phone and visited them, one by one. She finally had some success.

She was told the family had moved the year before. They were no longer in shape to take care of a house and look after their 4 acres.

Bess' friends did not know where they had moved; just that it was in or near a retirement village. One thought a condo. Several did know that Bess was attending a two-year college in a county seat nearby.

Without the help of her parents Crystal wasn't sure if she could persuade Bess to give up her attraction to Greg. As she had read further into the news clippings she had found one which described an interview with Bess. Bess had nothing but good things to say about Greg. He had pulled out the charm. In the article Bess was pleading for the community to demand freedom for Greg. Freedom from both prison and trial. Quoting Bess the article read in part:

"It is ridiculous for this wonderful man to lose his wife and then be treated like a criminal. Both the press and the insurance company are ignoring his alibi. There is no reason to doubt him."

The interviewer asked Bess to explain her relationship to Greg.

"I am his sister-in-law from his first marriage."

"How did that marriage end," asked the interviewer.

"I was just a little girl when it all happened I hardly even remember my sister. I knew her as a beautiful teenager who paid little attention to me. She was always going out with friends. By the time I got to be school-aged, Amelia had left. She was teaching school before she married.

"If you want to know more about her, she taught school right here in the same town where I go to college."

The article said nothing about their parents. Crystal thought it over and decided that she should go to the insurance company mentioned in the news clippings. She would find out more directly talking with them and she would offer to testify against Greg.

When the insurance company clerk realized who she had before her, she alerted the manager immediately. Conferring with CEO's in the main office, the manager drafted a letter to Greg's lawyers stating the insurance policy was invalid.

"It is true," they indicated, "the marriage to Mildred was illegal as Greg was still married to Amelia. The policy refers to Mildred as Greg's wife and uses Branson as Mildred's last name. There is not or never has been a Mildred Branson, therefore, the policy is null and void."

Further, they pointed out that there had never been a missing persons report on Amelia. Therefore, the number of years that she had been estranged from her husband did not matter in regard to legal statutes of limitations. So far as the world knew, Amelia never disappeared. She had never been a missing person. She simply has not lived with her husband.

Crystal feared she should not go back to Fox Willow. But where should she go? Where could she go? As soon as Greg saw that letter he would be out for her blood. Reluctantly she called Ruby.

"Of course you should come here," Ruby advised. "This is your home now." Crystal's next stop was the large local chain store, Smartmart. There she bought a blond wig and a trench coat, a packet of men's handkerchiefs, starter fluid, plastic baggies, a red rubber contraption usually used for enemas and extra staples such as tooth brush and bottled water.

She had one more thing to do before she returned to Fox Willow. She had to save her sister. Thankfully the campus was minute and the student body small. It took two hours for Crystal to spot Bess coming out of a classroom. She carefully followed Bess to another classroom, waiting until darkness to make her move.

That evening Crystal watched as her sister crossed the beautifully groomed lawn to the library of the community college. Bess had left her unlocked car in the parking lot. Their parents had never locked the cars.

"Thank goodness, I don't need to look for a coat hanger."

Crystal hopped in the car and searched quickly. She found a registration in the glove compartment. It was made out to Greg.

"This is not good. So he is furnishing her with a car already. Well. this has got to stop." Crystal took the rubber tubing out of her bag and siphoned gas out of the tank into the enema bag. She added the gas to the tank of a jalopy parked next to Greg's, repeating this action twice. Turning on the motor she checked the result. It would be close. This has to work. She wanted the car to start, but not to go too far.

"If it doesn't work tonight I'll just have to stay longer," she decided.

Back in Jake's plush vehicle, she waited for Bess to come out of the library. As she followed Bess, Crystal realized her guess had been right. Bess was headed for a lakeside cabin that Crystal remembered with dread. Earlier Crystal had checked the campus directory and visited the apartment complex identified as Bess' address. The landlady indicated that Bess had given notice and moved out two weeks before, collecting her deposit. Bess was living with Greg!

It would only be a matter of time before she would be tortured and possibly murdered if she stayed with him.

"I have to get her out of here," Crystal vowed. As she followed the car, Bess turned onto the lonely road that led to the cottage. There was a good chance that Greg wouldn't be there. He ordinarily avoided sleeping at the cottage. Often he had left her tied up there overnight. He said the cottage was haunted and she must stay alone as a punishment for some ridiculous fault. Her hair was a mess; her skirt too short; her skirt too long; her hair too stiff with hair spray.

Bess' car should stop soon now; it was going a little further than Crystal had imagined.

"If she gets much closer, she can walk to the cottage," Crystal worried.

Just as Crystal thought this, she saw Bess' emergency lights come on. Bess pulled over and Crystal did likewise.

Crystal got out of her car carrying a man's handkerchief in a plastic baggie. The handkerchief was wet from the engine starter fluid Crystal had purchased earlier. Bess was also out of her car and leaning against it. Bess took something out of her pocket.

"Oh, no!"

Crystal had forgotten all about cell phones. She'd never used one. Few people she knew had them, but apparently Bess did.

Crystal quickened her step, hoping that the blond wig was enough of a disguise. Bess hadn't seen her in the years that they'd been apart, but they looked enough alike to be twins. Thankful she had waited until nightfall, Crystal approached her sister.

"Can I help you," Crystal asked. "You seem to be having car trouble."

"Do you have a cell phone? The signal is weak out here. I seem to be out of gas. I don't understand it. It was half full this morning."

"Maybe it's a leak in your gas tank. Can I give you a ride to a gas station?"

"The rule is not to get in a car with a stranger. Could I just try your cell?"

"I'm sorry but I don't have one. Perhaps there is a house you can walk to or I can call someone for you when I get back to town."

"The only house is at least three miles and there's no phone there."

"Really? I was asked to deliver some papers to a house on this road. A Mr. Branson. My employers are trying to reach him."

"He's gone to Hilton Head on business. What kind of papers?"

"I don't really know. I'm not from here. Visiting my brother. He's an intern in a law office and they keep him way too busy. He said if I would bring these papers out to one of the clients he could squeeze in a late dinner with me."

"The Anderson law firm?" Bess asked.

"Why, yes. How did you know?"

"Greg Branson and I are close friends. I was just going out to check on his cottage while he's away. Yes, please take me back to town to get gas. When you bring me back I'll show you the cottage. It's a bit rustic, but neat in it's own way. Oh, that is if you have time to bring me back. Maybe the gas station personnel will give me a ride."

"I have plenty of time. At least two more hours before Art will be finished."

When they got back to Crystal's car she opened the passenger door for Bess. As Bess bent down to get into the low seated, sporty car, Crystal thought of Jake's comment about hating the process for getting in and out. Just as Bess was bent almost double, Crystal reached across the unsuspecting girl, pinning her right arm and pressing the handkerchief over her mouth and nose. Bess succumbed quickly.

"Thankfully I didn't need to use the pepper spray", Crystal thought. It took a couple of awkward minutes to straighten Bess enough to buckle her in. Crystal reclined the seat even more and took a warm throw from the back to cover her sleeping sister. Then she took to the road as quickly as possible. She could do two counties before Bess woke up if she was lucky. Then she didn't know what she would do. She would have to really talk fast or put Bess out again and she hated to do that. Crystal figured she had at most two days to get back to the relative safety of Fox Willow before Greg found out about the correspondence from the insurance company.

Two hours later she called Ruby.

Ruby was slow to comprehend the gravity of the situation.

"Give me a minute. I have an idea. Tell me where you are. Then call me back in ten minutes or as soon as you can find a pay phone. Don't use this cell phone again."

Luckily, Crystal was only about 450 miles away. When Crystal stopped at the diner she saw three phone booths just outside. That was good, she would need sustenance. Crystal ordered food to bring to the car and called Ruby while the food was being prepared.

Ruby answered on the first ring.

"Don't use cell phone again, especially not Bess' phone, because Greg will have the number. We have to assume he can get information from the phone company and find out who she called. We are going to try to help you reach Bess, so that she will come with you willingly."

"It's good we have rich friends like Opal and Jake! Rex is on the phone with him now. I'm going to fly to airport closest to you on a private plane. You should reach it before morning light. Do you have a map?"

"I have Jake's car. He has it well equipped. It's parked a few feet away." Crystal answered.

"OK. So go to the airport and I'll meet you there with other reinforcements. I don't know who can come with me yet, but it might be Rex; maybe Jade. Anyway they'll be enough of us that we can convince Bess to come with us. If we can't convince her, we have no choice. I believe you when you say that Greg is lethal. We can persuade Bess to listen to you, but we can't force her."

"I understand. Do you remember the key I gave you not long after we met?"

"Certainly. For your storage box at the bank. Should I bring something from it?" Ruby asked.

"Please do. The box with the tapes and a VCR if you can. If Bess sees even one of the three tapes, she'll want to join us. Can you get in the bank tonight?"

"I'm sure Jade can. They're very close friends of the bank manager."

The rendezvous at the airport went as planned. As Crystal was instructed she waited in the short-term parking lot on the highest level. Ruby found her with no trouble, as Jake's car was familiar.

"Rex is with me; he is renting a van. Rex, Opal, Jade, Gilda, Amber and Lisa. Pearl's husband Paul also. They'll be a few minutes."

"Bess has been stirring. I managed to give her a few sips of water. Did you bring the tapes?"

"Yes, and a VCR."

Bess woke up when she was transferred to the van. Groggily, she was even more confused by her surroundings. The seats in the van's back two rows had been placed in a fold flat position. Bess was lying on the floor surrounded by five women who were sitting on cushions.

Rex was driving the van and Paul had gone on ahead, driving Jake's sporty car.

The women made a nice cluster around the still groggy Bess. The night sky outside was dreary. Inside the van it was even darker. The storm had been threatening for a few days now.

"What is this? Where am I?" Bess asked in alarm.

"We're not going to hurt you," Crystal said gently. "Far from it. We just need you to listen. I'm your sister, Amelia."

"You can't be! My sister is dead.!"

As Bess turned toward the voice declaring she was Amelia, she gasped.

Crystal was holding a flashlight, illuminating her face. Bess thought she was seeing things. These women had drugged her.

"I'm looking in a mirror," Bess thought. She reached out her hand expecting to touch the glass. Instead she touched the flesh of Crystal's cheek.

The shock brought Bess back to her full senses. She was angry.

"This is a trick! It has to be! You've drugged me. Unless — Mother, is it you?"

"We all three look amazingly alike, don't we Bess? Didn't you ever see pictures of me and wonder about our resemblance? I've had to hide these last ten years or I would have had the same fate as Mildred."

"No, you're lying. Greg would never hurt anyone."

"Right now we are just driving around, circling an airport," Rex said from the driver's seat. He hoped to calm Bess.

"There's a private plane there with a pilot on stand-by. It's the plane we took to come here. Give us three hours. We've checked ahead for a motel room close by and it is ours until noon tomorrow. We want you to willingly go there with us to watch some tapes your Sister has saved. After that if you want to return to your old life, the pilot will take you wherever you say."

"I'm sorry I frightened you," Crystal spoke again. " I didn't think you would believe me and come with me. I should have tried talking to you first. To be honest I was afraid Greg would be at the cottage. Then anything could have happened."

"You're the woman who stopped when I ran out of gas! I can't believe you'd abduct your own Sister."

"Come with us and watch the tapes - one of them, at least. Then if you still don't believe me, you are free to go. You can be on the private jet by noon if we go to the motel now."

Crystal's voice was pleading. It was also filled with a passionate urgency. Bess couldn't think. If she didn't agree they would just keep driving around until she did.

"Let's get it over with then. You'll never convince me that Greg is anything but a good-hearted, successful man. I'll watch one of your tapes; then I'm on that plane!"

Even though Ruby had the volume turned down low, the strange woman's screams brought shivers to the Queen Bees as they watched the tape. Greg was seen torturing the woman. Her cries were mixed with pleas and promises to cooperate. The video camera must have been on a tripod as both Greg's hands were visible as he wielded his small knife with malicious skill.

Although the woman was fully visible, only Greg's hands and arms could be seen. At first Bess thought it must be someone else - maybe the man here right now. A chill went down Bess' spine. Just then the woman cried out in agony, contorting her body. The thin ropes around her feet and hands held firm as she reacted to the sharp pain. However, as her body contorted, she bent at the waist and her legs jerked upward. A lamp fell into the sight line of the camera; then the camera fell backward showing a good part of the room. Then the tape went dark.

"That's the cottage!" Bess cried. "The little cottage he insisted I move to; rent free."

"He use to tie me up there and leave me alone overnight," Crystal interjected. "The other tapes are of me. They'll be hard for you to watch; we look so much alike."

Bess was still trying to process the tape she had just seen.

"Why would he save these? You could have purchased these at some illegal source on-line."

"He often made me watch the ones of me while tied up in the bathroom. He'd force me to take laxatives and tie me on the toilet and leave for hours while the tape was set for play, rewind, play. It took me years to find where he hid them and to make copies. The one you saw was hidden along with the ones I had seen."

"I'm sick to my stomach! If you need to watch anymore I'm taking a walk. How can you think this is contrived if you recognize the cottage?" Lisa was blunt as usual.

"The woman looked vaguely familiar to me," said Crystal. "I thought perhaps you would recognize her."

An old memory surfaced for Bess.

"She was still in high school when she was abducted, if she's the person I'm thinking of. He must have kept her for months; maybe years. They had posters out when I was in 5th grade. Our class made some using bright colored construction paper. We had copies of her picture - she looked young and happy with curly hair. If it's even her, he must have chopped off her hair."

"Greg had a fetish for hair. He always wanted mine long. He had perfected the cave man pull!"

Bess inadvertently brought her hand to her hair. She was shaking and pale.

"Then you think he killed Mildred?" Her tone of voice indicated that Bess had no doubt of this now.

"Probably for the insurance money. I don't know what kept me alive for so long except he enjoyed torturing me."

"Why haven't you sent these to the police?" Gilda asked.

"He threatened my family if I ever told. If you don't know his voice it is just a man talking.

"Even if he was arrested he'd most likely make bail. Even if I could live long enough to testify I was afraid no jury would convict him. In the business and social world he was a charming and well-to-do gentleman.

"When I finally ran I knew he would catch me sooner or later. I took the tapes planning to turn him in. I needed a few days to think clearly. The few days got to be a few weeks and then a few years. I'm ashamed that I kept this secret for so long. Mildred would still be alive if I had dared tell. I wanted to believe he had fixated on me. I convinced myself that now that he was looking for me to he was too angry to focus on anyone else."

Crystal continued, anguished.

"I didn't know anything about what he was doing until I saw the news clippings about the honeymoon and the bride falling down steps on the honeymoon. Then I recognized you in a picture. Seeing you, Bess, finally prompted me to act."

"I believed everything he said," Bess added. "I believed that you died of cancer. That's what he told me, saying that it was quick and merciful. He claimed you would not even tell us. The cancer was so advanced when you found out that you did not want anyone to know. You didn't want people crying over you and trying to convince you to have treatments to just prolong the inevitable. He claimed you poisoned yourself, taking so much of the cancer medication that you couldn't possibly survive the night. He described how painful your death was that one night and how he stood by your side. He even had an urn that he said held your ashes."

The group discussed what they should do next. They did not want Greg to get away with murdering Mildred. Rex promised to try to find out when and if he was accused of murder. Crystal agreed to turn over the tapes to the Fox Willow police commissioner and follow his advice.

Bess was offered a choice of living at Ruby's Inn or rooming with her sister at Amber's.

"What happened to our parents, Bess?" Pearl asked.

"Actually, no one knows where they are."

"What? Are they missing too?" Lisa inquired with her usual curiosity.

"Missing on purpose, you might say. It seemed the idea of a retirement home looked good to them until they looked at the cost. Now they've put out the word that they moved into a retirement home, but it's a hoax. They got tired of taking care of that big old house, and they found out the home would take virtually all of their savings. They'd be stuck there if they didn't like it. So, they decided to spend their money first . Dad said you could always go to a retirement village after you are broke; then you get better deals. They've gone to see the world. They gave me $10,000 which they thought was the limit that they could do under the tax laws or something. Then they took off. I was getting post cards and mail the day they left a city. They've been to London, Amsterdam and Paris - I don't remember them all. I think they were somewhere in Asia according to the last postcard. Since I can't have my mail forwarded here I hope the landlady will keep it for a while."

Since Bess had left with none of her things, she and Crystal made a quick trip to Pearl's boutique. They arrived just a few minutes after Jen left. Jaclyn was delighted to show them some of the new things they had purchased from San Francisco - no two alike. Jaclyn had suddenly taken an interest in the family business. Jaclyn was even more interested in her mother as a person with some kind of mysterious past but she didn't say so to anyone.

By the time Greg returned to the cottage and spotted the car he was lending Bess, the private jet was in the air, heading for Fox Willow. Annoyed, Greg hurried to the cottage, finding no sign of Bess there. Thinking she was still on campus, he called her cell phone. He had purposely not tried to call her the night before. Waiting was good for a woman; made them more appreciative, Greg believed.

"At least the more passive, dependent ones," he practically licked his lips in anticipation. He had to wait for any games with Bess however until this Mildred disaster was over.

"Another message!" Greg almost threw his cell across the room. She wasn't suppose to keep him waiting. He couldn't even punish her yet. His cell phone rang suddenly, startling Greg. He adapted his honey-coated voice and answered immediately.

"I missed you, sweet one. Where are you?"

Quickly, Greg realized the call was from his lawyer's office. Not from Bess. A receptionist informed him he was needed right away.

Greg wanted to take Bess to bed, then go out, alone, for a nice dinner before he drove back the thirty miles to his apartment.

"I don't understand why tomorrow morning isn't soon enough," he argued with the receptionist. "What's the hurry?"

"The boss was adamant. All I can tell you - a letter was hand-delivered here from your insurance agency. I signed for it, but didn't open it. Later I heard yelling and more yelling and my intercom rang. I was told to get you here 'yesterday'! I'd think it is something you'd like to see."

"Only if it's a check!" Greg said wearily, then remembered to thank the receptionist who often told him more than her bosses knew. Another advantage of a handsome face, Greg preened.

Later, he left the law office swearing! Amelia had turned up at the worse possible time. He knew it had to be Amelia. His lawyers had just quit, claiming his lies broke their contract. His tart, Bess, had disappeared. According to the copy of the letter burning in his pocket, there would be no insurance money.

It was the next morning before Greg thought of tracing calls that had emanated from Bess' cell phone. He had to get the help of a computer hack to access the records, but he knew where Bess had called. That was the best lead he had. He joined the other hunters traveling toward Fox Willow, a man with hate in his heart.

Chapter Twenty-Five
Groundwork

Even though the weather had been warm when Jen chose to bed down in the car, she had gotten chilled in the night.

"I'm glad I made that reservation for tonight," she thought. "Maybe one more night and I will have found Jill."

Gabe had come home unexpectedly just as Jen was leaving. She had not noticed the unfamiliar car that dropped Gabe off just as her cab rounded the corner.

Gabe, curious, had hopped in the Chevy and followed. When Jen's cab took an exit lane to the airport, Gabe returned home and called Mark.

"Why didn't you park and find her?" Mark wanted to know.

"The traffic was fierce. I've never been up there before. I figured you already knew. That's why I called you; to find out what happened. Why she took off in a hurry."

An hour later they were going through Jen's things, looking for clues regarding where she had gone. After making a turmoil in her room, Gabe looked by the phone. Jen had left a notepad with information on it about her flight and rental car.

"This should get us close enough to find her. Let's roll," said Mark.

It took two hours for Gabe to pack. He cursed his Mom who had not washed any of his clothes but left them jammed together in a clothes hamper. When he finally found them they were so foul he had to wash them himself.

He was to join Mark who had left to check out of his one-room slum and grab his things. Mark was in a dark mood. Rushing to get to his room he had run a red light and smashed his truck into a minivan. The entire passenger side of the van was smashed; the hood blowing smoke. A beefy man got out of the van and started toward him, but stumbled, obviously hurt. Mark followed his impulse. Run.

A good Samaritan had left her Ford idling on the cross street, heading away from the scene. She had just reached the injured man. Wasting no time, Mark reached the Ford and scrambled in the driver's seat, taking off like an Ernhardt. Afraid of being followed, Mark took a long route to the building where he and others of the less fortunate rented rooms.

Mark had forgotten that the handle of his suitcase was busted and the lock sprung. He had picked it up in a dumpy second hand store along with most of the clothing he now possessed. It had hardly gotten him as far as this pad.

There was nothing he could do about it now. He should have remembered to get a suitcase from Jen.

He made quick work of packing his things in a large black trash bag. On the way downstairs it split wide open from the weight of the illegal hot plate and coffee pot, hand cuffs and shotgun. Shotgun shells rolled down the steps and Mark was stumbling on them. Every time he got upright he stepped on another.

A spinster in the room adjoining his had been insulted by Mark every time they crossed paths. It was hard for her to avoid him as the bath was shared for the entire floor. She peeked out to see what the racket was about. Seeing Mark's efforts to regain his balance, she grinned. Back in her room she locked her door and called 911.

Finally the landlady appeared with a metal trash can and helped pick up the objects.

"These were illegal. I'm keeping them," she declared, storming into her office with the can of loot.

"You'll give me these and my deposit back or you'll be sorry," Mark ignored the shotgun shells and let the clothes he had gathered fall on the floor in his effort to follow her. His ankle ached and his left knee was screaming at him from the fall. She made it into her office ahead of him and locked the door.

Mark cursed and looked for a heavy object to pound the door open. Just as he picked up a lamp in the lobby he heard sirens. He tripped on the unplugged lamp's cord, falling again on his sore knee.

"Yee oww!" Mark screamed in chorus with the sirens. They were close now. He had to get out of here. Mark grabbed a few of his clothes and made the back door. He painfully hobbled through an alley. At the end of the block his luck changed. He saw Gabe in the old Chevy coming to meet him. Mark waved him down.

"Make a u-turn; the cops are this way."

"What happened?" Gabe asked.

"Just get us on the highway and shut up," Mark demanded.

Jen had come on a whim. Now that she was here, she had no idea about how to find Jill. Maybe a cup of coffee would take the chill off.

She saw two restaurants open as she drove along the main street. She choose the one closest to a vacant parking space.

Waiting for her coffee she heard a woman at the next table

complaining.

"The breakfast at the Inn is so much better. I don't know why they changed our reservation. They could at least serve us breakfast!"

The lightbulb went off in Jen's brain. The television clip where Jen had seen Jill was about an Inn with a great breakfast.

"That's as good a place as any to start my search," she thought.

When her take-out coffee arrived, she approached the women.

"I just overheard you speaking of an Inn. Could you tell me where to find it?" Jen had never felt so bold in her life, nor so proud of herself.

"Over on Willow Street. Drive past the statue at the corner of the park; Willow is the next street over. No need going there today though. They won't give you the time of day."

"I just want to drive by. I saw it on television." Jen felt uneasy lingering among the strangers.

The house was truly magnificent.

"Who would ever paint a house lavender and purple," Jen thought. "Only someone very daring."

She parked and walked to the door hoping Jill was one of the permanent residents she had heard one lady mention. There was no answer. Jen glared at the sign on the doorknob.

"Closed for Renovations"

No other information.

Not having any other brainstorms, Jen drove back to town and had breakfast at the diner she had skipped before. She strolled around the compact business district when she finished, enjoying the quiet of the little town and window shopping. When the stores opened at ten, she carried her browsing inside. After exploring a bookstore she went inside a boutique. The late Spring wind had chilled her and the bookstore seemed damp. The boutique, however, was warm and inviting. A young girl was the only clerk visible.

Jen was fascinated by a display of jewelry. She had never seen pieces like it.

"It's fabulous, isn't it? It's made by a local artisan, Opal Edison. Can I show you a piece?"

"No, not today. It is marvelous, though. I'd like to try making jewelry someday."

"You should meet Opal then. She's one of my Mother's best friends. I'm Jaclyn."

"I'm Jen. Well, I'd better be going."

"If you decide you'd like to meet Opal and maybe take one of her classes, take one of her business cards. Everyone likes her. I'm thinking of taking her Summer class."

Jen couldn't get over the openness of the people in this town. Maybe Jill was just passing through the day of the tv show. An overnight guest at this Inn. If that was so, Jen wouldn't find her and Mark would go bonkers.

Jen looked in a few more stores. She decided to drive by the Inn one more time. In spite of the seemingly hopeless search, Jen felt good about this trip. The small town and friendliness of the people was an experience that warmed her. Why, the bakery clerk where she had just browsed invited her to sit down in back and sample a free muffin with jam.

"The jam is Ruby's. From the Gem & Jams Inn. She is letting me sell it now that she is thinking of closing to the general public."

"It's certainly delicious. I'd like to buy some."

"Come back in a day or two. She's never let it out 'though she sells a little at her Inn. She makes it all herself, so she doesn't want to market it too well."

Jen decided on one more drive by the Inn. This time the driveways and curb sides were thick with vehicles.

"Well, some people are getting into the Inn," she observed.

Parking in a neighboring driveway, Jen explored on foot. The Inn took up most of the block. One other dwelling stood at a corner facing Willow St., as did the Inn. The house seemed empty. Jen crossed quickly into the back yard. Sheltered by shrubs she saw that they were pruned so as to create a path. Curiously, she followed the curving path. It led to a door almost invisible because of it's cover of a large leafed ivy. Jen could hear laughter and chatter in the yard in back of the Inn. However, the shrubbery and carefully placed fencing hid it from view.

Doubling back past the queer path, Jen walked deeper into the back yard of the corner house. She found a folding chair leaning against a patio table. Taking the chair to the tall hedge she climbed up on the chair. From here she could see the party taking place in the Inn's back yard.

Lo and behold! There was Jill! There was the entire scene Jen had seen on TV. The gazebo, the tea pots, the people. Yes, the same faces that were on TV, and Jill's still among them.

Returning to her car Jen waited inside until the party dispersed and Jill came out of the front door of the Inn. Jen resisted the urge to dash out of the car and run to Jill. Her partner in crime of old was surrounded by friends. It would be best to follow her.

Once Opal was behind the wheel of a whiz of a Jaguar, Jen was on her tail. Jill stopped merely four blocks away. She pulled into a driveway as a door in the three car garage seemed to magically open.

Jen pulled into the driveway behind the woman she knew as Jill.

Curious, Opal walked back to the minute rental car. It was unusual to have travelers on this street.

"Can I help you," Opal began, stopping when she recognized the woman getting out of the car.

"OH, No! Not you!" Opal managed to speak as her heart stopped and her throat went dry.

"Please, hear me out. I've come here to warn you. Mark just got out of prison. He's looking for you. He blames you and me for his conviction."

"What do you mean he's out? I've been keeping track. I have another two years before I need to - Opal stopped in mid-sentence. She had almost said 'tell Jake'.

"He's out on good behavior; two years early," Jen was quick to take advantage of Opal's pause. "I can't imagine Mark having 'good behavior' but that's what I was told. Mark is back with blood in his eye. We've got to stop him."

"Stop him? From what?"

Jen talked fast, worried that this woman that Jill had become would only give her seconds of her time. Jill's clothes were perfection. A cashmere sweater. Fashion jeans. Elaborate hair-do. House to die for and a Jaquar on top! Jen felt like crawling under a leaf!

"He wants to do another job. Wants us to help him. Then he wants to set you up for the fall this time. That or kill you himself. Please, at least talk to me. I can't stop him by myself. I have a good life. We need a plan to get him back in prison. Let me come in your house and talk. Or we can talk in either car. Please."

"We'll go inside. The third garage over is empty. Pull your car in there in case he's followed you." Opal tapped a portion of her key ring and the garage door began to open. After both had parked and Opal had closed the doors, she joined Jen.

"Do you have bags with you."

"Just a small one. I left in a hurry. He doesn't know where I've gone."

"What do you bet he's guessed? Never mind. Get your bag and come with me. Just please quit talking until I can be alone with my husband a few minutes. When you first meet him you and I will be old friends and you will be just passing through."

"Whatever you say, but let's talk as soon as we can."

"We'll send Jake for take out while we 'catch up'. Come in and meet him. He's a love."

Jake welcomed Jen heartedly.

"I seldom get to meet an old friend of Opal's," he cheerfully acknowledged. "This is an honor."

Behind him Opal rolled her eyes.

"So Jill is the Opal of the lovely jewelry," Jen recalled the forgotten days at the halfway house when Jill started sewing and jewelry making groups. "This guy married her without even knowing her name," she thought. Her old cell mate certainly played in a different league than Jen's.

"If you'd like to freshen up, I'll show you the guest suite," Opal offered. "You must have traveled a long way."

Jen had never been in such a beautiful home. The walls of the guest suite were painted a soft white and adorned with quilted wall hangings done in jewel-toned cottons. The quilt on the bed was a sampler, with dozens of intricately pieced blocks.

The shower had three nozzles projecting from three sides of the step-in enclosure. A touch of a button set all three massaging the bather from three directions. Jen turned the temperature as high as she could stand it.

"I never want to get out!" she thought.

A hair dryer on the wall provided a quick solution to her soaking wet bob. With clean clothes Jen felt like a new person.

Meanwhile, Opal pulled Jake into their bedroom.

"Please sit down. I have to tell you about this so-called 'friend' of mine."

"She seems Ok," Jake began.

"Just let me talk, or I'll never get it out." Jake pulled out the desk chair, turned it around and straddled it. Opal sat on the bed opposite him. He pulled his chair closer.

"I'll be blunt. In another lifetime she and I robbed a jewelry store. Or rather we attempted this and might have succeeded except I had taken the bullets out of her gun. Or what I thought was her gun. Her's turned out to be a water pistol."

Jake started laughing.

"And you were almost six, playing cops and robbers," Jake interspersed.

"Don't I wish," answered Opal. "She had promised not to take a gun and when she pulled it out I thought it was real and I panicked and ran. Unfortunately, she had two velvet pads with assorted diamonds already stuffed into the bag over my arm. I didn't have the sense to throw it down there. By the time I realized I had actually robbed a jewelry store I went to the nearest police station to turn in the gems. Unfortunately, I had done enough to earn a prison term. I spent the three years before I met you in prison in South Carolina. That's why I never want to talk about my past. Well, most of the reason. I met Jen in Juvenile Detention where I went for shoplifting."

Jake looked stunned.

"And now she has looked you up because...."

"Because there's more to my story. Give me a chance to look at you before I go on."

"Ok, my turn then. You could have slept better if you'd told me sooner. I married you for better or worse; for taking or giving and that means stealing or giving back. I've notice you doing about ten people's share of the latter for a lot of years now. So if you think I'm not on your side 100%, think again. I love you, Opal. What you've become has stemmed from all your experiences, even the hardest ones to admit."

"I was going to tell you in two more years. At first I didn't want the children to know and when they grew older I thought I'd just put it off until time for Jen's cohort to be released from prison. He's bad news. It was his plan for us to rob the jewelry store as a cover while he robbed a bank. He knew I was fascinated with sparkly stuff - Jen had told. It was his gun I had left bereft of it's ammo. In Mark's mind he'd have spent the last 18 years on a beach in the Caribbean instead of behind bars except for my little trick."

Jake took Opal in his arms. They had shared so many happy times. She was Opal, not some prison inmate. She was his soul mate and he hers.

"So now we have to do something about this Jen and this Mark.

Something to keep them out of our hair." Jake whispered in her ear as he held her.

"Jen seems to sincerely want to get Mark out of her hair, too. I told her I'd listen to her. Do you want to sit in? She might clam up, but I think she's at the end of her rope and will talk to both of us if I say that's the only way I'll listen."

"Four ears will be better than two. Mark could have sent her to set a trap. Let's both listen."

When Jen joined Opal and Jake in the kitchen she was surprised to find that they were both expecting to hear her story. A big pot of coffee and three cups announced the threesome.

"I don't know where to begin. I never visited Mark in prison, nor wrote to him. Gabe was a handful. Het had Mark's meanness streak from the time he could walk He had spent time in foster care while I was in juvenile detention..

"When my second boy was born Gabe loved picking on him. Sami's the second one. I kept tabs on Mark through a helpful woman who worked at the prison. When she called to tell me Mark's probation was approved I took Sami to my Mom. Mark never knew him but Gabe does. It's only a matter of time before he talks to Mark about Sami. Then Mark will hit the ceiling that I wasn't faithful while he pined away. Sami won't be safe. Except for him I wouldn't have bothered you. Mark can make me do anything he wants by threatening Sami and he'll know it. The only solution is for him to go back to prison for at least long enough for Sami to grow up."

"If he's on probation just coming here will violate parole and put him back to finish his term. It's crossing state lines," Jake offered.

"Oh, he's not coming here. Well, he probably would if he knew Jill - er   Opal was here. I didn't tell him I was even going anywhere."

"You're sure he didn't follow you?" Opal asked.

"Whenever he came to the house he drilled me about where you were. I couldn't tell him because I didn't know until I saw you on the TV program. I left on an airplane without calling or seeing either Mark or Gabe."

"How did you get to the plane?"

"Called a cab."

"Did you call from your house?"

Jen nodded. "For the plane tickets, too. I made a note about the plane times and connections. I think I threw the note in the trash."

"So if they're looking for you they might find the note? You didn't bring it with you."

"I meant too. I had to hurry to make the next flight or wait a day - I don't know. Maybe I dropped it on the floor as I rushed out. At the airport I couldn't find it but the clerk had the information under my name."

"I think we have to work on the presumption that they are on the way. Do they have weapons now?"

"None that I know of; Mark would have trouble getting a gun wouldn't he - on probation? Gabe isn't old enough to buy a gun."

"So the only possibility would be black market guns?"

"I'm going to call our friend Rex and get his ideas, OK?" Jake asked the women. "He's a retired Fed and he'll help us with a plan. Why don't we call for take-out tonight? Fish fries or Pizza sound good to you?"

"Call Pete's and order bar-b-q with the works. I think we all need a feast to think this through," Opal requested. Turning to Jen she added, "They'll bring cole slaw, baked beans, French fries, sliced tomato and pickle , three-bean salad and sweet baked potatoes. You look like you need a hearty meal."

Chapter Twenty-Six
Private Eyes on the Prize

Sean looked up at a private eye he had hired two years before. The well- muscled, jean clad man's face belied the youthful look of his lean body and casual dress.

"Well, it's taken a lot of leg work, but I think I have her!" The man reported.

"Finally," Sean said exuberantly! "Where?"

"I'll show you on this map. It's a little town called Fox Willow, located about here."

"What makes you think she's there?"

"A woman named Jade who answers her description has been there almost since you said she left Chicago. I traced her back from here to the coast. Sit back and relax if you want even a shortened version. She gave me quite a challenge."

Sean called for coffee and the two relaxed.

"You gave me the first lead. You had heard her say that she would like to take a cruise. It was laborious, but I went through records or every cruise ship leaving the East Coast at that time or within a month.

"I found only one 'Jade'. I didn't think it could be her because for that cruise one needed a passport. I traced back in the records and a passport had been issued to a Jade Dobson born 1947 in one of the Virgin Islands.

"Trouble then was tracking her when the ship docked back in

Baltimore. She disappeared at that point. I guessed she might have left with a man. So I traced every man on board that cruise ship. There were only seven that were traveling without a female companion. I actually visited all seven. Two were 'together' in the deepest sense of the word. They remembered her on board. Said she spent lots of time with two older women. Three of the men were gigolos as far as I could tell. Looking for a rich woman.

"The other two I visited and interviewed. They both had tried to hook up with Jade and had dined with her a couple of times. Both independently told me they were looking for shipboard romances. For one it was a last fling before he married the heiress his family had chosen for him. The other was just a plain ladies man. Jade had made it clear to each of them that she wasn't about to enter into a 'have fun, that's all folks' arrangement."

"This sounds like the right Jade," Sean interrupted. "She was sick of the life she had been tricked into."

"At that point I was discouraged, but a check came from you and I paid my rent and went back to work," the gum shoe grinned.

"The ship's roster seemed my only lead. Either that or look for a second cruise ship leaving about the time the first docked. The roster gave me names listed as cabin mates. When I saw two ladies rooming together, I remembered the info from the first two I interviewed. They had mentioned a couple of women that Jade spent lots of time with.

"A stop at the Dept. of Motor Vehicles and a stiff bribe set me up with an address in the Hamptons. I called you for more expense money and took to the road. Both women were friendly; welcomed me into their home. They were pretty old and had a live-in companion who obviously wasn't comfortable receiving a stranger, but we worked though that."

The PI blushed slightly. He didn't share that he was still seeing the delightful young woman, a cousin of one of the ladies who had befriended Jade.

"They remembered Jade well. Showed me pictures taken on the cruise and back in the Hamptons. Yes, they had invited Jade for a visit and she had accepted immediately.

"What they didn't know was where Jade went when she left them. I accepted their hospitality for several more days, hoping something would come to them. Each day I'd look at the photo album and ask questions about the pictures - who was in them and where they were taken. Most were taken on board and the people were, "a lovely couple, I think from Kentucy."

"No, that was the blonde woman. This couple was from Vermont."

"The third time through the album I started from the back. I pointed to a picture with streamers decorating the ceiling and balloons in the background. Three people, Jade and the two women, were in the foreground."

"Was this the last night celebration?" I asked.

"Oh, no! That was a party here in the Hampton's!"

"Yes, Jade would have left earlier but we convinced her to stay for the party. It was at the Jefferson's. A party to honor a close friend visiting them."

"The people who threw the party were touring France and couldn't be reached. My hostesses called three old friends and got us invites to teas. The first person we visited had the memory of a honeycomb. The second kept a box of old cards - well, I should say a tall shelf filled with boxes of memorabilia.. She had them all dated on the outside of the cartons, but things were thrown in pel mel inside.

"After stacking the Christmas cards and get well cards in the box top, we only had about a grocery sack full of various bills, thank you cards and invitations left - all in a jumble. It was time for the woman's nap and she was adamant about it - Doctor's orders.

I left in low spirits, but the lady came through after all. She had found the invitation and it had the name of the honoree: Joseph Richard Grason."

"What a relief! How did that help you, though?"

"Digging through public records didn't yield an address. However, when I went to one of the genealogy sites on the web, I had better luck. There was a Joseph Richard Grason and a Joseph Richard Grason, Jr. Jr. was born in this Fox Willow place, 1972 - then pay dirt!

Mother: Jade Dobson."

"So Jade has a son," Sean had chill bumps. "Her dearest and least likely dream came true. You've done a great job! If you ever need references I'm your man." Sean handed the PI a bonus check.

"I didn't actually go there and see her," the PI added. "Once I got this far I wanted to come to you as quickly as possible."

"That's good. I may go and pay them a visit. I'll have to think it over. It sounds like her life is pretty much on the plus side."

"Grason would be in his late seventies now and she has a teenaged son. If I were you I'd want to at least go hang around the place for a few days and make sure she doesn't need any help. After what you've spent on this search and my dead-ends! It's hard to just let it go!"

"I didn't take much convincing, did I," Sean laughed. "Let's both go! How does late tomorrow sound? I have some loose ends to tie up. Can you get the plane tickets and arrange a rental car?"

"Will do!"

With plane tickets and car rental reservations in hand, Martin considered accommodations for Sean and himself. Through an internet travel site he got phone numbers for a Courtyard Inn and a Hampton Inn in Fox Willow. Both proved to have no vacancies. One clerk suggested a B&B, highly recommending same.

The PI called the number he had been given for the 'Gems and Jam' B&B. He got a recording saying the place was closed for renovations until further notice. Flustered, he called back the Courtyard and got on a waiting list.

"Where is the closest motel with a vacancy for at least tomorrow night?" he asked.

Upon hearing that would be a long commute, he got in touch with the rental car company again and had them arrange for a super-sized RV. He'd sold his a couple of years ago because of the price of gas, but he loved to drive the mammoth vehicles. He called AAA. Yes, there was an RV park just outside of Fox Willow.

"I'll drive the RV and Sean can follow in the rental car," he said to no one but himself.

"That way we can get around the small town without the hassle of parking a house trailer."

Sean and Martin boarded the plane at mid-afternoon. Sean didn't much like the idea of the RV, but he was excited to see Jade even though it would be for the last time. His hope that she would be free to marry him had faded when he found out about the two Richards. He had that bittersweet feeling of happiness for Jade, yet sorrow that he couldn't be a part of her life.

Sean did not know that just as the plane approached the runway for take-off, Duke Daniels was in his office demanding to know how to get in touch with Sean. When threats to the secretary had not worked, Duke hung around the neighborhood until the offices closed.

Duke had not done any lock picking for years, but the skill came back to him quickly. Once inside the office, the secretary's desk yielded the information he needed. Back in Sean's office Duke found and read the PI's report.

"Well, bless her heart!" Beautiful Jade should be willing to fork over a steady income to keep the secret of her past revealed. Her husband might be too old to care, but she had a teen-age son. Who would have believed it?

"Maybe I should help the old guy get to Heaven's Golden Gate a little quicker," Duke planned. "I bet I could shock him straight to Hell with what I know about his trophy wife!"

Duke cursed, angry that he couldn't just call for a last minute plane ticket. He sold his clunker of a car and got a ride from the dealer to the bus station.

"Fox Willow and Easy Street, here I come!" announced Duke to the almost full moon which was dominating the sky.

"We need a reason for showing up in a little town," Martin settled back in his window seat on the plane.

"I thought of that," Sean replied. "How about genealogical research. We are distant cousins searching our common ancestry. Hopefully there's a library with some data and certainly some cemeteries."

"Good idea. My Mother was a Smith. There are Smith's in

every cemetery in the States!" Martin grinned. "Should let us get by in a small town without arousing suspicion."

"OK. Smith family are we! I'll say my maternal grandmother was a Smith if anyone asks! Now that we have that settled, I think I'll take a nap."

Chapter Twenty-Seven
Gathering of the Hunters

Some came by air; most traveled the highways. Some brought pleasant memories and reinforcements for those whose closely guarded secrets were exposed. Some brought danger and darkness; terror and treachery. Some thirsted for revenge. Some longed to see a lost loved one.

Some were motivated by sheer greed. Some by curiosity. Some by patriotism. Whatever their reasons they all were coming to Fox Willow. The hunters and the hunted. The friends and the foes. The chase had been maddening. Season after season had passed with no sniff of the prey. Now the chase was all but over. The hunters had tracked down their prey. They were coming in for the kill.

Rex and Mel sensed the danger. They were in place; ready when the Hunters arrived in Fox Willow. Of the number coming they had no idea. They only knew two of the secrets; three of the hunters. In the next few days they would need their wits about them and more than a little help from the friendly citizens of Fox Willow.

Bobby was the first to arrive. He had followed Pearl and Jaclyn, hoping to break the ice with Pearl. He checked in at the Hampton Inn out by the interstate and planned his next move. Maybe he could find where Jaclyn worked or hung out. Her advice would be helpful.

Jules arrived the same day. His reunion with Amber was joyous. Elinor had arranged for Amber to accompany her to the airport.

There, brother and sister stared at one another, Amber seeing her Pere; Jules his Mere. All at once the enormity of the reunion hit them and they fell into one another's arms. Elinor was even in tears, and glad she was doing the driving. As they traveled the short distance to Fox Willow, both brother and sister sat in back, hugging and talking. They had both reverted to French and Elinor knew not one word of what was said.

Part way there, traveling in his Audi, Greg was the angriest of the hunters. The henchman hired by Abbot was only a few miles behind Greg, in a black Lincoln. Devlin and Jack were also driving, but coming from another direction.

Unknown to Jen, Mark and Gabe were on the open highway, traveling at close to double the speed limit in her old Chevy. If they reached Fox Willow at all it would be sheer luck. Mark had busted his parole multiple times in the past hours. A speeding ticket would put him back in prison. What the heck. If he was going back he would at least have the thrill!

"If you don't slow down this heap is going to break apart," Gabe said. "Pull over. I almost peed my pants when you passed that semi. I've got to go. Now!"

"Ain't done no good to pass him if I pull over now," Mark complained.

As soon as they stopped Gabe took the keys.

"My turn to drive. I ain't ready to die yet!" Gabe said.

"Chump!" answered Mark, oblivious to the fact that Gabe was too young to have a licence. Mark's knee had swollen and he needed to stretch it out. He squeezed into the back seat.

Harry Atkins looked over the mess he had made. The travel

agent took a while giving up Jule's destination.

Harry had waited until two of the three women in the office of the little agency had left for lunch. Now he was way behind Jules. Well, when their lunch was over the others would be in for a surprise.

"I'd better not waste any more time."

Harry took what cash he could find and the woman's jewelry, throwing the latter in a waste basket when he got to the airport. He was barely in time. Jules was boarding the plane. Harry took the last stand-by seat in the back row center. The man by the window offered to trade seats. Harry guessed he was sympathetic to the woman on the aisle. She had seen the blood on Harry's shirt and was gagging and scrunched over so far she was almost sitting in the aisle.

Harry suggested giving the woman the window.

"I'd rather have the aisle."

The man pretended to sleep, which suited Harry fine. When the plane was in the air he boldly left his seat and walked up to first class. Once past the curtain he took a leather suitcase from the overhead. The sleeping man in the seat underneath looked close to Harry's size. Harry made it into the front restroom without interference from the crew. There he discarded his bloody shirt, ripping it up and stuffing the pieces in the compartment for women's use only. He washed up as best he could and put on one of the two dress shirts he found in the suitcase. Stuffing a tie and half the cash tucked in the lining into a pocket, he boldly left the restroom, and returned the suitcase to it's original spot over the sleeping owner.

On arrival when Harry saw the happy reunion of brother and sister he called Abbot immediately.

"What will you pay for the two of them?" he asked.

"I've waited too long not to watch. Just make sure they don't leave until I get there. I'll hire a private jet. How can I reach you?"

****

"Jack, this is my Sister we're talking about. Even if you and she had never hit it off, I'd ask you to help me. If it'll help I'll call Margie. She knows you're committed to her. I tell you, Rachel's in danger. I don't just sense it, I looked at the files. I need a back-up; a fishing buddy for a cover. We'll be home in four days, tops!"

"I'll go with you, but it may be the end of my marriage. Don't call Margie; I'll talk to her myself."

To triple the problem Margie wasn't home when Jack arrived. Devlin would be by in less than an hour. Jack had no choice except to start packing before he talked to his wife. He left messages for Margie everywhere he could think of. He absolutely couldn't leave without telling her what was going on.

He had finished packing when Margie arrived. The first thing she saw was the suitcase.

"Devlin called. He needs my help," Jack began.

"It's Rachel isn't it?" Margie asked without pausing for an answer. "I always knew she'd knock on your door one day. Go then! End it with her once and for all. Just don't come back until you have."

"It's not for Rachel. Dev has been like the little brother that I never had. Look at all the things he's done for us. He insists he needs my help."

"Don't lie to yourself, Jack. You want to know what happened to Rachel - why she left you without a word. You want to know what got in the way of the life you planned with her. Go and find out. I'll be here if you decide to come back."

"You know I'll be back. You and our kids are my life now. Rachel is dead to me; one way or the other."

"Then go and face her ghost! The sooner the better!"

Devlin was coming up their walk. Margie saw him from the window.

"He's here now. Don't ask him in. Just leave and let me be!"

"I'll call you then," Jack reached to embrace Margie, but she stepped aside.

"When you come home," she said simply.

****

Mason's private plane made one refueling stop. He had kept his pilot on stand-by since receiving the first call from Jonesy. The fact that Jonesy reported no empty motel beds did not bother him. His plan was to pick up Lily with Jonesy's help and get her back on the plane. They would be back on the island well before dawn the following morning.

When they stopped for fuel the pilot made the call.

"Is the money deposited?" he asked a bank official. Upon confirmation of same he dialed Lopez on a separate phone.

"A small private strip not on any map. It's just outside a small town called Fox Willow. Yes, there's a bank there. I'll meet you there for my final payment after you've seen the girl, Lily." (Pause) "Well, to give you plenty of time to find her, let's say 30 mins. before the bank closes tomorrow. The time should be posted on the door. When we get there tonight we can check it out separately."

Chapter Twenty-Eight

Ill Winds and Silver Linings

Lopez had never looked around a small town before. He had come in to Fox Willow as the pilot had suggested: to check the time that the local bank closed. He was disgusted to learn that he had several hours to kill. Well, he waited for many years, what was a few more hours? He had asked his henchmen to stay hidden, as he wanted not too many small-town Eagle eyed citizens to see either of them.

For some reason, Lopez was drawn to the park. The statute on the east end could have been made by one of the old Italian sculptors. The symmetry was incredible. Two adult foxes playing with their three young! What strength! What exquisite beauty! Lopez noticed another sculpture facing the opposite side of the square. He left the sidewalk and strolled across the park, circling between the two huge willows. Yes, there was another stature. Even more beautiful than the first. Lopez had almost missed it because of the willow trees, but caught just a glimpse of it between them.

This sculpture he liked even more. The two adult foxes were going in for a kill! They had cornered a large rabbit which obviously was exhausted from the chase. Frozen in time the two foxes had the advantage of the rabbit. The rabbit was cowering as one fox leapt through the air above him.

"Let's see, I'm the bigger Fox. The guy who works for me is the other one. And Lily is the rabbit. Lilly will be the one cowering before us before the night is over. At last, I will end this, and end it tonight!"

There should've been little satisfaction in finding Lily after all this time. Two of his sons were dead and one in prison. His fourth son still refused to have any interest in the business. His empire had crumpled. His influence was at an all time low. That was partly because the word was out that he'd been unable to find his Lily. Now it would be known far and wide that he was the Godfather. His rule by intimidation was not over! It was just beginning.

Lopez strutted around the stature, staring at the details. Finally he tore himself away, and resisted the impulse to go in a local restaurant for breakfast. He did not want to be sitting next to a small town busy body. Instead he got back in his rental car and drove to a neighboring town where he ordered the largest breakfast on the menu.

Jonesy met Mason as soon as the plane landed on the narrow private strip 40 miles from Fox Willow. The pilot asked to come with them.

"I need to get something to eat," he improvised. "Maybe they'll have a movie house or something! I don't want to just sit here and do nothing."

"That's exactly why you're earning so much money!" Mason told him.

"There's plenty of food in the refrigerator right on the plane. There's also a microwave to warm it up. I may need to leave here instantly and I don't want to have to look for you in some movie house. That was not the deal."

The pilot cursed as they drove off without him. He should've gotten a cell phone number for Lopez. The guy sure didn't believe in giving out his number. Well, it was Lopez's hard luck. At this point, the pilot did know anymore than he had told Lopez anyway. He could have surely used an extra cash however. Perhaps not all was lost.

"As deserted as this place looks now," he thought, "someone could come along at any moment. I could even take a real chance and fly to another airport." The pilot decided to get something to eat and think it over.

Jules and Amber were still exchanging lifelong reminisces about their experiences since they were in France. Jules told Amber all about the experiences he had with her brothers and father after she left with her mother. Most of them were happy; some sad. Their father had lived to be in his 60s and had always hoped to see Amber and his wife again.

Georges had met the worse fate. He had been captured by a German unit on patrol. While Pierre watched, Georges had ruffled the feathers of a guard. This was an obvious suicidal attempt on the part of Georges. Death was better than identification as an underground participant. As a prisoner, his fate would have been inevitable.

The wound with which the German soldier inflicted Georges must've been excruciatingly painful. Jules did not describe this in detail. He had watched his brother die. There was no point in giving Amber anymore information. He need only to tell her that his brother was very brave. Claude had traveled separately from the others, going back to assist the French Underground. Jules had no further knowledge regarding Claude.

Pierre had lived until a few years ago. He had married and had three children. So far, there were no grandchildren, as Pierre had married late. Getting reacquainted with Amber was even more exciting to Jules and telling her what news he had. He wanted to know all about her family -- her husband, children and grandchildren. They arranged a reunion the coming summer so he could meet as many as possible. He was especially interested in the time that she and her mother lived in New Orleans. Amber had scrapbooks, with lots of photos and notes about their experiences. Both had mixed feelings when looking at the pictures of their mother's wedding. At the time their father would have still been alive, but there was no way for her mother to know that. After Amber left New Orleans with her husband Alexis had finally agreed to marriage with the man she had been close to for several years. Jules was excited to hear about the restaurant, and his mother's success as a French cook.

About ten o'clock Gilda and Lisa stopped in 'The Baker's Bakery' to 'sit a spell' and talk to Brenda Baker; wife, co-owner and assistant baker.

"It's got to be a really special cake." Lisa said. "Something fancier than Ruby would make. Rex is really a great addition to our little abode. We want to welcome him properly,"

"Well, you could have given me a day or two notice. I'm a baker, not a magician! You said by 4:OO o'clock" Brenda was teasing. She had no problem with rush orders.

"Is there a convention of some kind out at the motels? Why are all the strangers buzzing around town. Have you ever seen that guy staring at the sculptures out there? He's dressed like in the forties. Gives me the creeps." Gilda shivered.

"It's been like that all morning. Strangers all alone or in pairs window shopping mostly. If there's a convention out by the interstate we haven't heard. They most often order extra pastries for their continental breakfast bars when they have big meetings." Brenda observed thoughtfully.

"If it's a convention I think Gilda would know. Can you make us a nice cake in time or not?" demanded Lisa.

"I have layers for four cakes in the oven. They're all vanilla, but I can make up a four layered with chocolate icing and a nutty caramel center filling covering the lowest layer."

"Decorate it really fancy please. It should say 'Welcome, Rex'." Lisa added.

When Sean saw the size of the RV Martin had rented, he almost told the man to take it and go on a camping trip. It was like announcing on a great big billboard:

"We are in town looking for someone! Has anyone seen my sweet, lovely Jade?

"Did you have tee shirts made too?" Sean asked good-naturedly.

"What?" Asked Martin.

"Nothing. Just kidding. I don't think I've ever seen an RV this large."

"They don't make 'em any bigger," Martin said proudly. "You'll sleep like a baby tonight."

"Well, I'll follow you to the place to park it. There is a legitimate place, I hope."

"Only a few miles from here and almost on top of Fox Willow. I had to pay extra though to have the RV brought here to the airport."

Harry Adkins was transporting Abbot from the same airport and sitting on his horn. The RV was blocking the lane three cars up while Sean and Martin talked. Sean dashed back and got into the idling rental sedan. Once past the airport access roads Harry passed them both and went on cruise control at exactly 12 miles above the speed limit.

"Now what is it that you were saying?" Harry asked Abbot. Abbot was in the backseat mumbling incessantly.

"Lovely young girl. At last I've found her. Skin like rose petals. Hands so gentle when she washes the blood from my face. Little Suzette. Little Suzette."

Harry suddenly wondered if he was working for a man that was bonkers. Surely he didn't think the mark wouldn't have aged. Looking back over his shoulder he saw that Abbot was sleeping.

Talking nonsense in his sleep. No need for alarm.

Lucky for Harry he pulled in at the first of the two motels. Martin continued on in the RV with Sean close behind. The RV park was the far side of town from the interstate and the route marked on the map went right down Main St.

"Look," Lisa called to the Bakers as she and Gilda were leaving. "It's a parade."

The RV was so long it almost encompassed the entire block. Martin almost turned it over when making a right turn in the narrow streets. He had lost his touch. He made it though with several tries. As he straightened out he heard clapping and cheers. The street corners were filled with onlookers. So much for planning a low profile, Sean thought.

Harry had moved from smooth talker to intimidator at the motel desk. He was doubly glad he had changed to the borrowed shirt and tie.

"I KNOW we have reservations," he shouted. "Get me your district manager on the phone,"

Partly because he was shouting and a line was forming behind him, the clerk gave him one room.

The man with the loudmouth had his feet up on a lounge

sofa and was snoring loudly. The clerk got rid of them and hoped someone would cancel.

"I said two rooms!" Harry was shouting.

"There's only one ready now," the clerk improvised. "If you'll please take your friend there to sleep we'll call when we can give you another." Like never! The clerk was rethinking his decision to give them a room at all.

Chapter Twenty-Nine

The Sting

"You're having fun with this aren't you? You don't even seem surprised!"

"I wondered if you'd ever spill." Jake said. "Dick told me years ago, right after he got the promotion to Police Commissioner of Fox Willow."

"Told you what?" Opal gasped!

"Some clown named Mark put a hit out on you. A petty parolee that had been Mark's cell mate told all. He wasn't out a month before he stood guard for a convenience store robbery. He was caught on the surveillance Camera and was trying to plea bargain. He told on this Mark fellow."

"Why didn't you tell me?"

"You were in labor with Olivia at that time. The cops all thought it was nothing serious. Mark didn't have connections. No one visited him. He had a public defender who was so clean-cut it almost wasn't fair to the perp. He didn't have a penny for a cigarette, much less money for a hit."

"So you just pretended you didn't know all the years?"

"I just put it out of my mind. If we talked about it the children might overhear. It was your secret to bring up if you wanted to. I think I loved you even more for becoming this wondrous, exciting woman.

"By the way, I called Dick. He'll be here early in the morning."

"How about a back rub?" Opal asked. "We need to get some

sleep before long."

"Maybe I'll let you sleep in a little while," Jake muttered.

After hearing Jen out, Dick took charge.

"First of all, I want the three of you out of here today. I'll have men watch the house. No need for Mark finding out you're the wealthiest kids in town.

"Sergeant Rigg's mother's house is a few blocks from here. I'll write down the address and phone number. Give it to Mark when you call. Mrs. Riggs is in Florida and planning to move there. She took all her valuables and her best furniture already. She left some old stuff so the realtor could show it with furniture."   "Amber says houses sell better if they are furnished when potential buyers are looking." Opal said.

"Hides a lot of cracked plaster and other problems, she means." Dick grinned.

"You're going to a lot of trouble for me," Jen said.

"No trouble. This is great. How often do we cops get to set up a criminal before he's in the act. We rarely have a crime here in Fox Willow, especially not one that is solved before it starts." Jake cackled and Dick joined in the laughter. The two women were more serious.

"I'm glad you two are sure this is going to work," mused Opal.

"Let's put on more coffee and give Jen a chance to call Mark." Dick rose, stretching.

They all took a short break.

"I can't reach either Gabe or Mark." Jen said.

"Try about every 30 minutes and let me know if you reach either," Dick suggested. Meanwhile Dick made several phone calls, one of them long-distance asking for a courtesy drive-by. By 8:30 a.m.

they had their plan laid out. They all went down town for breakfast and to give Jen the layout of Fox Willow and the bank. By 9:30 a.m. Dick received a report from afar. The conclusion of the courtesy drive-by was that both Mark and Gabe were on the road. Not only was the car gone, a neighbor had watched as Gabe loaded a suitcase and a couple of boxes into Jen's old Chevy and took off.

Shortly before 11:30 a.m. clothing, family pictures, and books were relocated to the Rigg's house. The bank president was then advised of the scam. He approved the plans heartily. About 2:30 p.m. packages of marked bills were placed in each teller's cage with actual money only on top and bottom. Pale green paper, cut the size of dollar bills, made up the bulk of the packets. Meanwhile, a local restaurant owner was making a special lasagna sauce in his home kitchen. His wife was baking an unique and delicious cake.

A report from the phone company arrived at Dick's office at 4:24 pm. An individual, sounding like a man, had called Jen's home phone number. This person used the access code to listen to messages that had been left on that phone. The report indicated that he had read messages from a pay phone booth 225 miles from Fox Willow.

" The arrival time of our friends is estimated at between 7 p.m. and 8:30 p.m. Jake's truck and Jen's rental car are the only visible vehicles we want left in front of Rigg's house unless Rex is here 'visiting'. If anyone wants to back out of this, now is the time," Dick informed the others. He was all business now.

Shortly, a plains clothes officer in casual attire delivered lasagne in a large, microwave-safe container. The lasagne looked as if about a third has already been devoured.

Rex stopped by soon after and picked up Opal and Jen. They

went to the pub downtown for dinner. They consumed nonalcoholic beer in mugs as a precautionary action. If Mark and Gabe arrived in town thirsty and came into the bar they would see the women out partying together.

Once back at the house there had been no sign of Gabe or Mark. The threads that were strategically placed to announce any surprise entry were unbroken.

When Jake arrived 'home' they set up a card table and played gin rummy. Finally! The anxiously awaited pounding on door was loud enough to knock the door down if continued long. Jake answered immediately, coming face to face with Gabe.

"I'm looking for my mom, I had a message that she's here." Gabe's voice was bold and curt.

"Son, you got my message." Jen said, jumping up and running to the door. "I didn't mean for you to come. I just wanted you to know where I was."

Jen went close enough to Gabe that the others could not see her and put one finger in front of her lips, signaling quiet around these folks..

"Did your dad come?" Jen asked.

"He's out in the car. Go out there. He wants to see you!"

"Sure honey. You come on in. Meet my old friend, Jill. She goes by Opal now. I'm thinking of changing my name, too. I like Jewel a lot. Don't you think it suits me?"

"Don't keep dad waiting. He's in a bad mood. Would one of you show me the bathroom?"

Outside, Mark greets Jen gruffly.

"Why did you leave without me?" Mark demanded.

"I wasn't sure it was her. I just got a glance on a TV program."

"You want me to believe that dumb old Jill was on TV?" Mark was at his most sarcastic.

"The program wasn't about her. It was about some fancy place to stay, on the local news channel, one of those fillers, I think. I was just running through looking for something good to watch. They were talking about this fancy place and there was Jill sitting there or at least one of them looked like Jill. I decided to check it out. So I called the TV station and asked the name of the place, saying I wanted to stay there.

"It turns out I got lucky. Jill and I have it all worked out. We can't tell you in the front of these guys. Jake is Jill's husband and she wants out. He won't work a regular job; claims he's going to be a wood-carving artist. He carves little whistles out of willow bark. She wants to split and go with us after we do the heist. They are always short on money, and she's tired of it."

Mark was tired enough to be led inside, although he looked pretty grim as the introductions took place. Jake slapped him on the back, welcoming him. Mark was leery; however he gained confidence after a couple of beers. He was actually jovial after they let him win a couple of poker hands.

In spite of his age, Gabe had done most of the driving. Anytime Mark was behind the wheel Gabe couldn't sleep for sheer fright at the older man's recklessness. Gabe refused to join the card game, falling asleep on the old sofa.

After the fourth beer, Mark asks where he can sleep.

"I didn't hear anyone invite you to stay over," Jen complains "There are some motels around. I would have kept the reservation I have, had I known you were coming. Jill invited me to stay here, though, so I cancelled the room at the motel."

"If you have a room here, I'll just sleep in it too," Mark was too tired for amenities. "You don't think I'm going to wake the boy, do you? He sleeps like a half dead old man."

"Sure, you're welcome to stay here," Jake interceded. "We only have two bedrooms, but the bed Jen is using is a double. If she doesn't want to share with you, there's an old cot here in the hall closet."

"The double bed will be fine," Mark gives Jen a side look that says 'don't you dare contradict me'. Showing him the room and bathroom, Jen cautions him,

"Take a shower at least! You absolutely reek!" Her suitcase and a couple of items of her clothing were lying around. Mark flipped her the car keys.

"Go out and get my things then - better take your suitcase. My clothes are loose on the back seat. My suitcase busted. I'm not taking a shower and putting these things right back on."

Jen pocketed the keys and tossed him a thick terry robe.

"I'm going to bring in some clean clothes for Mark," Jen reported as she walked through the living room carrying her empty suitcase. Jake looked at Rex.

"Are you thinking what I'm thinking?"

Accompanying Jen, they searched the Chevy for weapons. Finding a handgun under the spare tire, Rex disabled it and returned it to it's hiding place. Oddly, they found no ammo.

Before Rex returned to the B&B, he and Jake checked the surveillance system set up in the small house.

"Are you sure you don't want me to stay?" Rex asked. "We could say I was too drunk to drive so you hid my car keys."

"We'll be fine. The two cops listening from next door will be monitoring constantly. They'll rush over if any fracas starts up over here."

****

Jen was the first one up. She uncurled from the rocking chair, stretching sleepily. Mark was jack knifed in the bed, snoring loudly. Jen pulled the quilt tighter around her, then remembered! This is Freedom Day! Freedom from Mark! She dashed for the shower.

Jake and Opal were already out of bed and dressed when the alarm woke Mark. Gabe was still sleeping on the sofa. Opal had the coffee brewing when Mark walked into the kitchen.

"I could sure use a cup of that java," he commented. "The smell is enough to make me thirsty."

"I was just about to make the doughnut run. How about it, Mark? Want to ride with me?" Jake asked Mark.

"Sure, why not?" Mark answered with a grin. Opal shakes her head. Mark thinks a moment; then realizes that with Jake gone they can discuss the heist.

"On second thought, I've been in a car more hours than I'd like to think. I need to stretch a while. Get lots of doughnuts."

At 8:45 a.m. Jake left the two women alone with Mark and Gabe. He was reluctant to do so, but the plan would never get off the ground if the four couldn't confer in private. If Jen was not on the up and up, it will be three against one for Opal. Jen even knows about the surveillance cameras!

"I'd best hustle!"

"OK, woman. Spill!" Mark said when alone with Jill. "Jen says you want to work with us. Before you needed a lot of persuasion.'

-274-

Opal describes the local bank.

"It's a very casual set-up. No bars that the tellers stand behind. It's more like an open counter. They have drawers on their side of the counter top where they keep money.

Jen walks in, towel-drying her hair.

"Let's do it today and get out of town before many people have a chance to see us. Gabe will stick out like a sore bomb, with his tattoos and that haircut." Jen urged. "Besides, you hog the whole bed. I finally moved to the rocker, but I wouldn't say I slept well."

"Today's too quick. It's already too late to be there when it opens." Mark argues.

"The bank stays open until four. Only one teller and the drive up window lady stay after three."

"You just looked for a day. How can you be sure?" Mark wanted to know.

"I've been here for years!" Opal attests. "Life is so dull here, I even watch the grass grow."

"So, you're more cooperative now that you've lived in a dump like this! Lumpiest bed I ever slept in! Worse than prison."

"One condition! Absolutely NO loaded weapons!" Opal said.

"That's the trouble with doing the heist today. Have to find a pawn shop and pick some up. Couldn't bring them across state lines, not in Jen's old heep. It could've broken down on our way. That's another thing. We need a good getaway car."

"Maybe I can get Rex to lend us his. Tell him I want to show my friend Jen around the countryside. You may as well give up the idea of guns. There are no pawn shops for miles and Jake and I don't have any guns. Can't you just use your hand or something in your pocket?

Even if you find a pawn shop in this state you have to register ahead. There is a waiting period before you can pick up the gun. Don't remember how many days, but it's a long time to be hanging out in a burg where everyone wants to know everyone else."

Gabe is waking up.

"Did you say guns? I got that covered. The pistol is under the spare. The ammo is in the back seat inside the stuffing that old man put in there when the old seat got moldly. Only enough to load up once though. How's your aim, *Dad?*" "I said no loaded weapons or I won't call Rex. Just leave the backseat in place. If you don't agree, no getaway car."

For a moment Gabe looked ready to strike. Mark gave a slight shake of his head.

"I'll stick with Mom's car," Gabe said. "I just filled the tank a few miles ago. We can't leave it here anyway. Even a small town cop can trace us from the car."

"Okay, we'll use the local car for the heist and leave the heap not far away. Jill, we need you to draw a little map from here to the bank and mark a good spot in walking distance to the bank to leave Jen's clunker. You two will pick us up as we come out of the bank and take us to our vehicle. We'll hop out and meet you in a burg away from here - in an hour, maybe two. Jill you know the area. Any idea where?

There's a small pub in Skywill, about 45 minutes from here going South. They don't actually open until about 6, for the night crowd. But they don't lock it up either after the two cooks come. We can probably get take-outs there and collect some cash from them when they open the cash register. It's called Louie's. There's only one business street in the burg. Can't miss Louie's; it's on a corner and has a little terrace they use on warm nights."

"Call that Rex guy to bring the car. If we're going with this today, we have to hustle."

"You're okay with no guns, then?" Opal asked.

"Looks like we don't have a choice." Mark answered quickly, fearing Gabe would argue.

"Okay, maybe Rex will bring the car over now and I'll ask Jake to give him a ride back after he has a doughnut. Here comes Jake now.

Rex walks in a little after Jake. He tosses the keys to Opal.

"Take care of my baby. I fueled her up. She is ready to roll."

"Have a doughnut and a cup of coffee." Opal offers Rex a chair as Jake comes in loaded down with baked goods. A little after ten A.M. Rex and Jake, their tummies filled with cream donuts, take off in Jake's truck.

"We're getting our hair done," Opal announced. "Not here - next town over at a big mall where no one knows me. I need to change my color in case someone spots me driving get-a-way. You two had best shower and shave. Gabe you stink so much they might pick you up as a vagrant before you get to the bank. Also, you might see if any of Jake's jackets or sweaters fit. That skull and cross-bone shirt won't cut it around here."

"When will you be back?" Mark asked.

"Never!" announced Opal. "I don't want any nosy neighbors seeing me in my new hairdo. We'll be watching when you go in the bank and drive by just as you come out. Jen will be in seat behind me. You get in back with her; Gabe take the front passenger seat!"

Gabe grimaces. He motions Mark to join him.

"Since when does she give the orders? I thought we were getting rid of her!

"She's our navigator on this job. She's got it figured out good! We can do her in when we don't need her."

"She's a looker, alright. What a stack! Maybe we should keep her around a day or two. I'd sure like to do her. Show her who makes the rules while I'm at it."   Mark cackles.

" I'd like to watch that!" We'll keep her as long as she's cooperative. Maybe she'd like to help me out a little, while you're doing it the other way."

"OK, you guys; thanks for helping us clean-up in the kitchen! You have Jen really trained, don't you?" Opal asked as she walked into the living room. "Here are your maps. I made one for each of you. Let's go over these before Jen and I leave."

Opal spread her sketches out on the card table no one had removed since last night. I have an idea. When Jen and I see you go into the bank, what if we pull up to the drive-in window, blocking it for anyone else and distracting one of the two clerks. I'll hand her a withdrawal slip for a couple of thousand and she'll open her money drawer. If Gabe steps through this little slinging gate they use to get back to the safety deposit boxes, he can come up behind her. She's an old spinster. I think she'll actually like being in a man's embrace."

At that all were chuckling.

"Take one of Jake's ties in there to tie across her mouth. She'll have big white bags that some of the businesses use to transfer payroll cash. Tell her to fill it up with big bills. Mark, you'll have to take care of the other one. She'll have the most cash. I'd suggest one blow so that she's unconscious. She'll be the most resistive of the two. I marked on the map the spot she'll go for - the button for the alarm. Don't put her in the hospital, OK? Just keep her away from that button."

The audio reveals whistling as the men took turns shaving and showering, Gabe going first. All cleaned up and in Jake's best rugby shirt, Gabe found the lasagna in the fridge and popped it in the microwave. He ate heartily, and most of it was gone by the time Mark came from his shower. The audio picked up more gross language concerning sharing and sharing alike regarding the lasagna.

At 1:15 p.m. the phone rang.

"Don't pick up. It's not for us ," Mark cautioned.

The answering machine blurted loudly.

"Hey Mark. It's Jake. Are you still there? I'm delayed and won't be back till about three. There's lasagna in the fridge. Oh and when I got the doughnuts I got a chocolate cake. If you go out the back door, there's a screened-in back porch. The cake is in the old fridge out there. Help yourself if Opal hasn't already fed you! " Eating the lasagna had just made Gabe hungrier. He and Mark both dashed for the back door. The fridge out back was packed with a variety of beer. On one shelf a humongous cake was sitting atop four six packs of LaBatt's Blue.

Between the laced lasagna and tainted cake, plus a few beers to wash it down, each culprit left the house in good spirits. When they got downtown, Mark said,

"Give me the gun!"

"You said you were carrying it. I thought that meant you got it out." Gabe was alarmed. He feared going in 'naked'.

"You said you had it covered." Mark hissed.

"Well, *Dad,*" Gabe said, his usual sarcasm literally dripping.

"We have to go back! There're too many people around here to dig under the spare and the stuffing that fellow put in flies like cotton tree lint."

Mark looked at his watch.

"No time now! Let me out here and you park in the area she designated on that little map. Get the gun but don't bother with the mess to get the ammo. We'll take them by surprise!"

"I thought you told me to always fire an early warning shot up in the air," Gabe protested.

"This won't be the first time I hit a hick town bank without any weapons. They won't know we don't have the gun loaded. Besides you look like you're carrying half the time. Just think about how sweet it'll be tonight."

Gabe felt uneasy about this change in plans. He almost went back to the house to empty the backseat of its ammo. However, that fellow Jake could come back there any time now. Gabe had done lots of petty mean things, but the first time he offed a guy he wanted a size advantage. Jake would be more of a challenge that Gabe had time for today, unless he could shoot from several feet away.

"That probably wouldn't work, either," Gabe admitted to himself. "I hope Mark is a better marksman than me."

Even if Jake wasn't back the stuffing was a nuisance. The stuff flew everywhere. He couldn't dig out the ammo on this busy street without attracting lots of attention.

Anyway, Mark was right. There wasn't time.

"Mark will pull it off without me if I don't get moving!" He felt better once he had the pistol in his hand, loaded or not. The stuff in the cake was doing it's thing, unknown to Gabe. He felt up on a cloud, but thought it was a high because of the bank heist. Man, this was the moon! He had done a couple of convenience store jobs, but never robbed a bank.

By the time Gabe got to the bank he was feeling better and better. The gun began to twirl in his right hand. He spotted Mark and gave him the nod. As planned Mark entered the bank first.

The euphoria had hit Mark the hardest. His speech was slurred. The bank teller he was walking toward thought he was purposely walking like Charlie Chaplin to amuse her. She giggled as he approached, almost stumbling.

Gabe followed Mark inside seconds later. He was surprised to see a couple of extra people standing around. One was filling out a deposit slip at a high counter. Another had taken a chair over by the window and had a pamphlet advertising something in her lap.

Mark's voice began echoing throughout the room.

"Hands over your head and hands over your head and everyone er ever un o ya down on de floor. Dwn on da floor; we mean business and I do mean business."

Mark staggered, almost falling. A plainclothesman abandoned his deposit slip and caught Mark's arm, holding him up right.

"I have de gun," Gabe announced, twirling it in the air to attract attention. "Do as he says. Get down!"

Gabe raised his arm high showing off the gun and began twirling it again. Suddenly the gun flew off Gabe's hand. It flew through the air, hitting Mark on the nose. Blood gushed out! Mark fell to his knees.

As Mark fell his hand glanced across the ankle of the plain clothes policeman.

"An ankle holster! What luck!" Mark slid the gun out of the ankle holster. Planning to scare everyone into compliance he clumsily tried to stand as he shot into the air. Just then Lopez was entering the bank for his rendevous with the pilot. The bullet hit him is right in the temple. Two policemen appeared from behind closed doors. Mark and Gabe were secured and handcuffed, their rights read on the spot. They were charged with armed robbery, second-degree murder, and manslaughter!

Lopez was dead by the time he hit the floor. The crime lord who could not be caught by authorities across two continents was taken down by a petty thief's stray bullet!

Chapter Thirty

The Surprise Party

The RV Park proved to be close to Fox Willow, but no one else was at the Park.

"If you're going into town, ask around to see if anyone could tell us how to contact the owner of this park. There's no sign of him here." Martin suggested.

Sean sighed. Martin might be a good private eye, but he wasn't very good as a travel agent. He should've found out that this place was closed before he rented the RV. Now he needed some kind of electrical hookup done by the owner. Sean got back in the sedan, leaving Martin to deal with whatever had to be done to the RV. All kinds of connections beyond Sean's interests or comprehension had to be made.

Gilda was getting anxious. The party was about to begin. She had streamers everywhere, tied from arbor to arbor; from shrub to shrub. The garden looked gala. People were beginning to come.

"I'm sorry you weren't willing to postpone this. How many did you invite?" Ruby asked as a couple arrived who Ruby hardly knew.

"Gilda went wild." Lisa admitted. "She was asking everybody she saw in town this morning to come to the surprise party."

"The major problem is, where is Rex? He hasn't been seen all morning. Not since last night, actually." Lisa was beginning to worry. "Mel, you're supposed to take him out to check on a used car this morning and bring him back at two-thirty."

Mel was quiet. If he knew anything about Rex's whereabouts,

he wasn't saying.

Ruby was going about her business as if nothing had happened unusual. She was even ignoring Gilda and Lisa. She had tried desperately to talk them out of the party.

The first people to arrive were Amber and her brother, Jules. What a miracle! It was so wondrously great for Jules to have found Amber and for Amber to have her brother. Even better, she had found that one of her brothers married and had children. Amber was an aunt, and even a great aunt!

"How wonderful!" Ruby thought when she saw them. She felt her loneliness for her family eating at her .

"Well perhaps I will see some of them again," Ruby mused. "After this past week, I have to believe anything can happen!"

Gilda ran up to Ruby.

"Have you heard from Rex? Do you guess he'll be here?"

"For all I know he could be anywhere. He was quiet about what he was doing today. That is very unusual. I still don't think it is a good day to have a party. Can't you tell these people to go home."

"Home? Of course not. We've even ordered a beautiful cake." Gilda stomped away, wishing they had listened to Ruby earlier. It was much too late to cancel the party now.

Gilda wondered when Brenda and Tom Baker would arrive with the cake. She hoped they would get there before Rex. Because of Lisa's insistence that morning, they both were coming and joining in the fun. Well, Gilda hoped it would be fun. It would be kind of a downer if Rex did not show up at all.

More Queen Bees were arriving, along with members of their families.

Ruby hid in the kitchen. She had a headache that was stifling. There was so much going on today. The last arrivals had told about a huge RV driving through town having difficulty turning off Main Street on to Church Street.

"The driver was a stranger. He turned that RV a hundred times I'd bet, inch by inch. He came as close as a strand of thread to eliminating the statue of the playful foxes with their kits."

"What else can happen today?" Ruby complained. Little did she know. The trailer park didn't even open for another week. Luther, who was owner and sole operator of the small six vehicle park was still on the road with his Winnabago.

Ruby put in a call to Dick's office.

"I think Luther has a sign that the Park is closed. I'm sure he wouldn't want anyone out there messing with his set-up." The clerk took the message laughing about the trouble the driver had taking it through town.

Looking out the window Ruby saw Opal. She arrived with a stranger and was making introductions. It had to be the woman Rex told her about last night when he arrived back at the Inn in the wee hours.

"Lisa, Gilda, come and meet my old friend, Jen. She loves to party and I thought you wouldn't mind. She met Rex last night over at the house. He doesn't have a clue about this party, does he?"

"We hope not," said Lisa. "We are planning it as a big surprise."

****

Sean was looking around town for Jade or some clue for finding her. Pulling out the packet of information that Martin collected, Sean realized that all he needed was a local phone book. Parking in front of a restaurant with a telephone sign in the window, he ordered a sandwich and stepped into the phone booth while waiting for his food. Taking the sandwich with him, Sean found the Cape Cod within moments.

"Now what?" he thought. Sean parked a few houses away and ate his sandwich.

He only had to wait about 30 minutes. The automatic door to the garage creaked as it opened. A dark red Buick turned toward town. Sean couldn't see the occupants well enough to know if one was Jade. However, he knew that there were three people in the car and one seemed to be a young boy. Chances were good that was Jade and her family.

Sean followed the Buick to a beautiful, huge Victorian home. The sign in the front announced "Gems an' Jams Bed and Breakfast". Sean parked two blocks away and walked back toward the house. With all the cars arriving it looked like a party. He could try crashing the party, but he wanted to stay in the background. If he just burst in on the fun, he would be spotted. He didn't want Jade to see him. He was on a secret mission to find out if she was okay. If he found her safe and happy he was leaving without even saying hello. No need putting her on the spot trying to explain an old 'friend' to her family.

Sean walked through the neighbors yard on the corner, wondering if he could see into the yard of the Victorian house from some point. Not being able to see through the thick hedge, he looked over at a Swamp Willow tree.

"I can climb that and look over the hedge since I can't see through it." Sean thought. Hanging his binoculars carefully around his neck, he climbed the Willow. Here he had a great view of the gazebo and garden where the party was gathering.

Meanwhile, Mason was watching the activity at the bank, with numerous people coming and going. A stretcher was brought out with the body on it completely covered. Some of the people from the bank were giving descriptions, asking if anyone knew who that guy was. Mason boldly walked up to the Rescue Squad vehicle just as they were about to lift the stretcher into the vehicle.

"Could I have a look? I was expecting to meet a friend here. I'd like to know if it's him."

The police officer overseeing the operation gave a nod.

"Let him look. If he can identify the body it will save us some time."

Mason swallowed hard. One side of the man's face was blown off. Even so, he recognized his long-time rival, Lopez. This could mean the end of this godfather's entire operation.

Not wanting to be associated with the gangster or hauled in for questioning, Mason lied.

"I'm relieved to say this isn't my friend. Sorry I couldn't help you."

Where to go next was the big question. Mason drove around trying to decide. He quickly found a street buzzing with activity! With all the cars in front o the huge Victorian house Mason's curiosity soared.

Driving by slowly he read the sign in front of the house. Lily's alias was right there! Jonesy had reported that the Fed questioning him had often slipped up and used the name, 'Ruby'. Yes, it was right there on the sign and not just the first name but the last name also. This was Lily's place! He would find her here!

Minutes later, Mason was exploring the back yard of the house next door to Ruby's. His explorations led him to lush arbors forming a path that led up a little walk. The wobbly path was concealed by tall arbors lush with green vines. Following it, Mason found it led to a door that was almost hidden from sight even when close enough to touch it. Curious, Mason tried the door and found it locked. He made quick work of unlawful entry and followed the stairs up to Ruby's rooms.

Mason had a strange feeling. As he looked around he saw no photographs. Eventually he spotted an album sticking partway out from the other books on a shelf. He slipped it out and took a quick look. It was filled with pictures; mostly of quilts. There were pictures of a few of people. One of them was certainly Lily. He would know her anywhere; in a photograph, in a video, anywhere. Lily was here! Mason was certain of it. Chills ran all over him! He felt cold and clammy, and he could not swallow.

Mason's hands kept shaking. He sat down in the most comfortable chair to wait for Lily's return. Freezing, he grabbed a quilt from one of the racks holding multiple pieced quilts. Eventually his shaking eased.

Soon, however, his curiosity was too much for him and he went to the side of the room overlooking the garden. Pulling back the drapes, he had a bird's eye view of the scene of the party. Most of the time he could not quite see Ruby from the window. By stepping out onto the little patio he had a much better view. In order to see more Mason tried to get as close to the edge of railing as possible, yet stay in the shadow.

Meanwhile Greg was driving all over town looking for Crystal and Bess. Upon seeing lots of cars and activity at a huge house, he paused.

"Maybe I should look here. It looks like this whole dinky town is gathering."

By the time Greg arrived there were so many cars in front of the house that he had to park almost a block away. Turning the corner as he walked back to the Inn, Greg spotted Duke, who was dashing through the hedge unmindful of the consequences. Duke fought his way through the dense hedge and saw Jade immediately. Recklessly, he dashed straight for her. Just before he reached her, Jake tackled him and Mel came to help secure Duke flat on the grass. Greg quietly slipped through the broken branches that Duke left in his wake, unnoticed due to the confrontation with Duke.

"Does anyone know this dude?" Mel asks, straddling Duke to keep the wiggling man in his grasp. Everyone was silent. Sean watching from the willow understands that Duke has followed him somehow. He shouldn't have come here. It looks like Jade has plenty of support in Fox Willow.

"These two men that came to her rescue are obviously good friends," Sean reasoned. Jade's problems with people like Duke weren't necessarily over but at least she had a support system.

An older man and young boy who had been pitching horseshoes on a far part of the lawn had come over quickly. They both put arms around Jade and found her a bench to sit down. Sitting on either side of her they turned toward her in a protective manner. These two were her husband and son. Had to be them. They not only matched the descriptions in Martin's report. Their actions spoke more than a written report can ever tell. Jade was still the same beautiful and desirable woman that she always had been. She just did not need him anymore.

Sean started to climb down the tree, but hesitated as more people were coming. Scanning a wider area with his binoculars, he saw movement on one of the little balconies that jutted out from all the double door sized windows on the upper level of the house. Someone else was watching the party from a high perch, but this fellow did not have the advantage of high powered binoculars. Sean was glad he had borrowed his PI's.

Sean heard a shrill whistle followed by Lisa running out the back door. Her whistle alerted the guests that Rex was coming. The partygoers quickly jumped behind hedges and chairs, ready to surprise Rex! Rex was accompanied by Dick. Hearing the whistle and sounds they couldn't identify, they came directly to the garden, through the doors Lisa had used. Everyone jumped out of their hiding places, shouting loudly,

"Surprise, Surprise!"

Mason bent further over the patio to see better. His Lily had her arm around this new guy they were all congratulating. If he had a gun Mason would have shot the new-comer then and there. No one could touch his Lily. His heart began to beat over time. His hands and feet turned ice cold. Mason doubled up with pain. He bent over the railing too far and fell headfirst down onto the cement patio. Sean was aghast as he watched the distraught scene that followed. Dick and Rex were describing an attempt to rob the bank that was delighting their audience. Several who saw Mason fall cried out, drawing the attention of most. Amber and Jules ran over to the man lying on the cement terrace, followed by half the crowd and one of the policemen.

The Baker's arrived with the cake and headed for the gazebo to put it down, with Harry following them so as to appear a legitimate guest. Duke broke away from the second policeman who had one handcuff fastened. In doing so he ran into Tom Baker, knocking the cake in the air where it landed on Harry, chocolate-coating his pants. The sirens of an ambulance added to the turmoil. Someone with a cell phone had called 911 upon seeing Mason's fall.

Harry cursed! He was looking for Abbot, who had insisted on being present when Harry eliminated Suzette. Abbot had gone berserk, however, and had eluded Harry. Harry spotted a man from the back with a shirt the same green as Abbot's. Harry came up behind Greg grasping Greg's shoulder. Surprised and totally livid with anger, Greg tried to trip Harry. Harry grabbed Greg, backing him into the hedge. Jake noticed the commotion and headed that way, joined by Rex. The crepe paper Gilda and Lisa had strung between the shrubs was tangled up as Harry and Greg accelerated their attack on one another. The garlands of bright colors were coming down all around and over the guests. The chocolate icing decorating Harry was now all over Greg as they wrestled. Crystal and Bess, seeing Greg, signaled to Amber. She grabbed Jules and the four left the party quickly.

The county sherif arrived with three deputies.

"I hope you brought lots of handcuffs," Rex observed, wisely staying out of the fight. Harry was getting the better of Greg when the deputies pulled him off and handcuffed both.

Lisa blew her whistle. She felt that if she blew loud enough, order would be restored. Just about this time, Devlin and Jack arrived at the B&B. Hearing all the noise, they came through the unlocked gate The two looked in amazement at the scene before them. There was Rachel right in the middle of the melee!

Chapter Thirty-One
Curtain Call

Abbot had wandered around the park and stopped in several stores. When approached by a clerk he responded in German. Abbot had watched the excitement at the bank with disinterest. He was looking for a certain young girl. When a group of school children walked around the corner, Abbot followed them into a drug store. One young girl had the coloring of Suzette. He touched her shoulder to get her attention.

"Get your hands off of me," she shouted at him. "I'll have you arrested. Get away from me now."

This wasn't Suzette. She had been kind and spoke gently. This girl didn't even speak the same beautiful language as Suzette. Abbot left the drug store. He had lately convinced himself that Suzette had never hurt him. Someone else had come there and attacked him while he slept. It couldn't have been his angel of mercy - the girl who had stopped the blood oozing from his wound.

Abbot sat down on a bench by the playground equipment, tired and confused. Wasn't he suppose to have a man working for him? How did he get here, to this town with the marble foxes? Where could he go to lie down? Suzette would show him, but he had to find Suzette.

Abbot dozed, still sitting on the bench.

Jaclyn wad called back to the boutique when one of the regular salesladies claimed illness. In truth the woman was nervous because of all the strange happenings, especially the commotion at the bank. Jaclyn let both of Pearl's workers go for the day and prepared to close early.

She hoped to catch at least a part of the big party. Lisa had invited her that morning.

Jaclyn noticed Abbot from the window of the boutique as he walked around in circles. The man was still in the park when Jaclyn closed the boutique. She walked over to him.

"You shouldn't be sleeping here," she said. "Is there someone I can call to come after you?"

Abbot stirred and opened his eyes. Before him he saw a young, fresh face with caring eyes. Jaclyn's soft touch as she woke him was all he needed to be certain she was Suzette. She must be. Suzette was the only person he had known to be so kind.

Jaclyn was alarmed when Abbot encircled her with his arms. She screamed a blood curdling scream.

Amber, Jules, Crystal and Bess were just entering the square on their way from the party. Bess pointed out the car window.

"That girl is in trouble." Amber automatically pulled the car over and Jules hopped our. Ari, who had been trailing Abbot as ordered, sprung to action. He had Abbot under control in quick time. Jaclyn looked confused.

"It's alright," Ari assured her. "He's my charge; he tends to wander in strange places and I lost track of him. I'll take him back where he belongs."

Ari ushered Abbot to a near-by car with Jules' help. Jules spoke in French.

"I have a photograph of this man," he told Ari. "If you are who I think you are, you've got the person you've been secking. If you have a piece of paper I can give you an address where he keeps things that never belonged to him. In return I want your assurance that he'll never be able to hunt his old enemies."

"I've heard he has been seeking certain persons involved in the French Underground. If you know of such persons you can tell them it's finally over. We'll see to any fallout."

The men shook hands. Jules stood by as Ari gave Abbot a calming injection. Ari called a number on specd dial on his car phone.

"All right! Bring him here."

Happy with his new orders, Ari picked up Sara and they disappeared .

As soon as they were alone, Jules took Amber in his arms.

"It's all over. Our old scout is on his way to a place worse than a deserted privy. I want to meet your children and grandchildren and to see Mother. Also, it's time for you to see you nieces and nephews. Blessed is this day!"

****

"The garden will never be the same. At least not this Summer." Ruby looked at her trampled rose bed and fallen trellises.

Maybe it's worth it," Rex interjected. "The man who fell from the balcony? You can definitely say he is the person you knew as Mason Peters?"

"Yes, beyond a doubt. Dick said the man shot at the bank proved to be Lopez. If no one else is after me, I guess I could go back to being Rachel, the new recruit."

"Thank goodness you said 'could' and not 'will'," Rex remarked. "Are you going to talk to your brother and his friend. They are waiting in the parlor."

"I want to, of course. The rules, as you know, say I have to wait for approval from Quinn."

"Not if you stay in character as Ruby. If it's ok with you, I'll explain to them that 'Ruby' would like to see them. First, they need to understand that any other person they have mistaken you for is not available."

"I'll go with you, then. I'll stand back while you give them the parameters."

Devlin reacted with poise.

"You really have a nice establishment here," he said. "My folks are due a vacation. Do you think they could book a week here?"

"I would be happy to have them. As soon as we can do something with the garden, we'll be reopening." Ruby said, fighting tears. She turned to Jack.

"Perhaps you have a family who would like to come also? The white-water rafting season is over this year, but the fishing's good."

"Yes, my wife and I have two little boys. They're still young, but my wife Margie talks about taking them fishing. She might like to see all of this for herself. It certainly answers a lot of questions for me." Jack knew he was stepping on shaky ground.

"Well, give her my regards," Ruby said. "Devlin, would you like a tour of the Inn? I'd love to hear more about your family."

Alone, the two embraced warmly without saying a word.

"So you're a detective for the Feds, now! What I hoped to be some day," said Ruby. "I've found a much better fit for myself, though."

"It looks like a little romance brewing, too," Devlin observed.

"Yes, pretty soon I will be known as Ruby Larson. I never was enamored with Fentasia. We are talking about a quiet ceremony, but there's no reason it can't just happen to fall on a date that we have guests in the Inn. Only thing, we don't want to wait too much longer."

Devlin grinned.

"I've got your brochures in my pocket. You can bet no one I know is going to drag their feet on this!"

"Do you and Jack want to stay overnight or would you rather wait until another time when we can speak freely?"

"I hope that's soon. I think I'll get Jack home and call back here for reservations. You can let me know the first week you can re-open."

Late that night Devlin dropped Jack at his front door. They had called Margie from the airport, alerting her that they would be late. She had asked no questions on the phone, but she heard something in Jack's voice. It was enough to hope.

She opened the door when she saw Devlin's car pull up to the curb.

Returning Jack's tender embrace, she commented.

"You found her."

"Yes. She owns a bed and breakfast inn. Her name's Ruby. Rachel's long gone. Ruby sends her regards and says she would welcome our family at her inn. Probably for an outrageous price, however." Jack laughed.

Margie hugged Jack tighter, responding to the warmth of his embrace. She joined in his laughter. Jack was finally her man and her's alone. Rachel was a childhood memory now that he had found her safe and thriving. The strong protective instinct he had for his wife and their children need no longer be extended to his childhood friend.

****

Dick took depositions from Jen, Jake and Opal.

"I don't think we'll even need these for Mark. He's violated his parole so much that he will spend many years back in prison. He assaulted his landlady, wrecked a man's vehicle, stole another vehicle - the list goes on. As for Gabe, I'm keeping him in my jurisdiction. There's a psychiatric facility near here with a locked forensic ward. They will at least see that he gets a high school diploma before he leaves. They only have twelve to sixteen boys at a time in the forensic set-up. Instead of a lot of confrontation they use lighter techniques. They try to find talents and skills that appeal to each individual enough to reorient them away from crime."

"They've had good luck with most, so far," Jake interjected. "I volunteer there once a week working one-on-one with a boy who has a real knack for carving. He's sold several pieces, which makes him really proud. Pearl's husband, Paul, rides up with me. He has a couple of boys interested in building full-sized model cars. It's a hobby Paul's always coveted but he can't afford the kits. The three of them are working on one car donated by someone. Most week-ends Paul goes up an extra day. When they finish this car they plan to sell it for a profit. They'll buy another kit and divide the rest three ways."

Jen didn't appear very hopeful.

"I can't think of anything Gabe likes except to eat, sleep and torment others."

Opal laughed.

"Maybe he'll become a chef!"

"Your joking, but maybe you've hit on something. Between about age eight and eleven I couldn't get him out of the kitchen. He hated all the canned goods and TV dinners I bought at the grocers and made up soups and salads to complement them. Most of them were pretty good, too."

"Maybe Ruby will volunteer there and teach jam making!" Opal laughed.

"What happened with the other guys you and the Sherif arrested?" Jake inquired.

"Greg had been indicted by a Grand Jury for manslaughter a couple of days before he came here. He had been given bail pending a trial date. Two officers came for him this morning. He'll have to await his trial in jail now.

"The one called Harry is still downstairs. His fingerprints indicate he is wanted in another state for assaulting a travel agent. The Feds want to talk to him first about this man he checked in with at one of the motels on the interstate. It seems the other man has simply disappeared.

"I've got another one named Duke, too. His fingerprints aren't showing much very clearly. He was one of the two involved in the rose garden fight and he is having trouble breathing. Preliminary tests indicate he'll need surgery - broken rib endangering a lung. He had a good bit of cash on him, but not enough for such a surgery. We may have him on a burglary charge too. He matches the description of a hitchhiker who stole a wad of cash from the trucker who gave him a lift. We've sent pictures to see if he can be identified."

A week later the Queen Bees gathered around the frame and began to quilt as if nothing had happened. They said their good-byes to Amber who was taking a couple of months to visit relatives, traveling with Jules.

"We're planning early September for our wedding," Ruby confided. "Be sure to come back by then."

"What happened with your friend, Jen?" Amber asked Opal.

"She's gone to her Mother's to stay awhile. Her younger son's there. She said she has a good bit of money. She was so fascinated with out quilts she is planning to open a small quilt shop. I promised if it gets off the ground that I'll come and give a lecture. Jen wants to call it "Jewels for the B & B: Body and Bed".

"How about your visitor, Bobby?" Amber looked at Pearl. "I thought he might be a little sweet on Jaclyn, though he seemed to old for her."

"It turns out he was adopted by his grandparents," Pearl answered. "He's looking for his biological Mother and thinks maybe Patricia, my Mom, fits the bill."

"Does she?" A chorus of voices asked.

"She will never tell, the condition she's in," Pearl mused. "I was old enough to notice if my Mother was pregnant at the time Bobby was born. Of course there were Summers she shuffled me off to Aunt Marie's. I think it's very unlikely and told the guy he'd be wise to look elsewhere."

Lisa came into the parlor, carrying a large envelop.

"The girl delivering this needs your john-henry."

Inside the envelop Ruby found a certificate of thanks and a discharge from service for Rachel O'Leary. There was a personal letter from a Senator and one from Quinn's boss. The latter released her from the Witness Protection program, but suggested she might be wise to keep her current identity.

"The far-reaching effects of the arrests made based on information you provided make it impossible to be certain that all danger is past. Two major mafia operations have been rendered ineffective.

Some of the territories these criminals controlled have been taken over by others. However, the organization and effectiveness of the new drug importers is loose and vulnerable compared to those now rendered ineffective. Your fellow citizens owe you a great debt of gratitude."

"I hope that's not bad news," Opal commented when Ruby returned to the parlor.

"Actually, it's better news than I ever hoped to have," replied Ruby, stifling a tear. "It's cause for celebration, but let's do it quietly; we've had enough surprise parties and fan-fare for a lifetime!"

A Message from the Author

The characters in this novel are all fictitious; any similarity to persons living or dead is purely coincidental. Ruby's jams are as imaginary as the woman. While all the ingredients she uses are edible, to my knowledge none of the recipes have been tested in the real world. Her method of finding blackberries should only be attempted in your dreams.

Several of my friends and family members read my first draft or selected chapters and gave me their comments. My thanks to all of them and especially to my daughter, Donna, for her initial edit and my friend Katy Sturm who encouraged me to keep Crystal in the story.

The cover depicts one of my wall quilts. I designed and photographed the quilt several years ago. For over twenty years I have belonged to a quilting bee that meets weekly. Also, I am a member of the local quilt guild and was one of the original National Online Quilters. These associations with other quilters have helped me grow aesthetically.

Other interests include garden and bridge clubs and more recently a couple of writer's groups. I have been writing for more years than I like to count, but only recently began to reach out to share my stories with others (mainly because computers have made editing and rewrites so much easier than my earlier experiences with typewriters). I hope that I sprinkled in a few laughs and provided a story you enjoyed.

Other Novels About Quilters:

Yes, these books are thriving - their numbers increase every year! The first one I know of is probably the best seller. Also, a movie was made based on the novel. *How to Make an American Quilt* by Whitney Otto made the best seller's list for several weeks running. In addition to a well-told tale, it has directions for making a quilt.

Jennifer Chiaverini has an entire series - at least a dozen - featuring the escapades of the Elm Creek Quilters. Ann Rinaldi, the excellent writer of young adult historical novels, has three books known as the Quilt Trilogy. Sisters start the quilt in the first book and the pieces are handed down to other generations as the books progress in time. They cover the revolutionary period, women in cottage industries later on and the experiences of a girl who lived with the Native Americans for a time, if my memory serves.

Sandra Dallas, Jane Peart, Aliske Webb and Lizbie Brown all have more than one novel to their credit - all in this category.

To me, *Under Cover: Secrets of the Fox Willow Quilters* is very much like a quilt. It explores people of varied backgrounds and cultures who blend into a network that is stronger than the individual people. A quilt reflects this same concept, as simple bits of fabric are pieced into a whole much lovelier and more useful than it's parts.

Made in the USA
Charleston, SC
22 October 2015